BEWITCHING THE WOLF

Blue Crescent Book One

SOPHIA MARTIN

ECLIPSE

Published by Eclipse Press

An Imprint of
ABCD Graphics and Design, Inc.
A Virginia Corporation
977 Seminole Trail #233
Charlottesville, VA 22901

Sophia Martin
Bewitching the Wolf

Print ISBN: 978-1-63954-009-9
v1

For everyone who has supported me, especially when I needed it the most.

Chapter 1

L eo Tyler could think of a lot of things he would
rather do than represent his pack of werewolves at
this government meeting as his Alpha had ordered
him to do. Walking on nails. Being kicked in the nuts. Swallowing wolfsbane. He disagreed with his Alpha, James, about a
lot of things, and had been relatively vocal about that since
becoming Beta after the death of his father some three years
previously. But the Local Government Area was apparently
insisting that their pack, as the largest group of werewolves in
the city, send a representative to their meeting about council
activities—something to do with afterschool programs, interspecies integration and helping children stay the course in
educational pathways—and James had been insistent that as
Beta, Leo go to represent the pack, as he himself was busy. As
far as Leo was concerned, it was more than likely that the
Alpha just didn't want to go himself and was fabricating some
prior commitment to avoid sitting through several hours of
government finagling. It sure wouldn't be the first time that
James had taken advantage of Leo's obligation to follow his

Alpha's instructions to avoid doing something he didn't want to do himself.

James had been Alpha for roughly fifteen years—more than half of Leo's life—and the older wolf, in Leo's opinion, had stopped proving himself worthy of the role some five to ten years prior—around the time Leo, a freshly minted eighteen-year-old, had taken off to see some of the world before the requirement upon him as heir to the role of Beta trapped him in Mystic City. He'd returned when his father became seriously ill, but Daniel Tyler had held on far longer than anyone had expected, leaving Leo in limbo as the almost-Beta of the pack for more than nine months.

Some of their packmates had had doubts about obeying the instructions of a Beta who had spent so many years away, which was ironic, considering they seemed to have no issue following the leadership of James, who in the time Leo had been out of Mystic City had seemed to completely abandon any effort to deserve the mantle of Alpha. He no longer trained to keep up with the strongest wolves in the pack, no longer joined them in their fight practice or the teaching sessions for the younger wolves about controlling their transformations or avoiding substances like silver and wolfsbane. Leo would hesitate to say out loud that James had gone soft, but it was hard not to think it in the privacy of his own mind. A Beta was supposed to be the second-best in the pack, not the enforcer for a wolf who had allowed his body and resolve both to sink into disuse. James commanded respect by virtue of leading the largest pack in the city, if not the state, but as Leo had settled into the role of Beta, as time went on and James began asking more of him, Leo was coming to believe the older wolf deeply unworthy of his own position. For starters, he should have had the balls to come to this stupid meeting himself, instead of making Leo do it.

Leo took a deep breath to steady his temper and climbed

out of his car. The sun was just starting to go down, the intense heat of the day finally beginning to fade. Warmth radiated up from the asphalt of the parking garage, and the city-centre smells along with that of hot tar were ripe in his nose. Underscored by... *something*. Something *else*.

He paused for a minute on his walk to the building where the meeting was being held, breathing deeply. Most werewolves had an excellent sense of smell, but Leo's was even better than most. He tried to separate out the scents of the city... cooking meat from the kebab store down the block, sweat from the gym on the upper level of the building where the meeting was being held, the overriding odour of hot tarmac. And that mysterious *something*, just on the edge of what he could detect. It smelled like... Christmas. Like cinnamon and nutmeg and warmth, and at the same time, like heat and seduction and a kind of frantic physical need he'd never felt before. He felt his wolf stirring beneath his skin, his body readying itself to fight, or maybe to fuck as though even his physical response to the *something* couldn't make up its mind what it was supposed to be.

Part of him was desperate to track down the source of this scent, but a glance at his watch told him he had three minutes to get into the LGA meeting or he'd be neglecting his duties as Beta.

Afterwards, he promised the wolf stirring beneath his skin. *Afterwards, we'll track it down. Just sit through a few hours of political posturing, and we can work out what the hell this is.*

The wolf was unsatisfied with this response, but Leo ignored it and made his way into the multistorey building where the local council representatives were gathering, forcing himself to stop paying attention to the information his nose was feeding him, which was specifically telling him that the scent was growing stronger. Stronger.

He wasn't the only supernatural representative at the

meeting, he realised when he entered the room. It was set up with rows of chairs facing a lectern with an aisle down the centre, the windows open to the dense city air. Even though they were facing away from him, he could recognise the scent of the two vampires sitting in the third row, the representatives of several covens of witches in the fifth, and the one other werewolf present, who was sitting on the other side of the aisle in the row front of the almost-empty back row where Leo slid into a seat. The other wolf seemed to sense his arrival at the same time and turned around to greet him with a friendly smile. Petra, if he was remembering her name correctly from the one or two times they'd met before, wasn't someone he knew well, but he made a note to say hello properly once the meeting was over. It couldn't hurt to foster some other werewolf connections, especially when their territories abutted that of his own pack, as Petra's pack's did.

The full room quieted suddenly, and Leo realised someone had stepped up to the lectern. And with the incredible scent dragging his attention forwards, he focused closely on the *something*, fixing on its source, on the path it took to reach him. And somehow, somehow, he had no doubt in his mind that it was coming from… her.

It would fit. She was… something. She was a witch; even in his altered state he could appreciate that. Magic hummed over her skin like static electricity. It wound through the gentle curls at the ends of her thick black hair, sparked in her eyes. To his frustration, at this distance, he couldn't tell if they were blue or green, and that lack of knowledge ground at his nerves. He wanted to know everything about her. Wanted to know what those perfect bow lips looked like when they curved into a real smile, not the practiced one she was maintaining as she spoke to the crowd. Wanted to know how they looked opened in a gasp of pleasure. In a scream. Wanted to know how her face changed when he made her call out his name.

"Good evening, everyone, and thank you for coming." She took a deep breath and looked down at her hands. "As most of you know, my name is Delphinia Greenbranch, and it really means a lot to us that you've all made the effort to attend. You may be aware that our coven, in partnership with the Department of Youth and Community, has been putting a lot of effort into the programs we're here tonight to discuss, and it is very satisfying for us to see that some of you are interested in what we've put together. I'd like to say a special thank you to the representatives of the supernatural communities who have made the effort to attend tonight. Valerie and Beau," she sent a smile to the vampires, "Lisa, Rupert, Alex, and Simone," another to the witches. "And in particular, our werewolf guests. It means a lot to us that you would consider being involved in something so far from your packs' usual methods." She made eye contact with the wolf in the row in front of Leo, sent her a grateful look, and then suddenly her eyes were on his, and the foundations of his world fucking *crumbled*.

He saw her eyes widen, was vaguely aware of the way her lips parted on an intake of breath, but he couldn't look away, couldn't take his eyes off the witch at the front of the room. Need swelled in his body, sudden as a lightning strike and potent as if he'd been starving for weeks and had just had a buffet of all his favourite dishes displayed in front of him. In his jeans, his flesh swelled irresistibly. *Need her. Need her.* He felt his canines elongating into fangs in his mouth as the wolf in him made its presence known. It was as focused on the witch behind the lectern as if he'd waved a blood-dripping steak in front of it. The look that Delphinia Greenbranch gave him— initially a kind of practiced appreciation that quickly morphed into what looked like dazed confusion—drew him in like a magnet. He wanted to fix anything that made her look uncertain—especially if it were related to *him*—wanted to change anything that made her even the least bit unsure of anything. Wanted to fix her entire life so it not only included nothing that ever made her worry even the tiniest bit, but also so that a large fucking chunk of it included *him*.

He suddenly wanted—*needed*—access to her. He wanted to touch every inch of her body, to take in the unbelievably perfect scent that was growing stronger the longer they spent in the same room, to weave his fingers into her thick black hair, to trace his hands over the curves that were all too visible under the dress she wore. Surely, she couldn't have thought that was appropriate attire for a meeting covering local government issues. Sure, it had a high neckline, but his position at the side of the room meant he could see past the lectern to register that it only reached partway down legs that her sensible high heels made look positively endless. Would those heels put her at eye height to him? She was clearly already tall, which was fantastic because it provided more skin for him to memorise with his touch, with his tongue. Were-wolves were usually tall, but Leo had always been at the upper end of the spectrum, which had been frustrating with many of the women he'd been with before, who had been too small, too fragile, to match him in any way, even those who were were-wolves themselves. He shoved the thought of them out of his mind; for some reason, he suddenly didn't want to think about anyone he'd been with before. He didn't want to think about the very idea of letting any woman close to his body other than the one whose gaze had finally broken away from his own.

"As you may be aware," Delphinia was saying, continuing as though she hadn't just paused for several silent seconds, "there are a number of local government districts within Mystic City. However, ours, consisting of the territories of two werewolf packs, the vampire coven and those of three witch covens, and the human territories, have the lowest level of continuing education of young people, both human and supernatural, of the entire city. So, one of the things that our program aims to address is the issue of keeping our youths in school. Obviously, there are various issues specific to individual races, such as the sunshine issue for vampires, but what we aim to do is to support young people to complete high school and potentially encourage them to consider further education."

She continued talking about the ways the programs were planning on keeping young people in school, but Leo barely heard her. His eyes kept fixing on tiny parts of her, like the prominence of her collarbone against her skin, or the curve where her ribs became her waist. The way she spoke with her hands made him imagine her touch on his skin. She was animated, clearly intensely passionate about the afterschool projects she was outlining, talking about ways to incorporate young vampires, who obviously couldn't be out in daylight, as well as witches, the supernatural race most historically integrated with the humans, and the werewolves, who were the least. Typically, the werewolves kept to themselves, keeping separate from many of the "normal" human ways of life. His own pack, Blue Crescent, existed as an entity in and of itself, taking care of its members as they worked to maintain it and provide for one another. Just the fact that James had sent him to this meeting was strange, given the way that the pack normally functioned as a purposely separate entity, uninvolved in the way the rest of the city ran. Was there something James was considering that he hadn't shared with Leo? Was he working towards integrating the pack into the wider society of Mystic City without even thinking to run the concept past Leo?

"The other part of this project that's important to discuss," Delphinia was saying from the front of the room, "is the fact that we're not talking about having separate programs for each of our different races. We're working to include not only humans but also all the supernatural races in all our plans. Obviously, everyone has their own specific challenges when it comes to being included in these programs," she gestured specifically to the vampires with a sweet smile that sent heat shooting through Leo's body, concentrating in his groin. "But we think it's important to try to raise our young people more inclusively than we were brought up. The separations between our various races are important to our identities, we don't deny that, but we think it would be a positive move if we started bringing young humans, witches, vampires, and were-wolves together to learn and grow together. We all live together here in Mystic City. We might as well start learning to exist collectively in a way that brings us all closer together."

There was a muffled hum in the room as people began speaking to one another, and he wanted to introduce his fist to the face of anyone who dared to interrupt Delphinia. She seemed prepared for it, though, smiling indulgently from behind the lectern.

"I know this is a fairly contentious suggestion," she said, and thankfully the room fell silent once more to listen to her, or else Leo might have had to do something drastic. "And for that reason, later tonight, we're going to open the floor to anyone who has any particular issues they want the opportunity for us to address as a group. In the meantime, we have a couple more people we're planning to have speak this evening, but after that, if anyone else wants to get up and have their say, we look forward to hearing your opinions. For now, I'd like to welcome Marcus Heath to the stage."

She stepped back from the lectern and someone else stepped forwards, some human with too much gel in his hair. Leo hardly even registered that he was present; his eyes were fixed on Delphinia, taking her seat at the back of the room behind the lectern. The man sitting next to her put a hand on hers and, when she looked his way, gave her an encouraging smile, and Leo almost blew up. Another man, touching the exposed skin of this woman? He'd never been a jealous man before, had always been content to fill a minor role in the lives of the women with whom he had... well, maybe you could call them relationships, at a stretch. When they found men who could give them more than he was able, he had never minded stepping back from that role. But suddenly, there was nothing *minor* about the role Leo wanted to fill in Delphinia's life. He wanted to leave his mark all over her skin until any other man in her life thought twice about laying a fucking hand on her.

Maybe the problem was partly the absolute tease of a dress she was wearing. It was almost as black as her hair, high-necked, but tight enough that it clung to her perfectly curvaceous body, ending at her knees in a way that meant when she sat down, it rode up enough that he could see the skin of her legs almost to mid-thigh.

Leo wanted to be the only person who touched her bare skin. He wanted to see and touch and cherish every single facet of her body and memorise them with his lips and tongue. He wanted to learn her so intimately that nothing about her was unfamiliar to him. He wanted to leave his scent all over her so no one else ever got close to Delphinia Green-branch without knowing that Leo had been there first.

It was this thought that took Leo aback. He was thinking about having her around other wolves, wolves who judged people partly on scent before they'd even met them. She was a *witch*, for heaven's sake. Why would she be around enough wolves that it mattered that he'd put his scent all over her?

Unless...

Unless some part of him was considering introducing her to the pack.

Unless he was planning on bringing her *into* it.

At the very thought of bringing the witch now sitting at the back of the stage into the pack as his partner, something in Leo that he had never known was tense immediately relaxed. Something in him... *eased*. As though it had always been waiting for Delphinia Greenbranch, been waiting for the concept of bringing her into his life as the kind of a partner the pack's pseudo-marital system recognised as absolute, been waiting for the option of making her *his* in the most unquestionable of ways.

Her scent filled his consciousness, even though she was no longer at the lectern, Christmas spices and sex and heat and *woman*. How had he lived this long without taking in this utterly addictive scent? How had he lived so long without having *her*?

Before he knew what was happening, the meeting was drawing to a close, having cycled through everyone from humans to vampires discussing the options that would make Delphinia's afterschool program plan feasible, and the room was emptying. Leo found himself rising to his feet, ignoring the friendly smile of the wolf in the row in front of him as he strode forwards to make the acquaintance of the woman who, in his head, he had already claimed as his own.

He was... big. That was the first thing Della thought when the werewolf representative stood in front of her. He was so tall. Broad. His shoulders seemed to be bunching and unbunching as he stood before her, hands making fists and relaxing over and over. She cast her eyes over him slowly, taking in every inch of the man who had looked so disapproving during her meeting. His scowls from the back row, the constant drawing down of his eyebrows, had had her biting her lips with unexpected nerves every time she paused in speaking.

He was bigger than any human—or inhuman—had the right to be. His shoulders were so broad, she had to stop herself from imagining running her hands over the breadth of them. His hair was the colour of melting chocolate, and his eyes were a strange silvery green that, once she looked into them, seemed to almost trap her own gaze, like falling into a mountainside lake. Deep and warm and all-encompassing and somehow both safe and… exciting?

"Who are you?"

The words were out of her mouth before her brain had a chance to catch up. Her voice came out deeper than usual, husky, like she had just finished an extended session of screaming. *I'd let him make me scream,* a voice in her head said, tone as salacious as the content of the thought.

"Leo," he growled, then cleared his throat and tried again. "Leo Tyler." He still sounded angry, the frustration in his voice and face at odds with the anxious tension in his stance.

The name rang a bell, and Della took an involuntary step backwards. "The Beta from the Blue Crescent pack?"

"I… yes." She seemed to have taken him off guard by knowing who he was.

"We'd kind of hoped your Alpha might join us tonight," she managed, trying not to get lost again in the silver-green of his eyes. Had they become more silver? Her tone still sounded strangled. What was it about this man that had her so off-balance?

Her statement seemed to startle a laugh out of the man. He ran a hand over his short beard and her fingers tingled at the imagined sensation of hair scratching over her skin. His laugh was like glass mixing with gravel, but somehow… pleasant? Something in her got the sense that he didn't laugh often and immediately wanted to make him make that deep gravel-glass laugh whenever she could.

"You'd be lucky to get our Alpha off pack territory on a full moon night in midsummer, let alone for an evening of governmental discussion." He bit his lip, as though he'd said more than he intended. "It's Delphinia, isn't it?"

"Just Della is fine," she managed, trying not to let her perusal of his brick-shithouse body be too obvious. For once in her life, she felt... small. Petite. *Her*, who had been the tallest woman in her coven since she was fourteen. She let her hair slide out from behind her ear, appreciating the sense of distance, of protection, that the slight barrier gave her.

His hand rose as though he had no control over it, pausing before the sheet of her hair partly covering her eyes. Was that... a growl that came from him? In a move almost swifter than she could follow, he tucked her hair back behind her ear, then dropped his hand back to cross his arms across his impossibly broad chest. Della had to fight to regain her voice. For some reason, she was suddenly breathless, her eyes feeling as wide as silver dollars.

"Leo." His name slipped from her lips, then she bit her tongue, searching for something they could talk about. Some way to break this silence between them, when it grew more heated with every second that passed. "Um. What did you think of our proposals tonight? The idea of integrating the humans and the supernaturals? I know the humans in Blue Crescent territory tend to keep to themselves."

He blinked at her as though this was the first he'd heard of the idea, as if she and two other program advisors, as well as one of the other witches, *and* both the vampires, hadn't all weighed in on the topic for a good hour and a half.

"The way you were scowling the whole meeting, I presumed you didn't approve of the suggestion." She bit her lip suddenly when she realised the statement made it clear just how much attention she'd been paying to him when she should have been completely focused on the meeting she was supposed to be running. His quirked eyebrow seemed to say the same thing.

"Much as I appreciate that you noticed," he said, and was it just her imagination, or was his voice suddenly a degree more flirtatious? "It wasn't about your proposal. I was... thinking of something else."

"What's so important you couldn't pay attention to the meeting?" Della demanded and immediately regretted the question, because his deep-set eyes were suddenly fixed on hers with a kind of intensity she'd never seen before, and it was... hot. Surface-of-the-sun kind of hot. A soft throb in the pit of her stomach that was quickly migrating to the juncture of her thighs kind of hot.

What the hell was this? Della had never, as in *never*, responded this way, to *anyone*. Even the few men, both warlock and human, she'd allowed to take her on dates, even those with whom the date had gone further than the original drinks or dinner or whatever, had failed to elicit even a fraction of this kind of immediate response in her.

"I'm not sure you really want to know," Leo muttered, dragging her focus away from her suddenly tightening nipples.

If he'd known her, he would have known that that was exactly the wrong thing to say. Della had been known for her never-ending curiosity within her coven for years, and it had gotten her in trouble more than once.

Why did something in her tell her this was going to be another one of those times?

Why did the throb that had taken up residence between her thighs insist that it would be worth it?

"I think I do," she heard herself say, her voice again taking on that just-been-screaming husky timbre. She tilted her head sideways and her hair again slid free from behind her ear, but before she could tuck it away again, Leo had stepped close to where she stood behind the lectern—impossibly close, indecently close—and done it for her. Only this time, his hand didn't disappear after that briefest of touches. This time, his hand sunk into the thickness of her hair and his grip tightened until he'd tugged her head upright again, leaving his mouth so close to her exposed ear that she felt the rush of his hot breath on her skin when he spoke.

"All right, little witch, you want to know what I was thinking about? What was distracting me so I couldn't pay attention to your meeting?"

With the microscopic amount of movement permitted by his grip in her hair, Della managed a semblance of a nod. Her own breath was loud in her ears.

"I wasn't thinking about afterschool programs, that's for goddamn sure," Leo growled, "because you smell like pure sex, and I can't get my damn mind off what you taste like underneath this tease of a dress. How long it's been since you were properly satisfied. How long it'll be before you let me get my mouth between your thighs and redefine whatever you used to think 'satisfied' meant."

"Delphinia?"

In a flash, Leo's grip had left her hair and Della was left reeling in something of an aroused fugue state as he stepped back from her, to stand to one side of the lectern as though he'd been leaning on it all along, moving so quickly it was like he was trying to hide that they'd been doing something wrong.

Had they? Was it wrong, the filth he'd just growled in her ear? Was it wrong that the words were humming through her body and, gods above all help her, she wasn't sure if she'd ever in her life been so aroused?

She didn't have time to consider it. Valerie, one of the two vampires they'd managed, with some effort, to convince to attend, rounded the corner into the meeting room, a smile stretching over her pale face when she spotted Della.

"There you are! Oh, and Leo, is it? You're from the Blue Crescent pack, aren't you? I hope I'm not interrupting anything."

"Not at all," Della said, hoping she didn't sound as off-balance as she felt. She smoothed her dress down her legs, suddenly hyperaware of where the hem sat just above her knees. It had felt perfectly suitable when she'd been wearing it in the office, but now she was aware of every inch of exposed skin. *I can't get my damn mind off what you taste like underneath this tease of a dress.* "We were just talking about how to go about integrating afterschool programs in Blue Crescent territory," she invented on the fly.

"Oh, you're keen to join with the programs, are you, Leo?" Valerie asked, the hyper-friendly vampire not seeming to find it odd that the werewolf had yet to move out from his position behind the lectern. Was he trying to hide that he was as aroused as she was?

"Very much looking forward to joining," Leo said, his voice as rough as sandpaper and deeper than the ocean. His eyes flitted over her just once more, but Della felt it down to her bones.

"Isn't that interesting?" Valerie said conversationally, leaning on the other side of the lectern. "I was under the impression most of the werewolf packs preferred to keep things very insular, very isolated from the rest of the super-naturals."

"Blue Crescent prides itself on becoming more open to new ideas," Leo replied, not missing a beat. "I'd love to hear more about Della's… ideas."

"Well, if you don't mind doing that another time, might I steal her for a moment? Beau and I need to be back at the nest shortly, and I wanted to have a quick chat about the logistics of including young vampires in programs during times when the sunlight hours are long."

"Sure," Della said, her breathing finally steadying. She darted back behind the lectern long enough to collect her notes, carefully not making eye contact with the massive werewolf still standing there and tried not to gulp audibly as she moved past him. When she heard his own harsh intake of breath when the skirt of her dress brushed his legs, she risked a glance up at his face and almost swallowed her tongue. His eyes were fixed on her like she was the finest work of art he'd ever seen, his irises flashing to a far deeper silver that told her the wolf in him was fighting not to make itself known.

"We're having another meeting," she managed, just barely. "In two weeks. Same place, same time. Maybe I'll see you there?"

"Count on it," Leo said, that sandpaper tone back in his voice, the intensity in his eyes enough to set her absurdly aroused body aflame all over again.

"That's… good," she managed weakly, before Valerie was slipping a stone-cold arm through hers and leading her from the room.

Chapter 2

There was no way Leo was waiting two weeks to see Delphinia Greenbranch again. He couldn't. He just... couldn't. Now that he had her scent in his nose, knew what that thick black hair felt like wrapped around his fingers... she'd awoken something in him. The sight of her, the scent of her. The way she talked so passionately, so confidently about her plans for the programs she was developing, but let her hair fall in front of her face when she was talking to him, like it was providing some kind of shield... Two weeks? There was no way in hell he was waiting that long. He was going to track her down and find out if his uncontrolled filthy mouth—something which had *never* happened to him before with a female he didn't even *know*—had managed to alienate the most beautiful woman he'd ever seen.

But first, he needed to explain to his Alpha why he'd all but signed up their notoriously insular pack to be involved a human-supernatural program designed to introduce young kids of different species to each other's ways while keeping them from dropping out of school at the earliest available moment. Though some members of the pack admittedly did follow the path of further education and training and were even involved in Mystic City's government or one of its universities, most finished as much high school as they felt necessary—which often wasn't all of it—then functioned within the pack, contributing to, and being supported by their communal way of life. Putting time and energy into keeping the young wolves in school—let alone the issue of doing it in programs that purposely integrated them with humans and other supernaturals—was going to be a hard sell to James and the rest of the pack.

Leo had been anticipating having at least a day or so to prepare for the inevitable argument, but when Emmett and Raj showed up at his door the next morning before he'd even finished his coffee, he couldn't say he was particularly surprised. News travelled fast in the pack.

Leo, Em, and Raj had been best friends since their school days, gravitating towards each other as the kids who made trouble tended to. Since then, they'd fallen into their own roles within their trio—Raj, who was over six and a half feet tall and never short of a ludicrous suggestion for something that would inevitably be a good time but have repercussions he chose to ignore until they were upon him; Emmett, the peace-keeper of the three of them who was usually the one who talked Raj out of whatever strange idea he'd decided was the best way to drag some fun into their usually work-focused lives; and Leo, who did his best not to abuse his power as Beta when dragging the three of them out of the trouble that following through with Raj's ideas got them into. He was aware that he was probably the worst friend of the three of them, since his commitments as Beta often interfered with plans that they'd made or even took him off-grid for a day or two at a time, but he still did his best to keep up with their nights out at the pub or staying in watching football. He lent an ear or a shoulder of support when one of the others needed it—more often than not Emmett, who had a habit of falling in love with every beautiful woman he came across and out of it just as quickly—or even just training together or assisting when each of them led the training sessions for the rest of the pack, as they'd been doing for a couple of years now.

The three of them were each formidable enough fighters that they no longer often found themselves in scraps with others, but when one of the older wolves had seen them holding off a larger group of wolves from the Apex River Pack with whom Blue Crescent shared a border—if Leo remembered correctly, because they'd crossed the border to try out a pub in Apex River territory and Emmett had tried to put the moves on one of the locals' girlfriends—they'd been conscripted into regularly contributing to training sessions for the other fighters within the pack and eventually, leading them. Though territory lines within Mystic City had been drawn when the city was founded and remained unchanged, border skirmishes between wolves, who were notoriously volatile, were not unheard-of, so as many of the pack as wanted to train to fight attended the sessions that were run several mornings a week. More than a few of the older wolves were surprised to see the group of young troublemakers assisting in running the sessions, but by doing so the three of them—even Leo, who had thought he was viewed as more responsible since he'd taken up the role of Beta—had garnered significantly more respect from the rest of the pack.

The whole Apex River debacle had earned Leo an extreme dressing-down from James, and he'd taken it on the chin and made Emmett buy drinks for all three of them the next time they went out as recompense.

Today was a different situation completely. The hammering on the door when Leo was only halfway through his morning coffee could only have been one of his two best friends, and when he opened it, he found both leaning on the doorframe.

"Morning, Beta," Emmett said, using the title he knew frustrated Leo to no end. "What's the story?"

"Story?" Leo blinked.

"Give the man a chance to wake up before you start the interrogation, Em," Raj said, as he pushed past Leo to enter the house. "He's hardly conscious."

As usual, once inside, Raj sprawled on Leo's sofa, the massive wolf taking up almost the entire couch. Emmett and Leo shared an unsurprised but amused glance before they each took the easy chairs that also faced Leo's TV, leaving the three of them in a semi-circle that Em broke by dragging his chair into position to face Raj and Leo more easily.

"So, what the hell, man?" he asked. "You're putting us in with the humans now?"

"Ah," Leo said, thinking longingly of the half-full cup of coffee currently sitting on his kitchen bench before turning his attention to his packmates. "You heard about the meeting last night."

"We heard about you committing Blue Crescent to being involved in some kind of integration program," Raj said lightly, as though it were nothing.

"There were some good points made," Leo said, not sure whether he should put some effort into sounding apologetic as practice for what was sure to be almost the exact same conversation he would have with the Alpha. Would that play better with James? Mostly, he admitted to himself, he was considering what would make it easier to spend as much time as possible in Delphinia Greenbranch's company without negatively impacting the pack.

"They've been making points about integration for years now," Raj pointed out from his position on the couch, "And you've never been particularly interested in it before."

"We have humans living in our territory," Leo said without much conviction. "They contribute to the running of the pack."

"All right, then we have all the involvement with humans that we need," Emmett said. "Why the sudden interest in signing us up for more?"

"It's not just humans," Leo replied. "There were vampires there... another werewolf. From Apex River, I think. Witches. The meeting was run by a witch."

There was a moment of silence before Raj said, "Shit, man. You're involving the whole pack in this program because you want to tap the witch who's running it?"

"What? I didn't say... it's not just..." Leo heard himself sputtering. "It's not about the witch," he added finally, hearing the helplessness in his own tone. "They made some really valid points. As a pack, we've been so isolated for so many years. We live and work among the humans, some of us even with the vamps and the witches as well. Doesn't it make sense that we'd actually put some work into allowing our pups to understand what they're getting themselves into when they sign up to be involved with other species?"

"Don't try to bullshit a bullshitter," Raj said with a significant degree of amusement, stretching out so his bulk covered even more of the couch. "The minute you mentioned her, your eyes shifted."

"*What?*" That hadn't happened to Leo since he was a pup still learning to control his changes. Sure, every now and then he'd feel his irises going slightly silver, but he'd always been able to tamp down on it. Control it. It hadn't happened completely like that, without his active control of the shift, in years. "You're kidding."

"Why would I joke about that?" Raj asked.

"He's telling the truth, Leo," Emmett put in. "What is she, your mate or something? Or are you just that hard-up that you'll go gaga over the first pretty woman to look your way?"

"Wh..." Leo had to work hard to control the surge of anger that rose at the idea of anyone, even one of his best friends, thinking something like that about Delphinia. He focused on the first half of what Emmett had said instead. "You know I don't believe in that crap."

The myth of each werewolf having a single ideal mate somewhere out in the world was nothing but a fairy tale they told pups to lull them to sleep, as far as Leo was concerned. To the best of his knowledge, no one in the pack had come across this fabled perfect mate, or even knew of any wolf who had. "She just," he finished lamely, "she just smells incredible. I've never... I've never known anything like it. It's like sex and Christmas all wrapped up in one. I just talked to her, that's all. But once I had her scent... I couldn't stay away."

Emmett laughed. "Kind of sounds like the mate myth, man."

"Hell, I'd wrap the pack up in this afterschool program crap too if I knew I'd get my mate out of it," Raj laughed. As a librarian, though, he spent significantly more time around books and fairy tales than either Leo or Emmett, though, so his believing that the story of finding one's mate might be more than a myth was somewhat unsurprising. "James isn't going to be thrilled, though," Raj added with a dark chuckle.

"When is James ever thrilled?" Leo asked, choosing to ignore Emmett's comment. The truth was the most popular version of the mate myth *did* make mention of a wolf being inescapably drawn to their mate's scent. He shook the thought from his head. It was nothing but a story. He'd track Delphinia down, potentially repair any damage he'd done by speaking to her the way he had last night and find a way to get her and her incredible scent out of his system so he could think properly around this need to be near her that had been hounding him since she walked away last night. That was the extent of his plan, and at this point it should be—it *was*, he insisted to himself—all that he needed.

But before he did any of that, he was going to need to justify his decision to involve the pack in the program to James.

———

The Blue Crescent Alpha didn't often leave the Italian restaurant-and-bar he'd made the seat of his power. He didn't seem to notice the parallels to the classic practices of the patriarch of a mafia family, or if he did, he didn't seem to care. Most of Leo's meetings with James happened in the back room of Horatio's, regardless of the time of day, and James had long since clearly disregarded the societal convention that would disapprove of him having his ever-present glass of whiskey at hand before noon.

It was probably—*probably*—not just the influence of the whiskey that had him so furious with Leo, though. To be fair, Leo thought, he might have been equally surprised—if not, perhaps, as openly outraged—if he were in the Alpha's position. Leo was aware that he had never given the impression of having an issue with the pack's insular nature in the past. Why would he go to the effort that it would require to change it now?

James, however, was on the far edge of furious, and had been since Leo had entered Horatio's, answering the Alpha's obviously unimpressed summons.

"What the fuck, Tyler?" James asked, the moment Leo had entered what he thought of as James' room in the establishment. It featured the table behind which the Alpha sat as well as a few others, like a smaller version of a restaurant, and always held a few of James' closest followers lurking around the Alpha.

"Do you know what you've done?" James continued.

"I figured that's why you sent me to the meeting," Leo said. For once, the vaguely deferential role that he'd made a habit of taking around James felt uncomfortable, like a too-small pair of shoes. "Why would I have been there if you weren't interested in being involved?"

"To make it clear to them that we damn well *weren't* interested," James spat. "Instead, you've all but committed the entire pack to involvement in this bullshit. I mean, integrating our pups not just with humans, but vamps and witches? Why the fuck would you think that was a good idea?"

"More than a hundred humans live in pack territory," Leo reminded him. "Some of our pack go out and work with them, and the witches and the vampires, every day. I kind of figured we were halfway to integrated already."

"They live *independently* in our territory," James emphasised. "The deal is that they keep themselves to themselves, and we don't make an issue out of their presence."

"We have to live in this city," Leo pointed out. "We have to deal with the humans and the other supernaturals every day. What harm does it do to let the young ones make some connections outside the pack?"

"It's not how we do things around here," James said flatly, taking a gulp of his drink. He sat forwards in his chair. "And just because you inherited the role of Beta, doesn't make you untouchable, Tyler. You'd do well not to forget that."

"I didn't even commit to anything," Leo protested. Was James really threatening him? With what? To demote him from the role of Beta? To evict him from the pack altogether? Those would be massive repercussions to ensue from something as minor as telling a single witch, in the presence of a single vampire, that Blue Crescent might be interested in being involved in their programs. "All I did was say we were potentially interested in being involved in the program. I didn't promise her anything." *Except that I want to introduce her body to my mouth in the most uncivilised of ways*, some part of his brain reminded him, and he pushed the thought away as fast as he could.

Apparently, not fast enough.

"Her?" If James had been in his wolf form, Leo had no doubt his ears would have pricked up. "Is this about a fucking *female*, Leo? Is that's what's stolen your common sense, some goddamn woman?"

"No, of course not," Leo snapped, but it felt like a lie to even say it. It felt wrong. Like he was somehow betraying the draw he felt to her—betraying *her*—with the denial.

How could he be feeling this way over someone he didn't even know yet? Hell, since when did he feel like this, feel anything *like* this, over a woman at all?

"I should fucking hope not," James said with another sip from his glass. He gave the appearance of having relaxed somewhat, sitting back in his chair, but his eyes were still coldly calculating as they surveyed Leo. "If there's some female involved, get her under you and out of your system, and then bring me back my Beta with his fucking brain intact, all right?"

Even though his own half-formed plan had been some-what similarly worded, the same thing in Leo that had balked at denying Delphinia's sudden importance to him wanted to snarl at the suggestion of getting her *under him and out of his system*. Wanted to growl at the very thought of any other male picturing Delphinia in an intimate moment, even if the man involved with her in that moment was him. Those moments should belong to him and him alone, dammit. Not to even start with the idea that having her under him would get her out of his system at all.

Unless...

He'd had those kinds of interactions with women before, when falling into bed together once had been enough to sate the attraction and they'd parted ways afterwards without needing more from one another. Was it possible that this insane draw to Delphinia Greenbranch could be satisfied in the same way? That if he could just find a way to be with her, sate the incredible urge in him to bring her so much pleasure she lost her breath from screaming his name, maybe he'd be able to excise her from the massive portion of his brain that she had suddenly occupied without warning? Maybe he could stop worrying that other men were noticing her perfect curves and get rid of his constant concern that she wasn't being properly cared for, that no one was taking responsibility for making sure she was eating properly or getting places safely when she went out.

The confusing, uncomfortable thing in his belly that had relaxed when he thought about introducing her to the pack as his partner almost went into meltdown at the very idea. Clenching his teeth, Leo ignored it. If he wanted to prove to Raj and Emmett that this insane attraction wasn't proving right their belief in the mate myth, having a one-and-done interaction with Delphinia would definitely be one way to do it.

Tyler, you are a colossal asshole.

It wasn't like he would go in with any pretenses, he argued to the part of himself that was disgusted by the very thought. If they were both on the same page from the beginning, what was wrong with it?

"Just find a way to tell them we're not interested in being part of their integration programs," James said derisively, bringing Leo back to the conversation he was still meant to be having with his Alpha. "I don't care how you do it, but Blue

Crescent is not interested in 'integrating' with anyone, let alone a mix of vamps, witches and humans."

"I—" Leo started, then cut himself off. This was how it worked. The Alpha made a decision, gave instructions, and the Beta carried them out. If part of him wished for an Alpha who took the wishes of those he led into account a little more, well, that was his own problem. "Yes, Alpha," he finished, forcing himself back into the uncomfortable deferential role, and stood to leave.

Now he had two reasons to need to find a way to get in touch with Delphinia Greenbranch.

Chapter 3

D ella was in her office when the call came in. Perhaps calling it an 'office' was a little ambitious; in reality, it was the second bedroom of her townhouse, crammed full of paperwork and discarded ideas she'd had the wherewithal to put on paper if not to carry out, usually after a glass or three of wine. There was a bed somewhere under the scattered papers, but it had slowly been overcome in her attempt to keep relatively clear the enormous wooden desk where she spent so many of the limited hours that she wasn't in the Youth and Community Department's main building where she worked.

The problem with bringing a significant amount of her paperwork-dense job home with her, as well as sitting on the Council of Witches as voice to express the opinion of the younger members of her own coven, for which there was a lot of paper-based prep work that needed doing, was that she alone was responsible for, she suspected, the destruction of literally thousands of trees. Not to mention the fact that once she'd discarded something into the morass of paperwork on the bed and floor of the room, finding it again was often more of a challenge than solving the issue for which she needed the paperwork in the first place.

She was considering whether she should use whatever part of this weekend she could spare from work to make a start on organising this room, at least as much as was physically possible, when the phone rang. She glanced at the screen, presuming it would be some sort of coven business needing her input—which, unfortunately, being one of the only government employees in the coven, seemed to be a steadily increasing occurrence—but the number wasn't one she recognised. She glanced at the clock, only partly surprised to see that it was approaching eight o'clock at night, and hesitantly lifted the phone to her ear.

"Della Greenbranch," she answered.

There was a brief silence from the other end.

"Hello?"

The caller cleared their throat. "Della, hi. My name's Leo Tyler. We, um, met at the meeting about the youth programs the other night." His voice was harsh, and it shot her right back to the moment he'd wound his fingers into her hair—a move that she would have considered unacceptable from someone she'd only just met if it hadn't felt so goddamn right —and his words sliding into her bloodstream and sending her internal temperature skyrocketing. *You smell like pure sex, and I can't get my damn mind off what you taste like underneath this tease of a dress. How long it's been since you were properly satisfied. How long it'll be before you let me get my mouth between your thighs and redefine whatever you used to think 'satisfied' meant.* Just the sound of that dark, deep voice coming through the phone, sounding, if she didn't know better, almost kind of… hesitant, was enough to send her heartrate into overdrive and centre her throbbing pulse directly between her legs. Just where he'd, what, threatened? Offered? Promised? To put his mouth.

"I remember you," Della said, cursing herself when the

slight shake of her voice revealed just how clearly she remembered their sudden, unexpected and unbelievably erotic interaction. She tamped down on the urge to clear her own throat, worried that it would give away the nerves suddenly coiling in her stomach at the prospect of speaking to this man again. Would he whisper more filth in her ear even if they were just talking on the phone? Was that just something he *did*? Or was she a special case, the desperate attraction he claimed to have to her an honest and, dare she hope, *unusual* occurrence?

"Delphinia. Della." Leo heaved in a deep breath, and she pictured him dragging a hand over his eyes. "Look, I owe you an apology. Accosting you like that the other night... I had no right to do that. To speak to you like that. I'm..." There was a pause, as though he was gathering himself. "I want to apologise."

"Apologise?" Della's mouth said, without permission from her brain. "You're seriously calling me at eight at night for the express purpose of apologising for holding me by the hair and telling me you wanted to put your *mouth* between my *thighs*?"

"Not exactly," he hedged. "I mean, it would have been earlier, but it's proven particularly difficult to get the phone number of a government employee, even when it's her work number."

"That's on purpose," Della said, pleased to hear herself sounding even slightly authoritative. After the media storm following the Dane debacle, she'd gone to some effort to make herself difficult for strangers to contact; it was good to hear that it had been effective. She added, "You know, it's partly to stop strange men from ringing me after hours."

"Good," Leo said. "You shouldn't ever have to deal with something like that." He seemed to notice the hypocrisy of his statement after he'd said it, and added, "Without a good reason, I mean. I mean... was there a lot of that, that you had to deal with?"

"Enough," Della said succinctly. "After the first time I appeared on TV, I had to change my number. Lots of men, human and supernatural both, seem to think that just because you care about kids, you're desperate to make an effort to have theirs."

From the other end of the phone came a sound that sounded almost like… had he just growled?

"Now why would you tell me that, when I'm trying to be a gentleman here?" Leo asked. "How can I think straight about apologising to you when you've got me halfway between jealous and furious?"

"You asked," Della protested helplessly, then steeled herself. "And who said I needed you to apologise anyway? The way you talked to me the other night, I-I didn't mind it. I liked it." The last sentence was so quiet, it was halfway to a whisper.

The noise he made this time was less of a growl and more of a hum of pleasure, the kind of sound she'd expect from a man—from a werewolf—if she was running her fingers over his heated skin. "Ah, Della," he said, and his voice was even darker than before. "I can't have this conversation over the phone, where I can't see your eyes, where I don't have your scent all around me. I called just to say sorry, just to ask if we could start over, but it doesn't sound like you want that, do you, sweetheart?"

"Not—not if it means you never talk to me like that again," Della said softly, wondering where the abject hell her brain had gone, saying things like that to a man she didn't even know. This wasn't a warlock from her coven chasing her to give him a shot, somewhat pre-vetted by their association through the coven. This was an unfamiliar werewolf from a pack that was notorious for keeping to itself—its Beta, no less. He might be an asshole, or abusive, or drunk on his own power and assuming it would be enough to get him under her skirt with minimal additional effort. An impression she was hardly refuting with her lust-drunk mumblings.

"Let me take you out to dinner," Leo said. "I'll talk to you like that all night if you want. We can scandalise the waiters and give them a good story to tell in the back."

"Leo—" Della said but was interrupted by his pleasure-hum again.

"Yes, gorgeous, keep saying my name. I'll have you screaming it if you'll let me."

"Leo!" Della said, trying to ignore the hot pulse thrumming between her legs, the way her nipples had puckered to tight points. "I'm trying to tell you something."

"Go ahead," he said, but his voice still held that deep-as-the-ocean tone to it, like every word she'd said was pulsing in his bloodstream as much as his were in hers.

"I'm… busy. At the moment. Very," Della managed around the rush of heat that came at the thought of him being as affected as she was. "I have a lot going on, I don't have a lot of nights off. So, if you want to go out, it'll have to be tomorrow night, or else not until the night after the next meeting."

"Tomorrow night," Leo said, and you would have thought she'd handed him a plate of gold nuggets at his tone at her agreement. "That's fine. I don't care what I have on, I'll clear it. Tomorrow will work just fine."

"I don't want to be a bother," Della said.

"Never," he interrupted. "Don't say that. Don't even think it. You could never be. Just—text me your address so I know where to pick you up."

"Oh, I don't think so," Della said, her sense of self-preservation finally making a belated appearance. "Tell me where you want to go and I'll meet you there. I like your filthy mouth just fine, but I'm not about to tell you where I live before we've even gone on a date, Leo Tyler."

He seemed to heave in a breath on the other end of the phone. "That's good. That's sensible. I-I'm glad you're being safe, even with me." The timbre of his voice dropped again, and she knew she was in for it. "But if you do ever decide to show me where you live, Della Greenbranch, the offer's open for me to show you just how much more I can make you like my filthy mouth."

Della's breath whooshed out of her in a rush. "Are you like this with everyone you're attracted to?" she blurted. "So dirty before you've even decided if you have enough in common to *like* each other?"

There was a long pause on the other end, and Della realised she was gripping the phone so tightly her fingers were aching.

"No," Leo said eventually. "Never before."

They were both quiet for a long moment, and she heard his slow, steady breathing on the other end of the line.

"Leo," Della said, knowing full well she was just saying it because of his response before, but unable to stop herself. "I have to… I have to go. I have a grant application to finish tonight. Just text me when and where to meet you tomorrow, all right? Now that you've tracked down my number."

He huffed out a quiet laugh. "What time works for you?"

"Any time after six is fine. I-I'll make it work."

"I'll text you," Leo said. "Sleep well, Delphinia."

"Good night, Leo," Della managed and, after a long beat of just listening to him breathe, hung up the phone.

Her hand fell into her lap as though the bones in her arm had suddenly disintegrated. The heat running through her body was like someone had dosed her with some sort of arousal juice, at about ten times the maximum recommended dose. She hadn't even laid eyes on the man tonight, and some-how, he still had her as worked up as if her nerves had been connected to live wires. Without conscious instruction from her brain, her thighs were clenching together and relaxing in an unfamiliar rhythm, as though she was desperate to feel something between them. And she *was*. She'd never had such as intense reaction to a man before, the sense that if she didn't somehow get closer to him, she might just cease to exist. The draw between them was like a string connected below her bellybutton, and it was tugging, tugging on her in a strange pull towards this man she barely even knew. If talking to him —the way he spoke to her—hadn't felt so strangely, incredibly *right*, the whole thing would have been an order of magnitude or two more disturbing. As it was, she was unnerved, sure, but not enough to stop her from meeting him tomorrow night.

Knowing this would mean she stayed up until the early hours of the morning to finish her grant application, she picked up her phone again and dialled one of the few people she knew would always accept a call from her, even at this time.

Magnolia answered after only two rings. "Della! You caught me at exactly the right time. I'm just on my way home from my shift." Maggie was a nurse at the local hospital but, though she often finished late at night, insisted that she didn't need a car; public transport was just fine to get her to and from work. If she'd been a supernatural, it might have bothered Della less, but as it was, she insisted on casting protective spells over the diminutive human at least every few months.

"Mags," she said, "hold on to your scrubs, all right? Something very weird has happened..."

Chapter 4

Leo had never been the kind of guy who went to a huge amount of trouble for a woman. What dates he went on—when he and whoever had picked him out of the pack to spend time with didn't just shoot straight past the civilised conversation part of the evening and directly to the incoherent moaning part—were usually casual and casually organised, a drink somewhere local, maybe a movie if they'd connected over a discussion of those. In truth, he'd never really needed to put in a whole lot of effort; when he did relatively infrequently give in to the urges of his body, not to mention his wolf, it had never been that difficult for him to find someone who was happy to keep things casual and go their separate ways after a couple of nights together.

But that level of qualified borderline disinterest wasn't going to fly with Delphinia. *Della.* She'd answered the phone as Della and sent what felt like every single drop of blood in his body shooting to his groin at the thought of growling the name while he was bringing her pleasure. It was a good thing he had made the call while he was home alone, because he had no doubt his eyes were glowing silver as the moon from the moment he heard her voice. Hell, from the moment he started digging for her number, the memory of her scent haunting him like a particularly insistent ghost.

He'd had every intention of apologising, then requesting to meet sometime to discuss the pack's involvement in the youth program and using that time together to not only explain James' position—because *that* wasn't going to make him feel like the world's biggest asshole at all—but also to desensitise himself to her somehow. He'd decided that his reaction to her, to her scent, at the meeting, could be nothing but a one-time failure on his part to adequately control his wolf when exposed to a beautiful woman. If he saw her again, he'd be able to manage it better. To find a way to get her out of his system if that was required. No matter how vehemently his wolf protested at the mere concept.

But this... this state of affairs had been truly unexpected. Was he seriously taking her on an honest-to-the-gods date, just to tell her the pack wasn't interested in being involved in her program? Just to see if he needed to find a way to get her into his bed for a night for the express purpose of hamstringing this borderline obsession he seemed to have developed with her? Something in him—his wolf, him*self*—just desperately wanted the chance to take her on a damn date, no agenda, just Leo and Della and a candlelit dinner and a bottle of wine and him spending the entire night trying to be a gentleman so that when he dropped her home, she might give him the chance to disprove the impression. He growled as blood rushed to his already painfully thickened cock. *For her*, the wolf was insisting. *It's for her.*

"Too fucking right," Leo snarled, "and that's the goddamned problem."

Because just as something in his chest relaxed somehow when he thought of having the right to bring her home and introduce her to the pack as *his*, his conversation with James had brought up another issue he hadn't properly considered. Blue Crescent wolves didn't integrate. They didn't fraternise outside the pack except when it couldn't be avoided. Blue Crescent wolves' partners, if they had them for the long term, were either other Blue Crescent wolves or, at a stretch, a wolf from another pack. Otherwise, there was a kind of one-night-stand culture that was probably perpetuated by neither the pack's Alpha nor Beta settling down with a partner of their own. If someone spent a brief time with someone outside the pack—a human, a witch or warlock, hell, even a vampire if their tastes ran that way—it was viewed through a sort of don't-ask-don't-tell lens, with the understanding that such associations were temporary.

The idea that he could bring Della into the pack and introduce her—a government-employed witch whose major focus was interspecies integration—as his partner, let alone if Raj and Emmett started talking about the whole mate thing again… the entire concept was ludicrous, and he'd been a fool to ever entertain the thought even.

Deep within him, his wolf howled, his canines lengthening in response to the thought, claws threatening to burst free from his fingertips. The very idea of letting Della go… the wolf was furious, desperately denying the impossibility of keeping her in his life. *I'll find a way*, a part of him insisted equally desperately. *I'll find a way to have her and keep her and make her mine. How could I even consider letting her go?*

An unwelcome memory of the man sitting beside her at the meeting putting his hand on Della's skin rolled through him, and he clenched his fists so hard, his elongating nails broke skin. Was he really prepared to let her go, let her find someone else, let another man have the right to put his hands all over her the way that Leo was craving to?

Too much. It was too much. He'd only met her the once, and just because merely talking to her on the phone was enough to get his cock hard as a rock and aching like never before, just because her scent blew his mind and his wolf was desperate to get his skin on hers, and she actually *liked* the way his mouth had run away with him after the meeting, and then again on the phone, and produced something more suited to a porno than an introductory conversation...

He just had to take her out for dinner, explain that the pack wasn't interested in being part of her afterschool programs, and maybe, just maybe, if there seemed to be even a chance of success, see if she might be interested in something casual enough between them to fulfil the requirements of the pack while at the same time getting this goddamn *obsession* out of his system.

Which meant planning a date, and not just a drinks-at-the-local-bar kind of date as per usual, either. Thus, the reason that he was, for almost the first time in the years since he'd taken on the role of Beta, coming close to what could be defined as 'pulling rank'.

Penny was one of the few Blue Crescent wolves with a job outside of the pack and its immediate requirements. She was a chef at a restaurant just outside of Blue Crescent territory, Maison, for which the waiting list for a table was several weeks long at a quiet time. But when her Beta rang and asked her to see if they could fit in a table for two that very night, she couldn't very well refuse.

Leo was going to make this a date that Della would never forget. Because something in him insisted that he never would, either.

Della was spending way too long getting ready for this meeting with Leo Tyler. Not that a beautiful dress, excellent makeup, and flawless hair weren't more than warranted when the meeting-date-thing was happening at Maison, of all places. How long had he been planning this, in order to get a table there? They'd only met—if you could call their first interaction so simple a word as a *meeting*—a few days ago.

Maybe, something in her whispered snidely, *he would have taken anyone there. Maybe you're nothing special to him, just a convenient body.*

Memories threatened to roll in, but she blocked them out, remembering Leo's voice on the phone when he'd growled out, "Never before." She couldn't let memories of Dane poison the strange but powerful connection she seemed to have with Leo. She wouldn't.

Just thinking of Dane brought a sour taste into her mouth, and she shoved the idea out of her head, running her fingers through the waves of her hair. She checked the time, realised she should be getting going if she wanted to get to the restaurant on time, and sat down to buckle her shoes. The heels were perhaps a touch excessive, but she'd bought them with one of her first pay checks after climbing out of the financial hole of dealing with Dane, and they represented her pride in her own achievements as much as her confidence in herself and, dammit, her desirability as a woman. *Confidence shoes*, Mags called them—in part due to her tiny stature, the little human had more pairs of shoes like these than Della could have worn in three months.

Although that might have been related to the fact that Della didn't incredibly regularly put herself in situations where confidence shoes were required. Sure, she went on dates—drinks with a co-worker here and there, or someone she'd met through friends, or a couple of times one of the warlocks in her coven or another to which they were close. Almost always someone to whom she had a prior connection, a way of knowing things about them or at least partially vetting them before she stepped out the door to meet them. Not that that would have protected her against Dane, who had been universally regarded as the nicest of guys before Della knew him. But it was something. Something more than going into a situation blind, and it gave her just the tiniest feeling of power in the interaction.

Not today.

She knew nothing about Leo, beyond his position as the Beta of Blue Crescent and that filthy mouth she inexplicably found so appealing. There was no information on which she could base an understanding of this strange connection she felt to him. He was a mystery to her, and while part of her was, if she was being honest with herself, completely terrified, another part of her was... excited? Intrigued? Maybe even slightly aroused?

It didn't make sense. This was breaking all her self-imposed rules. But then, what part of this made sense?

She stood, balancing herself in her confidence shoes, and collected her bag, wiping sweaty hands over the front of the deep blue dress. Sitting here considering it wasn't going to make a difference. She'd agreed to this date disguised as a meeting, and she was going to see it through, enjoy dinner without wondering who Leo had been planning on taking to this reservation, and work out what the hell she was going to do about the draw she felt to him.

Of course, she hit traffic. Extra traffic, because there were roadworks she hadn't been aware of. She'd factored enough time into her planned transit for a slow run just in case, but not enough for traffic to be so backed up that she had to actually stop repeatedly along the way. And then there was the time it took to find a parking space in that part of the city, and by the time she walked into the restaurant, she was twenty minutes late. She'd sent an apology text message when it had become clear she would be delayed but hadn't known by how much. Her perfectly styled hair had fallen out of the waves she'd put it in due to constantly running her hands through it in frustration and anxiety, and she had to stop herself from doing it again as the man at the door asked if she had a reservation. She gave him her own name as well as Leo's, but he barely got out a word before Leo was there, wrapping a hand around Della's and pulling her past the host stand. His hair looked as wild as hers and his eyes were glinting silver. When they got to the table, she hardly registered it, because she was still staring at him. He, too, had dressed up for the occasion, an open-necked button-down shirt under a suit jacket that struggled to contain his bulk.

He stopped beside the table, not letting go of her long enough for her to sit, and just stared at her.

"I'm so sorry I'm late," Della managed through lips that felt frozen and warm all at once. "There was traffic I didn't count on, and I couldn't get a park once I got here. I didn't think to factor that in. I'm sorry."

"I thought you weren't coming," Leo said, his voice halfway to a growl. He still had barely taken his eyes off her except to navigate between the restaurant's other patrons, feasting on her appearance in a way that made her glad she'd taken the time with her makeup and picked one of her most flattering dresses. For some reason, though, she had the sense that he'd have looked at her the same way if she'd been wearing pyjamas with her unwashed hair in a messy ponytail.

"Of course, I was coming," Della managed. "I told you I was."

"You look—" He ran a hand over his mouth and chin, shaking his head, then seemed to realise they were still standing next to their table. "Here, let me—" He let go of her hand to step behind her and pull out her chair for her. Okay, so this really was a *date*-date, or at least, he was going to treat it like one. Warmth spread in her abdomen, trickling through her veins like a champagne buzz as Leo circled the table to take his own seat. He was still staring at her as he sat.

"Do I have something on my face?" Della asked after a moment.

"What? No." Leo suddenly seemed to realise what he was doing and picked up the menu in front of him. "I just—you look lovely. I like your dress."

"Oh, this old thing?" Della joked, letting her hair fall forward to cover her face before she could consider the defence mechanism.

As he had the last time they were face-to-face, Leo reached out immediately and tucked her hair back behind her ear, seemingly before he was even aware of what he was doing. Astonishingly, his cheeks coloured slightly above the line of his beard as he let his hand drop to the table's surface. Della wondered if her mouth was hanging open. It felt like it should be, her breaths gasping audibly in and out at the throb of pure arousal that shot through her at his touch. She couldn't seem to look away from his eyes, once again sparking pure silver.

"Does that make you uncomfortable?" Leo asked after a long moment. "Compliments? Is that why you do that thing with your hair?"

"I-I don't know," Della admitted. "I don't do this all that often." She swallowed and forced a flirtatious tone into her voice. "Maybe I'm just doing it so that you'll touch me. You always push it back."

Leo's voice went ocean deep. "Della, if you want me to touch you, you don't have to goad me into pushing back your hair. All you have to do is give me permission and I'll have my hands on every damn inch of your body."

Della's eyes fell shut as she heaved in another deep breath, her hands twisted together on the table's surface. Her eyelids flew upwards when Leo's hand covered both of her own.

"I'm sorry," he said. "I won't do that again if it takes your eyes away from me. That's why I do it—pushing your hair back. I-I have this need to have your eyes on me, Delphinia. I don't like the risk that they'll be covered up."

She stared at him for a long moment before she found her voice. "I don't do it to goad you into anything. I'm sorry. I'm sorry I made that joke. I don't even think about it anymore, the hair thing, it just happens. No one else has ever commented on it."

A slight smile spread over Leo's lips. "Maybe everyone else just isn't looking closely enough."

She found herself smiling back, that inexplicable thread that seemed to connect them tugging below her bellybutton once more.

The waiter approaching the table interrupted their sexually charged stare-off. "Have you had a chance to look at the menu?"

"Not yet," Leo said while Della was still struggling to regain the capacity for speech. "Could you give us another few minutes?"

Certain that if she waited more than a moment, they'd just revert to staring at each other once more, Della hurriedly flipped the menu open and tried to focus on the various delicious options it listed.

"How on earth did you get a table here at such short notice?" she asked, examining the main courses, and immediately cursed herself. She'd sworn to herself she wouldn't ask any questions that she wasn't sure she wanted the answer to, but apparently her mouth had other plans.

"One of the chefs is a Blue Crescent wolf," Leo said. "I spoke to her, and she had them fit us in at short notice."

"Why do you look uncomfortable saying that?" Della asked.

A small smile raised the corners of his lips. "You're very perceptive."

"That's not an answer."

"You're right, it's not." Leo looked away from her for a moment. "I'm the pack Beta, you know that. It gives me a certain level of... influence, I guess you'd say, among the wolves. But I try not to use that power for my own ends. It should only be used for the good of the pack, in my opinion. Penny couldn't very well tell me she wouldn't fit us in if it were at all possible. I wanted to bring you here, so I put pressure on her in a way she didn't deserve. In a way that power isn't meant to be used."

"You didn't have to do that," Della blurted. "I would have been just as happy going to some no-name burger joint. I don't need fancy."

"I'd do it ten times over just to see you in that dress," Leo said. "I thought you were beautiful before, but all dressed up like this..." His eyes flicked over as much of her as was visible above the table, and she felt his gaze like he'd traced fingertips over her skin. "You're a fucking work of art, Della."

She felt a shy smile spread across her face and couldn't stop her eyes from falling to focus on his hands in embarrassment at the extravagant compliment. "Thank you," she murmured.

Leo reached forward and, with one finger, tilted her chin back up so she was looking at him once more. "Give me back those eyes," he said, his voice softer now, gentler.

"Ready to order?" the waiter asked cheerfully from beside them, interrupting what would surely have devolved into another erotic staring competition.

"Yes," Della blurted, trying desperately to remember what she'd wanted to eat. "Leo?"

If she hadn't been paying such close attention, she might not have noticed the way his hand on the table's surface clenched into a fist when she said his name.

"If you are," he said.

They placed their orders, and then Della let herself meet Leo's eyes again. "After that, it seems like a bit of a letdown to ask you how your day was."

He let out a huff of a laugh. "It was busy. Our Alpha, James… he's a bit hands-off in the way he leads the pack. He's still happy to make decisions, but a lot of the legwork tends to fall to me. So, I manage a lot of pack business on his behalf." It didn't sound like he was a particularly big fan of this method of management, but the closed-off look on his face told Della that pressing him for details might not be a particularly productive idea.

"And when you're not doing that? Managing the pack, that is. What do you like to do for fun?"

There was a short pause. "It's not exactly for fun," Leo said slowly. "But by training, I'm a carpenter. So, I do a lot of fixing things for the people who live near me."

"Do you ever just make things for the sake of it?" Della asked. "For the enjoyment of it, rather than to fix someone's problem?"

Was that really a blush rising in his cheeks? "Sometimes," he admitted. "I make furniture. Mostly for the poorer families in the pack, so I know they've got something that isn't going to fall apart in a strong breeze. Tables, chairs, bookcases, that kind of thing."

"It doesn't sound like you're particularly good at spending time just on yourself," Della noted. "It's always for someone else, isn't it?"

"The furniture—eventually, I guess," Leo said. "But the process of making it, that's just for me. It's easy to get lost in the creation part of it, making something useful out of… not quite nothing, but close enough that it feels like it."

"What about before you were Beta?" Della asked. "Before you had so many people to look after."

"I never really thought about it like that," Leo said. "That the job is looking after people."

"What did you think being Beta was?" Della asked with a smile.

"Mostly imposing James' will on people who would very happily continue to do otherwise," Leo said with half a laugh.

Della paused, wondering if she should ask this question or if it was crossing a line. He'd looked so closed-off before— should she just leave it and change the subject? But in the end, she couldn't help herself, or her rampant need to learn more about him and actually try to *understand* this man. "It sounds like you don't exactly enjoy what you do. Why do you do it?"

He looked at her consideringly for a long moment. "It's my job," he said simply, after the silence had stretched so long that Della regretted ever asking the question. "My father was the Beta before me, and my grandfather before him. I took an oath when I inherited the position. My role is to help bring the Alpha's instructions to fruition. James is the Alpha, so it's his opinion that's important. His vision for the pack is my responsibility to carry out."

"It just doesn't sound like you particularly enjoy, or maybe approve of, the way he runs the pack?" Della said, phrasing it as a question and knowing she was treading on dangerous ground here. "I guess I'm just wondering… why don't you find a way to change it if you don't like it? Speak to him or see if your packmates feel similarly and bring him a collective opinion. Find a way to act, rather than just allowing things to continue as they are."

To her surprise, this garnered the same humourless half-laugh as before. "I hate to say it like this, but, Della, you just don't understand how the internal politics of werewolf packs are run. You're not in one, so that makes complete sense, but it's an alien concept to someone on the outside. There's a way that things are done and organising a community protest isn't one of them. The Alpha's word, even if you don't agree with it, is tantamount to law. If I go against him, he can kick me out of the pack with barely a thought, Beta, or no. I would go from being responsible for hundreds of people to being totally packless—an Omega, is what we call them. It's not particularly polite," he added with a heart-melting smile. "I probably wouldn't repeat that term to anyone if I were you."

"Your secret is safe with me," Della promised. She took a sip of her drink, which she hadn't noticed arrive. Had the glass of wine been there since she sat down? She blinked at it, then focused back on Leo. "Would it be so awful for that to happen, though? I know you'd miss your position and what it means you can do for your packmates, but at least you'd be free of an Alpha who it sounds like he treats you like some kind of—of enforcer."

"There are so many things wrong with that, I don't even know where to start," Leo said, but there was no malice in his tone. At some point while they'd been talking, their food had arrived too—how had she been so focused on him that she missed that? "It's not the position I'd miss, not at all. In a lot of ways, it would even be a relief to be free of the responsibilities of being Beta. Not to be responsible for the welfare of hundreds of people. But then I wouldn't be able to… to help them anymore. To fix it when they have problems. I mean, what if the next Beta was like James? He would get to choose who came next if he expelled me from the pack. And he could pick someone who didn't give a shit about our people, and then where would they be? I can't risk that for them." He took a bite of food, looking like he was gathering his thoughts. "Then there's the Omega thing. Wolves aren't meant to be packless. It's not good for them, physically or mentally. And I could apply to join another pack, but the process is long, and they'd want a full report of why I was expelled from Blue Crescent. It would be hard enough to join a new pack even without having the mark against my name of being a Beta who abandoned his duty."

"But you wouldn't have abandoned it," Della protested.

"That's how it would be interpreted," Leo explained. "I told you, there's a specific way things are done in werewolf packs. We're traditional people, wolves. Conservative. We like to stick to tradition. And if you've only just recently shown a great disrespect for the traditional way of doing things…" He shrugged, but his shoulders looked tight. "No other pack would want me."

"I can't imagine that," Della blurted, her stomach hurting somehow at the evidence of his pain at the thought.

"What?" Leo asked.

"Not—not wanting you," she managed quietly. "They'd be fools not to accept someone willing to put himself through so much for his people."

"Is that why you're looking at me like that, Della?" Leo asked, half his mouth quirked upwards in a smile. "My community-minded attitude?"

"How am I looking at you?" Della asked.

"Like you're hungry," Leo said, voice deepening once more. He raised an eyebrow, somehow turning it into the sexiest facial expression the world had ever seen. "Like you're hungry, and I look like a meal."

Della sucked in a breath, trying to ignore the pulse of heat throbbing through her that he seemed to be able to call up at will. "Maybe I am hungry," she said, gesturing to the meals they'd hardly touched. "This food is spectacular, and I've barely managed to eat any of it."

To her surprise, his heated expression faded immediately

—the heat was still there, but muted, and almost hidden under something she couldn't identify.

"I don't like the idea of you being hungry," he said with the air of someone admitting a secret. "I don't know why, Della, but it does something to me, the idea of you not being… properly cared for."

"I care for myself, Leo," she said in a kind of confused protest.

"What if I wanted to do it?" Leo asked, his voice soft. His gaze was trained on her with the precision and intensity of a military sniper, the colour of his eyes flicking deeper and deeper from green into glowing silver once more.

Della shook her head to clear thoughts of Dane from it. "I don't know," she said, focusing somewhere in the region of his collarbone. "That's a pretty intense question to ask someone on a first date, Leo," she added, hearing the note of desperation in her own voice.

"This whole night has been intense," Leo said, his voice harsh. "We were intense the moment you got wet hearing me talk filth to you behind the lectern at a public meeting. This night was intense the second you put on that dress for the express purpose of making my dick hard, Della. Because it worked. It fucking *worked*."

Her mouth dropped open and she gasped in a breath, arousal and disbelief powering through her in equal measures.

Leo's hands, flat on the table's surface, clenched into fists and he reined himself in with a visible effort. "Della, I don't think I've ever told anyone else the things I've told you tonight. Maybe we're just intense people. Maybe we're just intense together." He squeezed his eyes shut for a long second, and when he opened them, the green tinge had returned to them. Still mostly silver, but no longer the colour of the rising moon as they had been before. "I can try to keep it in check, if it would make you more comfortable."

"No," Della blurted before she could think it through. Shock and arousal and distant memories of the past swirled through her brain. "No, I don't want you anything but genuine. But, Leo, I can't—" The words stuck in her throat at the concept of discussing what had happened with Dane. She cleared her throat. "I'm busy," she said instead. "I told you this was my only night off until the next meeting. I was up until almost three o'clock this morning finishing a grant application. And that's not unusual for me. I don't have time for this to be something *intense*. Maybe in a few years when the council's agenda is a bit more advanced, but I can't get into a *relationship* right now."

His expression as he looked at her was completely inscrutable. The silence stretched out, long and heavy.

"I'm not really a relationship kind of guy," Leo said eventually. "So, you probably don't have to worry about that too much with me. But, Della, I want to keep seeing you. Even if it's just the infrequent night you have off. There's something here, you can't deny that, and I want to ride that out."

For a long moment, Della just stared at him. "Okay."

"Okay?" Leo repeated, like he couldn't believe what he was hearing.

"Okay," Della confirmed. "It sounds like we're on the same page. That's… good." She pushed her chair back and stood. "I'm just going to duck to the bathroom."

"Della—" Leo said, coming half out of his chair with a look of near-panic in his eyes.

She laid a hand over one of his. "Leo. I'll be right back. I promise."

In the restroom, she splashed cold water on the pulse points in her wrists and tried to calm her racing heart. What in the name of all the gods had she just done? Agreed to some kind of half-relationship with Leo? And in between the weekly or fortnightly nights she was able to offer him, would he expect to be able to be with someone else? Multiple someone elses? This man who wanted to *provide* for her—what the hell did that even mean?

She could not relive what had happened last time she attempted a serious relationship with a man to whom she felt a strong draw. Hadn't she and Dane started off as something casual too? And it had ended up with her in pieces on the floor. She wouldn't survive going through that again.

But she couldn't deny the profound draw she felt to Leo, the inescapable heat between them, even when they were doing something like discussing the politics of his pack. There was something between them, something she desperately wanted to explore.

The question was if she was brave enough to risk it.

What the hell? *What the hell?* What had he just *done?*

Was there any surer way of driving a woman away than telling her you weren't interested in a relationship? Especially when it contradicted everything you'd shown her so far?

He could not handle having driven Della away. If she ran, he would chase her. He'd never been surer of anything in his life. This thing between them… something in Leo *needed* to explore it, find out how deep it ran. And if that meant pretending he didn't have a profound and driving urge to be everything to her, for as long as it took for her to truly trust that he was here for the right reasons, he'd take that chance and be happy to have it. He'd take every free night she had and hoard those moments like a miser.

It was true, he didn't know much about relationships. In the whirlwind of his usual life, he'd never felt like he had enough to offer a woman, not to mention the urge, to attempt one. But with Della ... with Della, there was nothing he wanted more than the opportunity to try.

So, what the actual *fuck* had he just done? Opening up to her like he never had to a woman before about the pack and his place in it, talking filth to her the way the burn for her in his blood demanded that he do... it didn't matter than she'd expressed that she liked it when he spoke to her that way. He had no business using it as some kind of... of weapon against her hesitancy. He was better than that, wasn't he? *They* were better than that.

If there was a *them* at all after the way she'd practically sprinted away from him. Didn't she know what the threat of a chase did to a werewolf? His blood was thrumming with the need to go after her, to pin her body down, lift that mindfuck dress and show her that what was between them might be intense, but it would be *worth it* to explore where it went. He'd *make* it fucking worth it, every second of her time that she gave him. He'd take care of every need she had. He'd make her *his*.

He made the conscious decision not to analyse this need to possess a woman in a way that he had never felt before, which had suddenly made itself so profoundly known. He ground the heels of his hands into his eyes and let out the quietest groan he could manage, reminding himself that it would be beyond inappropriate to follow Della to the bathroom. She'd left her bag here. She'd *promised* him she'd return. She would come back. He just had to be patient, even if every second that she spent outside his field of view—in a dress that would draw the eye of any man with a pulse, no less—felt deeply, fundamentally wrong.

"Leo?"

Her voice—saying his name, no less—almost had him shooting out of his seat again. He gripped the edge of the table hard enough that it creaked as she hesitantly slipped back into her seat, giving him a shy smile that did nothing to remove the worry from her eyes.

"Della," he managed.

"Are you all right?" she asked. A crease had appeared between her eyebrows, and he wanted nothing more than the right to reach out and smooth it away.

"I'm fine," he said instead.

"Really?"

"You came back," he said, since apparently his brain had stopped controlling the movements of his mouth. "I'm fine."

This time, her smile looked slightly confused, although marginally more real. "Look, Leo—"

Panic spread in him, potent and hot. "Della, stop. If you're about to end this, at least give me a minute, give me a chance—"

"Actually, I'm trying to agree with you," she said.

For a moment, Leo was shocked into silence. Finally, he gathered himself enough to ask, "Which part?" *Please let it be the part about wearing that dress to make me hard. Tell me you want me as much as I want you.*

"You're right," Della said. "There's something between us, and I do want to… to see where it goes. To ride it out, like you said. But we need some… some ground rules if we're going to give this a shot."

"Ground rules," Leo said slowly. "What kind of ground rules?"

"We have to keep this casual," Della said. "Like I said, I don't have much free time, so that part shouldn't be too hard. But I'm not in a place for it to turn into anything serious."

Knowing he'd probably stumble over speaking so profound a lie, Leo kept his agreement to a nod. He would have agreed to go to the moon if it meant he had a chance to keep seeing her.

"No one else while we're seeing each other," Della said,

and Leo's vision went red so rapidly that he almost missed her adding, "I'm sorry if that's a dealbreaker, given how little time I have, but I couldn't handle that. Not after... I just couldn't."

He swallowed down his irrational rage at the idea of her being with another man long enough to say, "Della. That was never even in question for me. It's far from a dealbreaker."

Her shoulders relaxed just a little, and this time the smile she shot him was real, real enough that it shot a bolt of arousal through him. Was there anything this woman could do that wouldn't make him hard? Or harder, rather, since it felt like the majority of the blood in his body had been swelling his cock since he caught her scent before she entered the restaurant. He heaved another dose of it into his lungs, just to feel a piece of her in him.

"This is the last one," Della was saying. Leo refocused on her, on her perfect mouth. "I don't, Leo... I don't think I want everyone knowing. Not if we're keeping this a casual thing, a temporary thing. It doesn't have to be a secret between us or anything, I wouldn't do that to you, but I'm not going to tell my entire coven."

Leo swallowed, trying to read the complex mix of emotions running across her face. What was it that Della was worried about if people knew? The witches were generally a fairly accepting group; they surely wouldn't have a problem with her dating a werewolf the way his pack—or rather his Alpha—would make an issue of him being with a witch. Was she scared people would judge her for having a casual—or apparently casual, for as long as it took him to convince her to let it become otherwise—relationship? Little did she know, this "ground rule" that had her looking at him with such trepidation actually *solved* a problem for him, giving him time to work out how to convince the pack to accept his relationship with a witch. Because after tonight, despite his best intentions to make it into some way of *getting her out of his system*, he'd completely burned through the resolve he'd had to make this a one-time thing. He wanted—no, *needed*, with an intensity that bordered on painful—to see where this thing between them would go. To keep her for himself for as long as he possibly could.

"I'm," he cleared his throat, "I'm fine with that, Della."

Relief was like a physical blanket as it spread over her. Her shoulders dropped to their normal position and the crease between her eyebrows finally went away. A real smile spread over her lips, and he was struck by a desperate need to feel it against his own mouth.

"Was that your last one?" he asked.

"That's all the ones I'd thought of," she offered. "If we come up with more, though, we should leave it open."

"Deal," Leo said. He looked down at their meals, which were barely touched, to avoid staring at the swells of her breasts visible over her neckline. Once he was sure he could control himself—beyond the transformation of his eyes, which were surely still glowing bright silver—he met her gaze again. "So, is this the part where I finally get around to asking how *your* day was?"

Her laugh rang in his ears like a symphony.

"Della," he blurted, "I just want to spend some time with you. See where this goes. That's all." *Liar.* "I can't pretend I'm not attracted as all hell to you, but we can try to be friends as well as that. As well as… all of this."

Gods, he loved how one side of her mouth lifted a fraction of a second before the other when she smiled. He wanted to lick those perfect lips before introducing the rest of her body to his tongue. *Calm down*, he ordered himself. *Keep your shit together. Don't scare her away now when you've just made some headway.*

"I'd like that," Della said softly. "My day… my day was busy too." She let out a light laugh that rang like music in his blood. "How familiar are you with governmental procedures?"

He managed to keep himself in check for the rest of the meal, keeping their discussion to work and friends and his pack and her coven. Being a fairly high-ranking member of her governmental department apparently meant that Della was called upon for all sorts of government-related things by the members of her coven, most of them only tangentially related to the work she did, which only contributed to her busy lifestyle.

"But why would they expect you to know anything about small business licences?" he asked in disbelief, trying to control his arousal as she licked pastry crumbs off her lips from her dessert. "You work in youth and community."

"That was my response as well." Della laughed, sitting back from her plate. "But we eventually worked out which permits they needed to apply for."

"You couldn't just say, 'That's not my department,' and send them on their way?"

She shot him a half-smile that had more than a hint of flirtation in it. "You're not the only one who likes helping people when they can, Mr. Big Bad Beta."

"Keep looking at me that way, and I'll have you calling me that for a very different reason, Della."

She raised an eyebrow, her shyness from earlier completely forgotten. "You're very confident."

He signalled the waiter. "Let me get the bill, and I'll show you why," Leo offered with a smile that he could feel was all teeth.

He watched as she bit her lip and then, impossibly, she nodded. Those strands of hair slid forwards and, as if on cue, they both reached out to tuck them behind her ear again. Leo caught her fingers in his own and dropped their joined hands to the table. "Della, I'll keep talking filth to you because you've told me you like it, and because my mouth tends to run away with me when you're around. But I will never, ever go further than that unless you're one hundred percent on board. Do you hear me? Don't give me a *yes* with doubt in your eyes."

"There's no doubt, Leo," Della said, her voice breathless. "I-I want you. I want… whatever you want to show me."

Heedless of the other diners, Leo lifted her hand to his lips and licked a slow path down one of her fingers. The look on her face and the parting of her lips as she sucked in a breath was a hundred times worth the painful throb of his engorged cock at his first taste of her skin. "Whatever I want to show you, huh?"

"Leo," Della breathed.

"Excuse me?" the waiter asked from next to Leo, sounding hesitant to interrupt them.

Della yanked her hand back like she'd been burnt, but Leo held her gaze for a long moment afterwards, just to revel in her enlarged pupils and wide eyes before he acknowledged their server. Clearly, he'd been right in the prediction he'd made over the phone—they'd be giving the waiters some stories to tell in the back tonight.

He'd rarely been less cognisant of anything than he was of paying the bill and asking the server to pass on his greetings and thanks to Penny. His attention was so focused on Della shifting around in her seat like she was uncomfortable, her tongue repeatedly peeking out to wet her lips.

"I'm going to need you to walk out of here in front of me," Leo admitted when Della went to push her chair out.

"Why—" she started, but then he quirked an eyebrow and watched as her eyes widened in understanding of the condition she had put him in.

"I can only hide so much," he admitted with half a smile. "And you've got me about a million miles past that."

"Really?" she asked breathlessly. She sounded utterly shocked by his response to her, to her *scent* that felt like it should be permanently soaked into his skin by now.

"Della, you'd get me hard in a pair of old pyjamas, let alone that dress. I've been sitting here watching you lick those pretty lips for hours. I just got my first fuckin' *taste* of you. You've had me like this pretty much since the moment you walked in."

Was he imagining it, or was there just a hint of satisfaction mixed in with the surprise on her face?

"Stand up, then," she said, just the barest touch of a challenge in her tone. "I'll cover you."

Once I'm done with you, you're goddamn right you will, he thought but was too busy positioning his erection so it was as unobtrusive as possible and using Della's swishing hips as a visual barrier between his thickened cock and the rest of the high-class restaurant, which by now was thankfully mostly empty. Not that seeing the drape of material covering the swell of her ass did anything to help the situation whatsoever.

Once they were outside, he took a deep breath of the cooling, city-dense air, intending to calm himself down, but instead getting a deep lungful of Della's scent. He turned to face her, and something in his expression had her backing up a step.

"One thing you should know about werewolves, sweetheart," Leo managed, his voice almost a growl.

"What's that?" Della asked breathily.

"Only run from one if you want to be chased," he said, and this time it was a growl that left his lips. He could feel his canines pushing to elongate and he fought the urge.

Eyes on him, Della backed up another step.

With a snarl, Leo lunged forwards until he had her pinned against the building's brick wall, And the feel of her body against him was so perfect, it made him want to howl at the moon—softness and glorious curves that pressed against every hard plane of him. And the way his erection fit at the notch of her thighs... *perfect* was too small a word.

"Della," he ground out.

"Leo," she moaned, and every nerve in his body lit up like he'd been electrocuted. He couldn't stop his hips from rocking forwards into hers, grinding against the apex of her thighs, or the growl that escaped when he did.

"Where are you parked?" he demanded of her, begging his body to behave.

"W-what?" she stammered out.

"I need to kiss you, Della, and I've been hard up over you for hours. When I get my mouth on yours, it's going to be fucking indecent, and I won't do that to you on the street where anyone could walk past."

"In… in the parking lot on North," she stuttered, and Leo forced himself to take a step back from her, mourning the separation of their bodies.

"Show me."

A sense of pure masculine pride filled him when her legs shook as she stepped away from the wall. Without a word, he took her hand and let her lead him a few streets away to a carpark, stopping beside a small green vehicle. Her pupils were still so wide, he could barely see the colour of her eyes when she turned to him.

"This is me."

Checking only once that they were alone, he tugged her between the cars and once more aligned their bodies. Her moan could have brought him back from the dead with the bolt of electricity that it shot through his body, and without speaking, he wrapped a hand around the back of her neck and covered her lips with his.

The feeling that surged through Leo was like nothing he'd ever felt before. Arousal and possession and homecoming, all at once. Her hands fisted in his collar, slipped inside his jacket to twist in the fabric of his shirt, her body shifting where he had it pinned to the car, writhing against him as she met the press of his tongue with sweet swipes of her own. He was harder than he'd ever been in his life, and every time she dragged her tight curves over his bulge, it got worse, until he thought he might explode.

"Leo," Della moaned against his lips, pressing the juncture of her thighs so perfectly against his hardness. "Leo, I need—"

"I'll give you what you need," he growled, reclaiming her mouth with his own. *Every goddamn thing you need, I'll give it to you.* Dragging his hands down over the sweetness of her breasts and the curve of her waist and hips, he slipped one under the hem of her teasing dress and cupped her sex in his hand. Her gasp was like being granted entry to paradise, especially when he pressed down, and it morphed into a moan.

"Leo," Della breathed, desperation in her tone. "Please." Her head tipped back, exposing her throat, and the wolf in him wanted to howl at the show of surrender. He pressed a kiss there, dragging his teeth over the smooth perfection of her skin as he found the swollen bud at the apex of her sex and began massaging it through her panties.

"Wet little thing, aren't you, sweetheart?" he growled against her skin. "I wasn't the only one in that restaurant needing this. Sitting there with your wet little pussy soaking through your panties. Next time, you tell me, and I'll take you out the back and eat this perfect cunt until you scream so loud the whole building knows what I'm doing to you." He bit down on the skin of her exposed throat and felt the shudder roll through her entire body as she came, gasping and moaning and chanting—chanting his *name* in a way that made his chest fill with the most absurd amount of pride. "That's right, sweetheart. Say my name. Tell me who's making you come."

One final round of shudders rolled through her, and then she was grabbing at his wrist to slow his insistent fingers, pushing up on her toes and dragging his mouth down to hers.

"Leo," she gasped against his lips, panting for breath. "That was—" She shook her head, eyes wide.

"You're incredible," he murmured, stroking back the hair that had fallen over her face.

One of her hands fell to cup his bulge where it was throbbing in his trousers. "Can I..."

"Not here," he said, though denying her—denying himself —caused a bolt of physical pain to shoot through him.

"But you just—" she protested.

"Next time, Della. I won't let you get on your knees in a public parking lot, and you'd best believe the first time you get me off, it'll be in the mouth that's been teasing me all damn night."

Another shudder ran through her body. "Leo," she breathed, and he claimed her mouth again.

When they finally broke apart, he was impressed that he still had the wherewithal to deny his wolf's urging to tackle her to the ground and claim her for his own. Regular Della was incredible, but satisfied, grateful Della? It was like she was doing her best to convince him to go back on his word and see if her tongue felt as good on his dick as it did stroking into his mouth.

"It's getting late, sweetheart," he managed, stroking a hand over hair tangled from his searching fingers. "You should get home."

Her hand smoothing down the side of his face felt indescribably good, somehow soothing and arousing all at once. "I had... the most incredible time tonight, Leo."

"Me too." He kissed her once more, pulling away before it could become something deeper. "Now you'd best get in that car and drive away, because your backseat is too small for me to do all the things I want to you, but it's starting to look pretty damn tempting."

"Are you trying to convince me to stay or go?" Della

asked, laughing, but she separated herself from him and dug her keys out of her bag. She slid into the driver's seat, and he leaned against the open door.

"Text me when you're home safe, okay?"

"Same goes if you get there before me." She looked up from fastening her seatbelt. "We both know you have my number, after all."

Her teasing smile remained in his mind long after she'd driven away. But when he found himself with his hand on his painfully swollen cock that night, it was the look of absolute shocked abandon on her face when she came for his fingers that he pictured. And because, after a full evening with Della, once wasn't nearly enough, the second time was to the memory of the way she'd gasped out his name.

Mine, the wolf in him was growling the entire time. *Mine.*

Chapter 5

M aggie rang when Della was getting out of the shower the next morning. For the briefest of moments, she thought it might be Leo calling, though he had no reason to call her. They'd exchanged "home safe" messages the night before after she'd managed to walk in through her front door, legs still feeling slightly shaky from the strength of the orgasm he'd given her. Her cheeks still heated when she thought about it—mostly from the memory of the location where she'd allowed him to put his hands up her dress —but she somehow knew she could no more have kept his hands off her than she could have stopped herself from breathing. *Maybe next time I can keep my head in the game enough to insist on being somewhere private*, she thought with chagrin as she reached for the phone, blood already pounding in her veins at the promise of a *next time*.

A rush of disappointment flowed through her for just a moment when she saw Maggie's name on the screen, then a matching pulse of guilt at the response.

"Morning, early riser," she greeted her friend.

"Overnight shift," Mags explained, absurdly chipper for

such an early hour, especially after a full "day" of work. "You're lucky I didn't ring during my break last night; I was so keen to hear how the date went. But I thought maybe you might still be *busy*." She emphasised the last word with a laugh at the double entendre. "So, don't hold out on me. How did it go?"

"It was… good," Della said, thinking of the hours they'd spent talking as she tried to ignore her body's response to nothing more than his presence, his voice, his shifting expressions. *Sitting there with your wet little pussy soaking through your panties.* Blood rushed to her face again.

"You are *not* trying to leave me with nothing more than 'it was good', Delphinia Greenbranch," Maggie protested. "I haven't been on a date in months. Della, please. *Details.*"

Della tried and failed not to laugh. "Okay, so we went to dinner at Maison—"

"At *Maison*?" Mags interrupted. "You're kidding me. Your werewolf is one fancy guy. How'd he manage to pull a table there at such short notice?"

"One of the members of his pack is a chef there," Della explained.

"Perks of being the Beta of one of the biggest packs in Mystic City, I guess," Mags joked, and Della tried not to think about Leo's discomfort with having used his influence in such a way. Tried not to relive the ups and downs of their conversation, the way she'd been so absorbed in him that she hardly even noticed her food.

"Yeah, so we went to dinner. We talked a lot." She wrinkled her nose at the realisation that they'd never even come close to discussing the youth programs, which were ostensibly the reason for their meeting in the first place.

"And?" Mags demanded.

"He's a really interesting guy. Very… dedicated to his pack."

"You're really not helping me here, Della," the human complained.

"We kind of talked about being… together," Della said hesitantly.

"*What?*" Maggie screeched. "Okay, that is worthy of discussion. How did it go?"

"It was kind of intense," Della admitted. "He… he wants to give it a try. Maybe as much as I do. That was pretty flattering." It felt kind of egotistical to even say the words—that someone like Leo Tyler was attracted enough to her that he accepted her packed schedule and specific ground rules without question.

"Ooh, saucy," Mags said. "And?"

"And I had a little… just a little bit of a freak out about it. He's a very intense guy, and for a minute there the whole thing just reminded me of Dane, you know?" It was almost painful to let his name pass her lips. Almost scary, as though by saying it she might somehow summon him.

"I can see why," Mags said sympathetically. "Big, bad dude, desperate to be with you, and everyone knows werewolves are possessive motherfuckers. What happened?"

"I ran away to the bathroom, spent a few minutes calming myself down, and decided I want to give it a shot. I won't let *him* control me anymore, even if it's just in memory. That part of my life is behind me now." Her voice was steady, but her hands were still shaking as she wandered into the kitchen and set about making coffee.

"Oh, Della." This time Maggie's voice was rich with understanding. "That's really brave. I'm proud of you."

"Thanks, hon," Della said.

"So, what did you two decide? You're going to give it a shot?"

"I guess so," Della said. "We're going to keep it casual, and you know what my schedule's like, so we probably won't see each other all that often. Every week or two when I have a night off, but that doesn't seem to have put him off, which is a good thing."

"Damn right it's a good thing!" Mags crowed. "What about after dinner? The way you sound when you're talking about this guy, Della, plus the way you said he talks to you... did you drag him into the backseat of your car or something?"

Della made herself laugh, but she wasn't sure it sounded convincing. "Nothing like that. He walked me to my car, we kissed, and I came home."

"Seriously?" Maggie sounded absurdly disappointed, as if she was the one who hadn't been permitted to get her painfully attractive date off when he'd clearly been in a state of extreme arousal. "Well, how was it?"

"The kiss?"

"No, the drive home. Obviously, the kiss, Della."

Della laughed again, this time for real. "I don't even have words, Mags. I have honestly never experienced a kiss like that before. The back seat thing was seriously looking like a viable option, but he pulled back and told me to text him when I got home safe. Said we could do better than a carpark to go further." She heard herself sigh in a way that, in someone else, she might have described as *besotted*.

"*Damn*," Mags said vehemently. "Can I have one? Can you organise that for me, now you have a connection in the pack?"

Della laughed again. "I'll do my best. I don't know if you'd call it a 'connection in the pack'. I asked him if we could keep the whole situation quiet, for now at least, if we're going to give this thing between us a shot."

"What? Why? If I were you, I'd be shouting it from the rooftops. 'I have a sexy werewolf lover. Be jealous.'"

Della took a sip of coffee. "Maybe it's silly, but I just couldn't stop myself remembering how everyone looked at me... you know, *after*. Like I was broken. Like I was a victim.

And I don't want to jinx it, but when this thing with Leo ends —obviously it's a different situation, but I don't want people's pity all over again. I don't want to be the girl who lost her 'sexy werewolf lover'. So, I think it's better to keep it quiet."

"I guess that makes sense," Maggie said slowly, cautiously. "I mean if that's what you want. *I'd* still be taking out an ad in the Mystic City Times, though."

Della snorted. Knowing Mags, she honestly might.

They talked a little more as Mags finished her trip home and Della got ready for work, then signed off with a promise to catch up soon. Between their two competing work schedules, they often went weeks without seeing each other in the flesh, but rarely more than a few days passed without at least a phone conversation between them. It was almost time for Della to renew Mags' protection spells, too—which the little human insisted she didn't really need—so they'd need to catch up for that soon. She made a mental note to schedule it the next time the two of them spoke.

When she walked into work, she half expected people to look at her differently, as though she might have 'I was given an orgasm through my underwear in a public carpark' emblazoned on her forehead. No one looked at her any differently than normal, though, and she made it to her desk without incident. She unpacked her things and sent off the grant application for review before settling into the usual rhythm of her work. She might sometimes get frustrated with it, but Della honestly loved what she did. The way almost every part of her job was directed towards helping people, making the lives of all those living in Mystic City—not just her own coven or even other witches and warlocks—better. She considered stopping for lunch, but there was enough work rolling across her desk and into her inbox that taking the break seemed like a waste of valuable time.

She barely noticed when someone stopped next to her

desk until Petra, one of her closest colleagues and one of the only werewolves in the department, tapped her shoulder. "Della. Reception asked me to tell you that your lunch arrived. It's downstairs."

"What?" Della asked dumbly, her brain still trying to detach from the paperwork she'd been filling out. "I didn't order lunch."

"Well, Nathan in reception asked me to pass on that it's arrived." Petra shrugged.

Della pushed back from her desk. "I guess I'd better go see what's going on." *So much for getting more work done by skipping the lunch break*, she thought ruefully, thrusting an arm in between the elevator doors to stop them closing. She slipped into the almost-empty space without checking who was in there and glanced at the buttons to check that the one for the ground floor was already illuminated. Then she looked up and almost bit through her tongue in surprise.

Karl Waterford was standing on the other side of the elevator, his brutal stare fixed directly on her, like he was trying to burn through her with his glare. Though they were in the same coven, as well as working in the same building, Della had kept a firm distance from Karl since the Dane Incident—the man across from her had been her ex-boyfriend's closest friend in the coven and still, it appeared, was holding a solid grudge against her for her role in his downfall. How anyone, let alone a warlock, could be on the side of someone who'd done the things that Dane had been demonstrably proven to have done was beyond Della, but clearly Karl was capable of it.

"Nice to see you again," she ventured, wondering if this was the kind of rift you could heal with words. "It's been a while."

"Not long enough," Karl all but spat, and then the doors opened on the ground floor lobby, and he was immediately striding through them, putting space between Della and himself with the kind of speed usually seen in a competitive athletic setting.

Doing her best to shake off the unexpected encounter, Della rolled her shoulders and proceeded to the building's front desk. Nathan, the receptionist, shot her an appreciative smile followed by a quick skim of his eyes over her body that was probably meant to be subtle enough to go unnoticed. "Della Greenbranch," he greeted her enthusiastically. "Lunch delivery for you."

"There must have been some kind of mistake," Della said, taking the parcel he held out to her for lack of an alternative option. The folded note stuck to its surface flipped open and she ran her eye over it, thinking it might reveal the parcel's true owner. Instead, she read,

Della–

It sounded like you might not have time for a lunch break today, so I thought I'd save you the trouble. From a no-name burger joint, as requested.

–LT

Her breath caught in her throat. All right, this was… this was dangerously sweet. He'd even remembered her line about the burger joint. In a daze, she thanked Nathan and proceeded back to the elevator. Once upstairs, she took the parcel to the staff room, which was mercifully only sparsely occupied, and sat down to open it.

It was, of course, a burger, and an enormous one at that. It smelled so good that her stomach, which hadn't even been hungry a moment earlier, growled loudly.

She pulled her phone out of her pocket and pressed the number he'd texted her from last night.

He picked up with a cool, "Leo Tyler."

"It's Della," she said, then added, "Della Greenbranch," in case he knew more than one person with the name.

His tone immediately softened. "Della, after last night, do you really think you have to introduce yourself with your surname when you call me?" There was a hint of a laugh in his tone, and her cheeks coloured.

"I just got your, um, burger delivery," she said, trying not to let her embarrassment colour her tone. "I was just ringing to say thank you. You were right, I was too busy to go out and get lunch today."

"I was sort of relying on you not having brought something from home," Leo admitted. "Have you eaten it yet?"

"Not yet. I just got it."

"All right, don't thank me yet, then. Have a bite. It's from a little burger place I know a couple of blocks from the edge of pack territory." He said the words easily, as though everyone measured geography that way. "The chef was a friend of my dad's back in the day, so I ate there a lot as a kid. I don't think it's changed a bit since then. Which is a good thing because you can't improve upon perfection."

Della had unwrapped the burger as he spoke and now took a big bite. And he was right—it was spectacular. The perfect mix of simplicity and subtle hints of spice. Juice dripped down her chin, and she lurched forwards to avoid it getting on her clothes.

"What was that noise?" Leo asked with a laugh from the other end of the line.

She had to finish chewing before she could answer. "Your burger attacked me," she said, laughing in return.

"Oh, I should have warned you—they're juicy."

"So, I have just discovered. You were right, though, it's

delicious. Definitely better than anything I might have bought for lunch."

"I'm glad you like it. I didn't," he paused, "I didn't like the idea of you going without food. And we didn't exactly get to focus on what we were eating last night, so I kind of owed you a meal."

"You didn't owe me anything," Della said. "But it was very sweet of you, either way."

"So, your day's been as busy as you thought it would be?" Leo asked. She had the sudden thought that he was trying to extend their phone call. Why didn't he want her to hang up? It couldn't be for the same reason she wanted the call to continue—that she liked hearing his voice so much.

"Busier," Della admitted. "You could print an encyclopaedia on the amount of paper that's crossed my desk this morning. What about you?"

"I had to mediate an argument between two families that originated, I kid you not, over who had the better vegetable garden. Helped fix a fence. Delivered a few edicts from James. The usual."

She hesitated. Should she engage with the edicts-from-James thing or was that overstepping the boundaries of their fledgling whatever-this-was? She settled for asking, "So who did have the best vegetable garden?"

Leo snorted a laugh. "Honestly, they were both pretty terrible. The argument was dead before it began. It had to be settled, though, so I mediated their fight."

"Their *fight*?" Della repeated in shock.

"It's how werewolves settle things," Leo said casually, as though refereeing a sanctioned brawl were no big deal. "From challenges for Alpha all the way down. We're fighters. Teeth and claws only. It was over before there a chance for anyone to do any damage—I made sure of that. No one got properly hurt, just a few scratches. But there's no longer any bad blood between the families. They've worked out their angst, and we can all go on with our lives."

Never before, had the differences between them been presented to Della so sharply. Questions buzzed through her mind like flitting fireflies, but what came out her mouth was, "Teeth and claws?"

"Ah," Leo said, sounding like he was gathering himself to respond. "Well, you know how we can shift into wolves?"

"I was aware of that part of the whole werewolf thing, yes," Della said, careful to keep her tone light.

"We can also partially transform," Leo explained. "I'm sure you've noticed I can't seem to keep my eyes from changing when I'm around you. They're usually green, you know. At least around everyone else."

Della felt a buzz of satisfaction run through her at the reminder that she affected him as much as he did her but said nothing beyond a hum of encouragement.

"In times when a wolf is feeling something... intense, I guess you'd say, we can also grow fangs and claws. And if it gets really full-on, sometimes the young ones find themselves getting a bit hairy. They don't usually have the control to arrest their shift halfway, though, so it's not something you see all that often."

"Wow," Della said, a laugh in her voice. "I'm starting to think I should have done some more background study on werewolves before getting involved with one."

"We're not so complicated," Leo said. "I, for example, right now just want to know you're eating your lunch."

Della laughed. "Maybe not so complicated to you, but you've grown up with it."

"That's fair enough," Leo said. "Well, what about coven culture? I'm sure there are some things about witches that I'll find equally mystifying."

"Well, there are definitely no sanctioned fistfights," Della said, then caught herself. "Sorry. That came out sharper than I meant it to. It's just an… unfamiliar practice to me. Fighting at all is frowned upon within witch covens. When you have magic in play, as well as emotions running high, it becomes infinitely more dangerous to let those instinctive responses rule you."

"It's fine," Leo said. "You'll have to try harder than that to offend me."

"I'll work on it," Della laughed.

"So how do you solve disagreements within the coven if there's no fighting?" Leo asked, sounding genuinely interested.

"I mean, there are still fights," Della admitted, "they're just not legal. The ones that use magic, at least. The ones without are just frowned upon. But if you don't feel like brawling it out, you can take your disagreement to the Council of Witches, and if they can't come to a decision, it gets brought before the Elders."

"Kind of like courts of law," Leo noted.

"The Elders are pretty busy, so it takes a lot to get something brought up to them," Della said. "The Council gets a lot of low-grade stuff, though, and we have to rule on a ton of dumb arguments."

"Hang on. We?" Leo asked. "You're on the Council of Witches?"

"Hadn't I mentioned that?" Della asked, trying to scan her memory over their conversation last night. It was hard to even remember a lot of what they'd discussed because she had so frequently been distracted by Leo before her, his big hands, the curve of his lips, his eyes so focused on her.

"You talked about Council things. But I thought you meant the Youth Council at work."

"Yeah, I guess that could be kind of confusing," Della admitted. "But, yes, I'm on the Council of Witches as well. It's part of why I'm so busy. It's a bit like having a second job some days."

"How the hell do you have time to sleep?" Leo asked.

It might have sounded like he was joking, but something in his tone made him sound almost indignant on her behalf.

"Are you upset because I'm on the Council?" Della asked hesitantly.

"What? No. Of course not." He hesitated. "I just don't like the idea of you having to go without, in order to solve other people's problems. Especially if it's sleep you're missing out on."

"Why does that matter to you?" she asked, honestly curious.

"Della, unless it's me keeping you up late, I just don't like the idea of you missing sleep. I can't explain it." Quietly, as if to himself, he added, "I can't explain any of this."

Della tamped down on the thing in her chest that immediately tried to draw parallels to the control Dane had exerted over her sleep patterns in the past and focused on the other part of his comment. "And why exactly would you be keeping me up late, Mr Tyler?" she asked, keeping her voice innocent.

"Oh, that's where you want to take this?" Leo asked with a smile in his voice.

"I can't imagine what you're talking about," Della teased.

"I can make you come like a freight train without even taking off your panties, sweetheart," he reminded her. "Imagine what I could do if we were somewhere I could strip you bare. And if you think I'd be satisfied with just once, you're kidding yourself. I'll be keeping you up late because you'll be too busy screaming yourself hoarse to remember that time is passing."

"W-what about you?" Della managed to ask through a mouth that suddenly somehow felt both numb and hypersensitive, like she was craving Leo's lips on her own again.

"Not happy that I stopped you last night, are you?" He sounded strangely satisfied by the thought. "Don't worry, sweetheart, I'll let you take care of me too. I'm fucking obsessed with that mouth of yours. Watching you bite and lick your lips all through dinner last night had me so hard... you have no idea. The damn second we have the opportunity, I'll be putting you on your knees and working out every single ounce of this need between your pretty lips. And that's not even touching on what I'm going to do to you when I finally get your body under mine."

Della's breath left her in a rush. She glanced around and was relieved to see that she was the only one in the staff room. "What are you going to do?" she asked, barely able to believe she was doing this.

A hum of approval came from Leo's end of the phone call. "The longer I have to wait, the harder you're going to get it," his voice rumbled down the line. "I'm going to pin you down and show you exactly how bad I've been wanting you, Della. Take you so hard you feel me between your legs for a full week. And then I'm going to flip you over and do the whole thing again, just so I get to watch your ass bounce when I'm pounding into you."

"Oh," Della managed in a gentle moan, her capacity to speak having apparently gone on hiatus. She swallowed through a suddenly dry throat. "That... I think I'd like that."

"You'd more than like it, Della," Leo assured her. "I'm going to have you begging me to put you on your back every time you have a free minute. And that's a promise, sweetheart."

Della heaved in a deep breath and desperately tried to work through her suddenly fever-hot body and the pulse of arousal she could feel thrumming between her legs to find some equilibrium. "That's some big talk you have there," she managed after a moment.

"Are you just trying to get me more and more worked up to prove it?" Leo asked, his voice so low it was almost a growl. "Because it's working, sweetheart."

There was a brief silence between them as Della tried to catch her breath.

"I don't know if I've mentioned it, but I *really* like that dirty mouth of yours," she said quietly after a moment.

"Oh, you will," he promised. "But in the meantime, I'd better let you go before I can't restrain the impulse to storm your building and use it on you."

Della almost managed a laugh, but the mental image of Leo bursting into her offices to satisfy *her*—with his *mouth*, no less—had once again stolen her breath. "I guess I should probably finish this and get back to work," she admitted. "The paperwork is probably piling up."

"I'll speak to you soon, sweetheart," Leo said, the sound of another promise in his voice. "Enjoy the burger, Della."

"Bye, Leo," she said, and then he was gone, and she was left trying to control her pulsing arousal in the empty staffroom.

She was just cleaning up the detritus from her burger when Petra and a couple of her other co-workers came in and headed immediately for the coffee machine.

"Are you all right, Della?" Petra asked. "You're kind of flushed."

"Just, um, ate some spicy food," Della lied. "I'm fine."

She put the wrappings from her lunch in the bin, trying not to think about the feeling that maybe something significant had changed in the course of that phone call.

Chapter 6

Leo had to stifle the urge to send lunch to Della every day of the week. The primal satisfaction of knowing that at least one of her basic needs was being met was deep and powerful and ran through him for hours after their conversation over her burger. That, however, might come across as a little creepy, he told himself, so he settled for scouring pack territory for the restaurant he was going to get the next meal from. A few days from now would be perfectly fine, he told himself. That wasn't creepy, right? To send your new sort-of girlfriend lunch every couple of days, when you couldn't see each other?

And he was absolutely chafing at the bit to see her again. He'd thought—he'd told himself—he'd be able to handle it, the infrequency of their meetings, as long as he knew he'd get to see her again soon. But it had only been a few days, and though they texted every day, his wolf was howling with the need to touch her, to… to *claim* her. Their car park kiss, spectacular though it had been, had far from calmed his desire for her, the opposite, in fact. Every night he dreamed of the way she'd shuddered and shaken for his touch, imagined what would have happened if he'd let her undo his pants and wrap those pretty little hands around his swollen length. Imagined marking the front of her pretty blue flirt of a dress to punish it for making him so fucking hard. Pictured wrapping her legs around his waist and taking her up against the side of her car, thrusting into her gorgeous body until she was gasping and moaning and screaming his name for the whole damn city to hear.

It wasn't exactly making him pleasant to be around, this raging unfulfilled need. When Emmett and Raj showed up for their scheduled weekly sport-watching-and-beer-drinking session, which it was his turn to host, the thunderous expression on his face when he answered the door was so fierce, it caused them to exchange a look of concern. Didn't stop them from coming into his house, though, which might have been preferable. He wasn't particularly good company now, when his every second thought was of Della. He'd thought about cancelling but didn't want to disappoint Em and Raj. Now it was looking like maybe he should have.

"Geez, what happened to you?" Emmett asked, leading the way into the kitchen to the fridge where he knew from experience the beer would be. "You look about ready to start a fight, man. And I know for a fact James still has you delivering his messages, so if that isn't enough violence for you, it must be something big."

"Is it your mate?" Raj asked with a touch of sympathy, accepting a beer from Emmett, and removing the cap with his teeth.

"Nothing," Leo snapped, "and she's not my mate."

"You wouldn't mind if I asked her out, then?" Raj added. "She's smokin' hot, and if she smells as good as you say…"

In half a second, Leo had the larger wolf pinned against the kitchen wall, Raj's greater strength and bulk seemingly failing him. "Try it, and I'll feed you your own fuckin' claws,"

Leo growled, feeling his own fingernails elongate along with his canines.

Raj raised both his hands in surrender. "Joking, Leo. I was joking. How would I even know what she looks like?"

With a snarl, Leo released his friend from the wall and stalked back across the kitchen to accept the beer Emmett wordlessly held out to him, trying to control his breathing. Neither of his friends spoke as he got himself under control, finishing the first beer in a few rough gulps and gesturing for a second. Slowly, his adrenaline rush receded, and his teeth and claws returned to their normal state.

Leo and Raj blinked at each other for a long moment before the bigger wolf took a swig of the beer he'd somehow managed to hold on to and asked without malice, "What the fuck was that, man?"

Leo had no answer for him. "I don't know," he admitted.

"I'm not going to say the M-word again," Emmett said from where he was still standing next to the fridge. "But I honestly think it's an option worth considering, Leo. Especially if the idea of her with someone else sets you off like that. I've never seen you get all possessive like that over a female. You're usually the most easy-going guy around."

"I don't understand it," Leo said in a low voice. It was hard, even to his best friends, to make this admission of weakness. "She's just… I don't know. It's like my wolf's instincts are constantly trying to take over with her. I just want to know all the time that she's safe, and all her needs are being met, and —" He ground his teeth together. "I want her so goddamn badly, you can't even imagine it. I feel like a heroin addict or something. Reading a text from her is enough to get me hard."

"I get you, man," Em ventured. "We were all pups once, we remember it."

"It's worse than that," Leo said. "Five times, ten times worse than when I was going through the first change and trying to learn to control my instincts. I get one fuckin' breath of her scent and everything in me just roars into overdrive to have her, claim her, provide for her. I didn't realise how bad it was until we went to dinner, but my wolf is—my wolf is fucking obsessed with this woman."

"So, you didn't…" Raj raised his eyebrows suggestively.

"No, we fucking didn't," Leo snapped.

"Maybe it'll get better once you have," Em suggested. "The wolf will feel more comfortable and stop being so desperate to make a claim on her."

"But what about the rest of it?" Leo asked. "You think after I've had her, this need to fulfil every wish and require-ment she has is going to get *better?* I can't even imagine that." He clenched his fists, trying to control his wolf, who was all but howling at the idea of finally having Della beneath him. "But she only wants something *casual*. Says she doesn't have time for anything else. How am I supposed to keep it casual when I have this shit roiling around inside me? James told me to fucking get her out of my system', and I swear to the gods that was my plan to start with. But I don't even know if that's possible anymore. And it's not like I can bring her into the pack as my m—" He caught himself. He'd almost called her his *mate*. "As my partner," he finished lamely. "She's a witch. She's not one of us. It would all be different if she was pack."

"True," Raj interjected. "Pretty much any of our females would be keen as hell to let the Beta work out those urges on her, casual or not."

"Raj," Emmett said with the ease of long practice. "Shut up. You're not helping."

"He's right, though," Leo said. "Part of me wishes she was one of us, but then she wouldn't be… her. And that's who I want." He swallowed another slug of beer and was surprised to find that it drained the bottle. He set it on the bench behind him. "Look, Raj, I'm sorry, man. I didn't mean to go off at you like that. Just don't talk about her like that, yeah?"

"Sure," Raj said easily, striding across the room to clap Leo on the shoulder. "Now how about we take a break from the talk and watch the game? Get your mind off it?"

They brought beers through to the living room and settled in for the remainder of the match. Leo found himself wishing it didn't take so much for a werewolf to get drunk—he could have done with the release as well as the distraction. He tried to fix his attention on the game on the TV, but he kept finding his thoughts returning to that scent he was so primally, profoundly drawn to, to the way one half of her mouth lifted before the other when she smiled, the way she gasped in arousal when he gave free rein to the dirty words that were always dying to come out when she was around. To the way she moaned and shuddered when she came for him.

That recollection sparked a response so intense, he locked himself in the bathroom doing the breathing exercises they taught the pups to get themselves under control when they were fighting to regulate their shifts, missing the end of the game in the process. The next one had almost started before he deemed it safe to come out again, that he wouldn't morph into the same furious ball of unsatisfied need at the first provocation. He did better in the second game, possibly partially thanks to the beer he was drinking like water, fast enough that it was giving him a slight buzz. He saw Em and Raj exchange a glance when he reached for another—how many was he up to now? Nineteen? Twenty? Wisely, neither of them said anything.

They said their goodbyes with claps on the shoulder and Em offering, "Give me a ring if you want to talk, bro. I promise I won't even mention the M word."

"I might do," Leo said noncommittally, knowing he probably wouldn't. He'd felt stupid enough discussing it face-to-face in his own kitchen; he struggled to picture a situation where he was comfortable taking his friend up on his offer.

Once they'd left, he placed the myriad bottles into the recycling bin and put the living room back to rights, then sank into an easy chair, his head in his hands. Despite his near-frantic consumption over the course of the evening, his were-wolf metabolism meant he had barely enough of a buzz to prevent him from being confident driving. Years ago, as barely more than pups, he and Raj and Emmett had experimented to see how much they could drink before actually getting drunk. Even back then, not yet fully grown, each of them had had to consume straight spirits the way Leo had been drinking beer tonight to get properly intoxicated. They'd been prepared—kind of excited, even—for the experiences other species talked about, vomiting, maybe even passing out, the works. But all that had happened to Leo was waking up with a slight headache the next day. Sometimes the inability to become drunk was a blessing—it meant he could drink at a normal rate for hours without feeling it. Other times, like tonight, it would have been a blessing to have been able to switch off his brain, even just for a few hours. To turn off the thoughts of Della that had now been plaguing him, stealing his focus, for days.

Knowing it wasn't a wise decision but fully prepared to blame his inadequate beer buzz, Leo dug his phone out of his pocket and typed in a message to her. *Thinking of you tonight.*

Every night, he wanted to add, but mentally growled at himself. *Casual. Keep it casual.*

He started getting ready to go to bed when his phone buzzed with a reply. He nearly hurdled the bed in his eagerness to read what she'd sent.

I was actually just debating sending you something similar, she'd written, with a small smiley face after the words. *How has your night been?*

It was good, Leo typed. *I had some friends over to watch the game. You'll be pleased to hear one of the warlocks won Man of the Match in the first game. You?*

I'll admit I don't really follow much sport, Della replied almost immediately. *I was just finishing up some council stuff. One of the pages I needed took ages to load, so I had a chance to have a quick chat with one of my friends. I'm getting ready for bed now.*

A moment later another message came through. *Do you guys get excited if the award goes to a werewolf?*

There's a sense of species solidarity, Leo admitted, trying not to think about her in bed. He neglected to mention the celebratory shots that usually followed. *Youth Council stuff or Council of Witches stuff?*

A bit of both, Della replied. *I called it a night when my eyes started blurring. You can only look at a screen for so many hours of the day.*

One good thing about being Beta is that once I'm home at the end of the day, I can usually switch off, Leo typed. *Late night calls don't come often.* He didn't mention the fact that when they did, it usually meant James wanted someone to be taught a lesson, and often a violent one. For a moment, shame roiled in his chest.

That sounds like the dream, Della replied. *I'm falling asleep as I'm typing. I'm going to turn in now.*

Me too, Leo said, though the idea that she was lying in bed talking to him had been enough to set his heart pounding all over again. His cock stirred at the image. *Sleep well,* he added.

Sweet dreams, she sent back, with a winking face afterwards.

You too, he couldn't stop himself from replying. And he had a strong feeling that his would be of her.

Chapter 7

"You're obsessed," Maggie told Della over the phone.

"I know," Della said miserably. "But I can't help it. I can't stop thinking about him."

"You're a grown woman," Mags said. "You should have better control than this. You're not a vamp who's found their One. You're a witch, and as far as I know, witches don't have predestined mates they can't stay away from. So, him sending you food again and the two of you spending your lunch break talking on the phone shouldn't turn you into this kind of simpering mess!"

The reprimand was warranted. Della had completely zoned out while Mags was telling her about the interaction she'd had with a patient and it took her friend snapping at her to bring her back from daydreaming about the sound of Leo's voice, imagining what he looked like and what he was doing as they spoke. She was sitting out in her townhouse's little garden, crammed with potted plants she used in spells that required more than just raw magic, and just the touch of the warm evening sun on her skin had made her think of him.

"I know, Mags," she told her friend. "I'm sorry. That was shitty of me. I'll make it up to you."

"It's not about making it up to me," Maggie said, her voice softening. "I'm just worried about you. Is there any chance this is at least partly because you're burning yourself out working so hard? I just don't want to see you throw your heart into a relationship that's meant to be casual and then be crushed when he doesn't do the same."

"Or when it ends," Della sighed. "I know, and I'm trying to be good about it. It's just… it's like someone's cast a spell on me. I just think about him *all the time*."

There was a brief pause. "Is it possible someone has?" Maggie asked, not unreasonably. "There's got to be a way you can find that out, right?"

Della stopped stock still for a moment, amazed that she hadn't thought of that. "Mags. You're a genius. I have to try this. It could explain everything."

"I don't want to downgrade the genius of my own idea," Maggie said, a touch hesitantly, "But can you think of any reason someone would want to spell you to fall in love with the Beta of the Blue Crescent pack? I mean, who would stand to benefit from that?"

"I have no idea," Della said, "But feeling like this can't just be *natural*, Mags. Even when I was falling in love with… with Dane," she swallowed at the foul taste it left in her mouth when she said his name, "it wasn't like this. Not so intense, and definitely not so *fast*. I mean, we've been on one real date. We haven't even slept together yet. It's *absurd* for me to be this obsessed with him." She swallowed. "Or maybe, it's not real."

"How does the spell work?" Mags asked. "To check if there's magic being used?"

"It's not a particularly complex one, actually. You just need an open flame and a sample from whatever you're testing to see if it's been spelled. I can probably just use a few strands of my hair."

"Oh, not a raw magic spell then?" Mags asked. "I don't like the ones with ingredients so much. They feel too much like cooking, but, like, dangerous."

"Hey, cooking can be dangerous." Della laughed. "Remember that warlock you dated who almost burned down your apartment trying to make ravioli?"

Mags groaned. "Okay, but a different type of dangerous."

"This one's hardly 'eye of newt and toe of frog'," Della protested lightly. "You only need the flame because it turns green if the object or person you're focusing on is the subject of a spell."

"You have to burn your own hair, though," Maggie hedged.

"That's just a focus for the spell. It's just easier than cutting up a piece of clothing I've worn recently. Would you want to sacrifice clothes you like? And your scrubs don't count," she added quickly.

"All right, all right, you've convinced me." Mags laughed. "How about we keep discussion of the real 'eye of newt and toe of frog' stuff to a minimum, though, all right? I got my lunch break an hour late today because we were so busy, and I have no wish to see that food again so soon."

"How is it that you can handle people with their bones sticking out through their skin, but the idea of me casting a spell with 'ingredients' as you call them is enough to ick you out?" Della asked.

"I don't know, I can't explain it." Mags laughed again. "Part of my brain just finds it… unsettling, I guess."

"Well. I'll keep the discussion of it to a minimum, as requested," Della promised.

"So do you want to put me on speaker while you do this one?" Maggie asked. "I mean, you're only going to ring me right back with the results, *I assume*. Might as well cut out the middleman."

"Sure," Della said. "It might take me a minute to find the right kind of candle, though."

"I just got home," Mags assured her. "I'll start making dinner."

"Which reminds me," Della said as she stood to go inside and dig through her candle collection, "I have to redo your protection spells when we can organise to have the same night off."

"I would have thought all your nights off were going to your Big Bad Wolf," Maggie said cheekily. "You know I don't really need those spells, Della. I'm perfectly capable of taking care of myself, even without a werewolf obsessed with me to protect me from threats."

"It makes me feel better when you have them, if you're going to be riding the train at all hours," Della said. "The Big Bad Wolf can take a backseat to more important things, like keeping my friends safe."

"Oh, all right," Mags gave in. "I'll have a look at my schedule and see what night we can both carve out to have dinner and get it over with."

They chatted about unrelated topics until Della was able to find a proper spellcasting candle—and add buying some more to her list of jobs for the weekend—and set herself up in the small open space in her garden between all the potted plants.

"Okay, I'm about to start," Della said when they reached a break in the conversation.

"Give me a minute, I'll turn off the stove," Mags said. "All right, I'm completely focused. Ready to listen."

"You won't hear much," Della laughed.

"You think I don't know how spell casting works?" Maggie

asked. "Like, a third of our doctors are witches. This is not my first rodeo."

"Okay, well, I'll tell you when we have some results," Della said.

Calling up her magic from the deep well within herself, she flicked her fingers at the candle to light it, then drew her circle of protection and added the first strand of her hair to the flame.

Not all witches bothered with a circle of protection, but the extent of Della's power meant that without it, if she lost focus on a spell, there was a risk that a wave of raw magic could burst out of her, causing damage. The more powerful of the young witches and warlocks were usually instructed at an early age not to perform magic without them, and she tried to keep to the rule even when she was doing minor spells. Most of her spell casting these days was just encouraging her plants to grow, an easy way to siphon off excess magic when her stores of it were full to the point that it was starting to push her to expend some. Perhaps if she'd been brought up using it for minor things like lighting candles or boiling water without feeling like it was a waste of power, she'd find it easier to find ways to expend that excess magic, but as it was, she just had the most lush garden on the street—and her neighbours' plants did pretty well out of the deal too, on the days when she couldn't get rid of enough power to get her stores of it under control again just by encouraging her own plants.

She focused her magic and her intention on the few strands of hair she fed to the flame and breathed in deeply, pushing her power into the fire.

The flame changed colour.

"It's… it's blue," she said out loud in complete shock. She knew Mags would hear the stunned disbelief in her voice.

"What does blue mean again?" the human asked. "I

thought it was just green if there's a spell on the thing you're focusing on."

"You're right," Della said in shock. "I've never even heard of someone getting a result of blue for this spell." She paused. "Maybe I did it wrong. Lost focus or something. Hang on, I'm going to start over."

She broke the protection circle and even collected a different candle, just in case that had affected the spell, then redrew the circle and started over, focusing as hard as she could on the pieces of her hair that she slowly pushed into the candle's flame.

Blue.

Again.

What the hell?

"It's gone blue again," Della said out loud for Maggie's benefit. "I've never seen this before. I've never even *heard* of this before."

"So, you have no idea what it means?" Mags asked. "It couldn't just be a trick of the light and it's actually green?"

"Here, you look." She snapped a photo of the candle flame, still bright blue, and sent it through to Mags.

"Yep," her friend's reply came after a moment. "That's definitely blue."

"I'm positive I did the spell right, at the very least the second time," Della said. "I mean, what the hell could this mean? It's supposed to be a simple yes/no spell. If your focus is being cast upon, you get green. If they're not, it stays red. If you do the spell wrong, you singe off your eyebrows. It's not exactly complex stuff."

"Well, I'm glad your eyebrows survived intact," Mags said, a laugh in her voice. She sobered. "What do you do with a result like this?"

"There's only one thing I can do, really," Della said. "I'm going to have to speak to my grandmother."

"*Ouch*," Mags said with feeling. "Well, I'm here if you need moral support for that, I guess."

"If I ring you in tears afterwards, at least it won't be any great mystery why," Della said, trying to keep herself positive despite the dread now coiling deep in her belly. "It's the best course of action, though. The old woman has more magical knowledge than all the city's witching libraries combined. She'll be able to explain what this means."

"Good luck," Mags said, sounding dubious—and with good reason. She was well aware of the relationship Della had with her grandmother. "Well, my soup prep has now gone cold, so I'm going to farewell you on this questionable note and finish making my dinner if you're okay?"

"Of course," Della said. "I have to get back to work anyway. There's a Council meeting the day after tomorrow, and I've barely started my prep."

"Well, make sure you get some sleep at some point," Maggie instructed her. "You're worse than me, and I do shifts in Emergency."

"I will. Good night, lovely. I'll talk to you later."

"Night, hon," Mags said, and then she was gone, leaving Della to ponder the mystery of the bright blue flame. She was so distracted by that—as well as the threat of having to visit her grandmother—that she barely got through any of her Council meeting prep. Eventually, she gave up and went to bed, and her dreams were full of shadowy versions of Leo and bright blue candle flames.

Della's grandmother had been one of the coven Elders for fifteen years before Della was even born. After Della's mother passed away, the visits to Grandmother Elise that had been infrequent turned into waiting for her father to finish work at that big, spooky old house every afternoon after school. Even as a ten-year-old, Della had apparently had plenty of flaws for Grandmother Elise to point out, which she had done with gusto. Della tried to focus on the positive part of her time at her grandmother's place. She'd paid close attention to the old woman's activities and learnt magic far beyond the education usually given to someone of her age. It was part of why, as an advanced witch with a significant level of power, she'd been elected to the Council of Witches at such a young age. When she'd told her grandmother about her appointment, it had been one of the few times in her life that Grandmother Elise had had nothing negative to say.

Her grandmother was highly sceptical of telephones, so Della sent her a message through a spell casting candle flame that she'd like to visit the following afternoon—knowing it would put her behind the 8-ball at work but deciding that clearing up the mystery of the blue flame was more important —and quickly received a reluctant acceptance in response. Memories of years of afternoons spent fumbling through her homework as Grandmother Elise either ignored or criticised her ran through her mind as she drove up the tree-lined driveway.

Grandmother Elise's house was exactly the kind of spooky-looking old mansion that witches of legend might have chosen to inhabit. It was ancient, with multi-paned windows looking down from the second storey like staring eyes, and a red door that had always reminded Della of a gaping mouth. It was in excellent repair, maintained as it was almost exclusively by magic, but Della imagined that when Grandmother Elise died and the spells eventually faded, it would crumble into a heap of tiles and brickwork.

The door swung open as Della approached it, and she suppressed a shiver. "Grandmother?" she called as she stepped through. "I'm here!" There was no response, which usually meant Grandmother Elise was in her workroom, so Della headed that way.

The hallways leading to Grandmother Elise's workroom were as crammed with pots of plants as Della's garden, but where she used mostly natural methods to encourage their growth, her grandmother's plants were all spelled to thrive in a dim indoor environment. It turned the corridors into a kind of indoor jungle, the air heavy with moisture and the smell of thriving greenery.

Della could hear Grandmother Elise chanting before she even got to the workroom, a spell for fertility that had fallen out of use in recent years in favour of a newer, simpler, but somewhat less powerful version. Someone must have come to her seeking the older, more potent one. Della knew better than to disturb her while she was working, so she stood in the doorway and watched her cast the spell. It involved far more ingredients than the newer version, a complex chant, and dedication to no fewer than three fertility goddesses. Once Grandmother Elise was finished, the room was left full of a sweet-smelling smoke that made Della slightly light-headed when she breathed it in.

Finally, Grandmother Elise broke her protection circle and snapped her fingers, immediately causing the smoke to disappear. "Good to see you finally decided to drop in," she said without looking at Della. "Are you going to stand there staring all day, or might you deign to help an old woman clean this up?"

"What would you like me to do, Grandmother?" Della asked. *And hello to you too.*

"Pick up a broom and get to work on the floor. You young things think everything needs to be done with magic. A little physical work will be good for you." She turned and surveyed Della from top to toe where she was still hovering in the doorway. Instantly, she was transported back to childhood, when she'd receive the same searching look almost every time she walked through the red front door. "And it looks like you could use it too," Grandmother Elise added in what may have been disguised as an undertone, but which Della was clearly meant to hear. She tried to tamp down on the deep sigh that threatened to break out of her and went to find the broom.

It was at the back of one of the cupboards, and heavily cobwebbed, proving that Grandmother Elise was not practicing what she preached when it came to cleaning without magic. Della swept up the rose petals and bits of eggshell without comment, though, collecting them into the corner of the room while Grandmother Elise returned her supply jars to the overflowing shelves that lined every wall of the room. Elise snapped her fingers, and the pile of detritus disappeared.

"Come, then," she ordered Della. "It's time for tea."

Della suppressed a shudder.

Grandmother Elise's teas were the stuff of legend in their coven. She rarely sold them, and when she did, they went like hotcakes. She had teas for pain relief, for patience, for efficiency, for contraception; all the ingredients spelled just enough to enhance their natural properties without impacting the user beyond their intended effect. Witches both from their own coven and from others visited her to beg for them, and Della had been gobsmacked to see the kindly old woman her grandmother became when she had one of those visitors. Then they'd leave, and she'd revert to the overly critical witch Della knew so well.

The teas Grandmother Elise gave her were always for things like achievement, or success, or increased magical power—after that one, Della had almost caused a hurricane trying to summon a light breeze one summer afternoon; she had flatly refused to drink it again. And they always tasted terrible, no matter how appetising the ingredients list sounded on paper. Perhaps Grandmother Elise took pleasure in it and purposely only gave her the ones she'd fight not to spit right out. Whatever the motive, tea with her grandmother, for Della, was more of a threat.

"Hmm," Elise intoned, surveying the unlabelled plethora of jars that lined one of the walls of the large, sunlit kitchen. She stretched to collect one that was almost beyond her reach and nearly set those around it tumbling to the ground.

"What are you doing just loafing around, Delphinia?" she demanded without turning. "Boil some water."

Della wasn't sure whether she'd be scolded for using magic or for doing it manually—probably either—so she filled the kettle and flicked her fingers at it, setting it boiling. Grandmother Elise sniffed at the use of magic but, shockingly, said nothing. She measured out the tea into the pot and poured water over it, then was silent for a long moment as it steeped, surveying Della once more where she sat in her accustomed seat at the scarred wooden table.

"Clear-sightedness, today," she said eventually. "You need it if you thought that haircut was a good idea."

Della glanced down at the braid that hung over her shoulder. "Thanks, Grandmother."

"Now what question did you have for me today? I know you only come to see me when you want something, not just to sit and drink my tea, though many others would pay through the nose for that privilege." She sniffed pointedly.

"I cast for spell detection yesterday," Della said, ignoring the jibe as she was long accustomed to doing. "And the flame went blue, not green. I was wondering if you knew what that meant."

Grandmother Elise picked up the teapot and poured for both of them, almost as though she was buying herself time. That was impossible, though. There was no way her grandmother would do something so… hesitant.

"It means there is magic being used on the subject, Delphinia, but not in the form of a spell."

Della blinked. "How is that possible? To have magic used on me, it surely must be a spell. Even raw magic spells make the flame turn green in a detection spell."

"You were the subject, then?" Grandmother Elise asked, raising a single eyebrow.

Della nodded.

Her grandmother fixed her with a beady stare. "There are different kinds of magic," she began, and to her shock, Della saw a hint of the kindly face she showed her customers coming through. "There's the kind we witches can access, the kind that changes a vampire when they are bitten, the kind that calls werewolves to change at the full moon."

Della stiffened at the mention of werewolves and took a sip of her tea to try to hide it. It was… surprisingly not particularly awful, at least on the scale of teas her grandmother usually made her drink.

"The term used in most literature is 'natural magic', which is accessible to witches, and 'supernatural magic', which exists on a plane to which we have no access, and only rarely affects individuals in our world, rather than the world itself. Supernatural magic controls the sun and the moon, the creation of creatures, human and inhuman, the evolution of life itself. All those things that are beyond our control as witches—permanent change to the laws of physics, creating and destroying matter, true emotion—are governed by supernatural magic."

"So, you're saying the *universe* is using magic on me?" Della asked in disbelief.

"That's one way to look at it if you need things simple," Grandmother Elise said, a hint of her usual acerbic nature shining through once more. "Why exactly did you think you might be under a spell?"

Della heaved in a breath and decided she might as well lay

it out. It seemed the best way she was going to find answers. "I've been having... feelings, for someone. And it seemed to me that they were coming on unnaturally fast and unnaturally strong. So, I thought perhaps there might be magic involved." She looked down at her tea. "I guess I was right, in a way." She could feel how lost and confused her own expression must appear.

Grandmother Elise considered her own tea for a long moment. "Yes," she said eventually. "Yes, there is magic involved. The universe's most complex magic. But no one is spelling you if that's what you're worried about."

"What do I *do* about it, then?" Della asked in desperation.

"Foolish girl, do you think I have answers to every question in the world?" Grandmother Elise snapped. "Supernatural magic is not to be tampered with. It controls the force of gravity, the power of a vampire finding their One or a werewolf their mate. Perhaps it is working on you now in a similar way. It's dangerous to interfere with this sort of thing."

"But I don't know what to *do!*" Della burst out. "Am I just supposed to... to feel this, to let myself be overwhelmed by it? How come the flame doesn't go blue any time anyone starts having *emotions*? Why is it just me?"

"There's magic at work, Delphinia," Elise said quietly. "Magic we cannot control. You're right—what you're feeling is beyond normal emotions. It's supernaturally controlled. You can't interfere with this."

"I don't know how to live with this kind of... this kind of *intensity*," Della said in desperation.

"Well, you're going to have to learn," Grandmother Elise said, rising from the table. "Now finish your tea and get going, girl. Some of us actually have work to do."

For a long moment, Della sat at the table in a state of something like shock. Her grandmother returned the jar of tea to her wall of similar containers and stood in the doorway surveying Della for a long moment.

"It may not get easier," she said, for once a trace of sympathy in her voice. "But you'll get used to it. You have my blood running through you. You are a Greenbranch, Delphinia, and we endure." With that, she left the room, leaving Della to clean up the detritus of their tea as usual, confusion making her head spin as she did so.

Chapter 8

Leo was pretty sure he was losing his mind. It had been almost two weeks since he'd seen Della in the flesh and his wolf was howling over the extended absence. He'd given in and shifted to run through the forest outside the city in his wolf form the last two nights, hoping to burn off some energy, but all it had done was make him more aware of his boundless hunger for her, for her touch, her voice, her face, that damned *scent*. If being *more* aware of it was even possible.

The meeting about the afterschool programs—which he hadn't mentioned to James he was still planning on attending, since he hadn't quite managed to mention to Della his Alpha's refusal to be involved in the program—was tonight, and energy was humming beneath his skin at the very thought of seeing her again.

To his shame, he was in the middle of delivering one of James' threats, a threat he himself would be the one to carry out if the woman in question didn't stop pushing the limits of the law regarding the sale of witch-spelled objects, when Della texted him.

I'll see you tonight at the meeting? she wrote, as though it was ever in question.

Let me drive you there, Leo texted back, once he was out of the woman's shop, leaving her pale with fear and promising obedience.

Almost immediately, as he was walking down the street to greetings from his packmates which he acknowledged with short nods, he received a response.

That would involve you driving me home after, would it not? Della asked.

I guess it would, Leo wrote, as though his wolf hadn't considered this already, and sent up a howl of approval in response.

He watched as the marker of Della typing appeared on the screen, disappeared, appeared again. It felt like he was holding his breath, even as he filled his lungs with air. He needed her, needed to at least have that time alone with her, see that she got home safe. Otherwise, he was pretty sure he'd wind up tailing her car when she left the meeting to ensure she made it through her front door without incident.

But if she invited him in… the wolf beneath his skin sent up a howl at the thought. The thought of being alone with her, in private, in her house… the thought of all the things he could do to her in a space where no one might walk in on them, where no one could accidentally hear—he clenched his fists and fought to keep himself in check. He must look a fright, he realised; the other people walking by gave him a wide berth and the acquaintances and shopkeepers who usually greeted him when he was in this part of the pack's territory were taking one look at him and cutting themselves off. He fought down the wolf that was trying to rise to the surface and glanced down at the phone still clutched tightly in his hand.

I have to be there a bit early to make sure everything is set up, she'd written. Was she hedging? He wondered.

I'm really good at arranging chairs, Leo responded.

See you around 5.30 then? she asked.

The wolf snarled in satisfaction. Leo had to stop his hands from shaking with the adrenaline that was suddenly coursing through his body.

What's your address? he asked.

She lived deep in the Avalon coven's territory, but from what he knew, it was a fairly safe area. Something in him, something that had without his knowledge been concerned she wasn't safe while he wasn't there to protect her, relaxed slightly. The rest of him was as keyed up as he'd ever been, the thought of once again being alone with her—truly alone this time, with no other restaurant patrons or potential carpark users to interrupt them—sending pulses of heat through his blood.

He'd be hard pressed to focus on the damn meeting before he could take her home, that was for sure.

Leo was parked outside the address Della had given him at 5.30 on the dot. He rolled his shoulders, trying to reduce the sudden burst of—was that nerves—that was fighting to dilute the mixture of arousal and anticipation thrumming through his veins, and knocked on the door.

"Come on in, it's unlocked," Della called.

Heat pulsed through him, and he fought it down. *Be civilised, Tyler. Don't leap on her the moment you see her.*

Della appeared through one of the doors that opened into the small entrance hallway, carrying a large binder stuffed full of papers. If he'd thought it was the flirty blue dress she'd worn on their date that had had his arousal skyrocketing, his response to her in a simple white business shirt and straight black skirt proved that thought entirely wrong. Lust roared through him like an open flame and before he knew what he was doing, he was stalking towards her, backing her against the wall next to the doorway she'd come through, pinning her with a hand on either side of her head. With a gasp, Della dropped her binder to the table by her side. A low growl rose from his chest as he took in a lungful of her scent. Their eyes met and held. Held.

"You shouldn't do that," he managed after a long moment filled only with their rapid breathing.

"Do what?" Della asked.

"Invite people in without knowing who it is," Leo managed. "It might not have been me."

"I'm a witch, Leo," she replied, her voice breathy. "I have sensor spells set up on every boundary of this property. I knew it was you the moment you turned into the driveway." She closed her eyes and took a deep breath, and when her chest brushed Leo's, they both groaned. He saw her hand clench into a fist at her side. "I was just collecting the last of the papers I need for tonight," Della added.

"Good," Leo forced out. "Do you have everything?"

"I think so."

"Then we can go." Neither of them made a move to shift from their position. He breathed in her scent once more—sex and spices, willing woman. She was wet, he could smell it. She needed him, and he couldn't take her right now.

"Della," Leo growled. "Della, the mood I'm in, if I kiss you right now, we won't leave this house for a week."

Surely, he was imagining the spark in her gaze at his words.

"If it wasn't for the meeting," she said quietly, "and all the people I've promised I'll be there, I'd take you up on that, Mr Tyler."

Leo dropped his head and took in a deep breath of her scent at the curve where her neck became her shoulder. She shivered, and his wolf rejoiced at the visible evidence of his effect on her. If only she knew, he thought distantly, the effect *she* had on *him*.

"I'll be bringing you home after the meeting tonight," Leo said slowly, trying to keep his voice even. "And, Della, if you want to say goodbye at the door and walk through it alone, I'll drive away and I'll take care of this," he pressed his body forward so she could feel the full length of his cock, swollen and aching for her, "On my own, thinking of you the way I have been for the past two weeks." He felt her sharp intake of breath as if it were filling his own lungs, and he took the leap. "But, Della, if you let me come through that door with you, you have to know I'm going to take it as an invitation to show you exactly what I've been dreaming of doing with this perfect body."

There was the briefest of pauses. "I want to know," Della said, swallowing hard. "I want to know what you've been... what you've been dreaming of. I want to know if your dreams have been the same as mine."

He couldn't help himself. With a growl, Leo dragged Della's shirt out of the way and sunk his teeth into the skin of her shoulder. Distantly, he was grateful that he had had the presence of mind to do this somewhere no one else would be able to see, but the forefront of his mind—the conscious, human part—was overwhelmed with the pure instinctual gratification, the primal joy, of tasting and marking his woman. She tasted like everything he'd ever wanted, like joy and sweetness and sex and the future he'd never even let himself imagine. He flicked his tongue over the place his teeth had dug in, soothing her, and revelling in her strangled gasp as her free hand rose to cling to one of his shoulders, dragging upwards and diving into his hair as though she'd drag his mouth to hers.

Gathering every ounce of his self-control, Leo managed to take half a step backwards. Enough that every facet of their bodies was no longer touching. Enough that he could see her face.

Della looked like the incarnation of arousal, cheeks flushed, lips bitten red. Gods, how he wanted to cover those lips with his own, but no. *Focus.* They had somewhere to be.

"Are you all right?" he managed to ask, though his voice was more of a growl.

"I'm…" Della said and paused. "Did you just leave a mark on me?"

"It's covered by your shirt," Leo said, trying to ignore the rush of primal satisfaction that filled him. "It'll be covered unless you're wearing a shirt with a *very* low neckline. And Della," he added, "the only person you're wearing that kind of shirt for had better be me."

He didn't expect the way she went stiff before him, all the rampant arousal disappearing from her features in the space of a second.

"Of course," she said, and there was a stiffness in her voice completely at odds with the panting, needy woman who had stood before him mere moments earlier. "We agreed."

He looked at her, brows lowered. "Della—"

"We're going to be late," she murmured and slipped from the cage his arms had formed around her to collect the binder and her bag waiting by the door.

It was mostly Della doing the talking on their drive to the meeting hall, telling him about the situations she was managing at work, her two co-workers who had hooked up and still thought no one else knew despite how obvious they were being, the frivolous issues that had been brought before the Council of

Witches for their next meeting. Leo was trapped in a turmoil of extreme arousal, fed by the way her scent filled the car and permeated every breath he took, and concern over the way she'd frozen up on him. What had gone wrong? What had he done that had put that haunted look into her eyes, and what did he have to do to fix it? Della seemed to be relaxing more and more as they drove, her voice losing its stiffness, her posture relaxing to the point that she even put a hand on Leo's thigh to direct him into the correct car park as they arrived at the meeting hall. Lust shot through him at her touch, but he tamped it down. It didn't matter how savagely his wolf longed to make good on the promises he'd made of what would happen when they got back to her house. First, he needed to solve this mystery.

Setup for the meeting was easy even if he had to tamp down on his jealousy when Della embraced another male in greeting—the same one who had dared to touch her during the last meeting if Leo wasn't mistaken—and welcomed him to Mystic City. Apparently, he'd travelled from elsewhere to be present tonight, and Leo had to stop himself from politely requesting that he go back wherever the fuck he came from.

Della even called Leo over from where he'd been helping set out the chairs to introduce him to the man. He sauntered over, sizing up the other male.

"This is Leo Tyler, the Beta of the Blue Crescent pack," she said. No mention of their involvement, he noted, though, of course, that had been one of their ground rules, hadn't it? That they keep their relationship quiet?

"Ian Ashbough," the other male introduced himself, extending a hand. "Tituba coven. I've come from Tirawi City for the meeting tonight—my coven is very interested in Della's ideas about integration. I think the model could be used in a lot of places if we can make a success of it here."

"It must be useful that you have nothing to lose if it fails in a city that's not your own, either," Leo said sharply.

Ian had the gall to look shocked at his words, but quickly collected himself. "On the contrary, I've been working closely with Della to make this venture a success. I've put my name to it in my own coven and Della and I have reached out to other covens to see if they're interested. I daresay I have significantly more to lose than a werewolf who can withdraw his interest in the program whenever it's convenient for him… or his pack."

How much did the warlock know? How *could* he know about James' instruction to withdraw Blue Crescent from any involvement in the program? Leo could barely stop himself from baring his teeth and snarling at the challenge. He reined himself in with a considerable effort.

"Either way," Ian said, clearly changing his tone with a grin at Della that made Leo grind his teeth, "I'm sure we all have enough invested that it's in our best interests to see the program succeed. Which I'm positive it will."

"We can only hope," Della said, smiling warmly at the asshole warlock.

"Do you mind if I borrow Della for a moment?" Leo asked, not knowing what he'd do if Ian expressed reluctance.

"By all means," the other male said, spreading his hands wide. "I'll go see if I can dig up that lectern. Pleasure to have you on board, Leo."

He left the room, and in a flash, Leo was a hair's breadth away from Della, crowding her into the shadowed corner to the side of the small, raised stage.

"Leo—" she managed to gasp before he was clasping her face in his hands.

"Tell me you've never let him touch you the way I have," he demanded, hearing the asshole in his voice but unable to conquer it.

"What? Leo, Ian doesn't see me like that," Della protested. "He has a girlfriend back in Tirawi City—"

"I can smell it on him, Della," Leo said. "He wants you, badly."

"Wanting and doing are two very different things," Della said. Her voice had gone soft. "Leo, you can't get this worked up about every male friend I have. I know werewolves tend to be possessive, but this is ridiculous. Not everyone is looking to fuck me."

Hearing her say the words burst some dam inside him. "You promised me no one else, as long as this lasts. Just remember who the male is who'd die to take you home tonight. Who's been dreaming of *fucking you* for two full weeks now without a break."

"I keep my promises," Della said, but he could scent her arousal at his words. She took a deep breath. "And I promise I won't introduce you to anyone I've been with without warning you first. And I expect the same courtesy from you."

"Of course," Leo said, locking the promise inside himself so he didn't go mad with lust imagining Della getting possessive over him, Della leaving marks on him to assert her claim... Not that she needed to. He shoved down that thought as well and pressed a kiss to her forehead, taking a deep breath of her scent and revelling in the touch of his lips on her skin. *More later*, he promised his impatient wolf, and stepped back from her.

"Thank you," he said, holding her gaze so she'd see the honesty in his eyes. "And I'm sorry. For... that."

"Let's just try and keep *that* in check until we get home, shall we?" she asked, a touch of flirtation entering her expression. If it was possible, his dick hardened even further.

"In the meantime," Della continued, looking around the half-set-up room, "I guess we have some chairs to arrange."

Her slightly cautious smile lit Leo up like someone had replaced his veins with strings of fairy lights. *Anything*, he found himself thinking. *Anything you need from me, Delphinia Greenbranch, and I will do it.*

So together, they set up the rest of the chairs. And when Ian returned, having successfully located the lectern that he drew along behind him on a floating magical tether, Leo managed to restrict his reaction to a single assessing glance that the warlock returned.

Their eye contact was broken when the door opened and the friendly vampire from the last meeting—what had been her name... Virginia—swirled into the room in a burst of oversized skirts and immaculately curled red hair. "Della!" she cried, apparently overjoyed to see the witch. "Sunset is getting earlier by seconds each day, so I thought I'd see if you needed any help setting up."

"I think we're doing all right, thanks anyway, Valerie," Della replied with equal cheerfulness. "You met Leo from Blue Crescent last time, didn't you? He stopped by to help us out this week."

"I could do all of this with magic in a tenth of the time if you'd let me," Ian said, a teasing complaint.

"A little physical labour is good for you," Della said. She sounded like she was teasing back, but there was something else there. "My grandma always said using magic for all your menial tasks was a cop-out. Not in those words, of course," she added with a laugh.

"Your word is my command," Ian said with a laugh of his own and a shrug, grabbing the last of the chairs and positioning them. "That was much faster than usual, anyway. I guess we have Leo to thank for that?"

"My pleasure," Leo said, his eyes on Della, revelling in the way she went slightly pink at his words.

"I've never known a werewolf pack to be particularly interested in integration," Valerie said, fixing Leo with her endless immortal stare and a bloodred smile. "Especially one as dedicated to independence as Blue Crescent. What has changed to bring you into our circle? Are the wolves suddenly looking to integrate with the rest of us for some reason?" Her perfect eyebrows were raised, but her mouth was still in that lovely, inhuman smile.

"I thought Della made some very good points last week," Leo said. "I'm still working on convincing my Alpha, but I'm pretty keen to be involved with what she's been talking about." There, that was all true, no lies in what he'd said.

"Ah, yes, Alpha James Norfolk. I've heard tell of his commitment to… living by his own rules, shall we say." If possible, her blood red smile spread even wider. She knew, then. What James did, the way he ruled, and the things Leo had to do as his second-in-command. The things he hadn't told Della about yet and wasn't sure he ever wanted her to know; the beatings, the threats, the way his role as Beta seemed to emulate a mob enforcer more and more as time went by. What was this, a threat from the vampire? To expose him to the witch he couldn't seem to get enough of as what he truly was?

Refusing to let his expression change, Leo repeated the line his father had taught him from his own days as Beta. "The pack comes first, Lady Valerie, and James has always done what he thinks is best."

"Is that so?" Valerie replied in a tone that said she didn't believe a word of it. "And none of that 'Lady' nonsense, please. I'm not here as a vampire Master, just an interested party intrigued by Della's coven's ideas. We've been friends since before she was elected to the Council, you know."

"I'm glad to hear it," Leo said. "Your coven's support for her program will mean a lot when it gets approved."

"At this point, all we need is enough groups to commit that we can get some decent funding," Della chimed in. "Every-one's input at these meetings is really valuable for ironing out the details, but we can't really go anywhere without larger-scale support." She smiled at him. "That's part of why we were so excited when your Alpha said he'd be sending a representative last time. The werewolves haven't exactly proven themselves keen to be involved."

"Well, I'm very glad I came," Leo said truthfully. He pushed down on the part of him that panicked at the thought of not having met Della if James had sent someone else to the first meeting.

"Me too," Della said, with one of the smiles that set his heartbeat racing.

At that moment, the door swung open again and a contingent of humans arrived, noisily chattering. With a last heated look at him, Della went to greet them, Ian trailing her.

When Valerie took a seat in one of the middle rows of the chairs they'd arranged and gestured for Leo to take the one next to her, he happily complied.

"My friend Beaufort, whose coven's territory is alongside your pack's, should also be joining us tonight," she said. Leo had a vague memory of there having been another vampire at the last meeting, but he'd been too consumed by Della to pay much attention. "I'd be happy to introduce the two of you," Valerie continued. "You might be happy to have some outside support when you go to *convince* your Alpha to be involved in this integration project. Or perhaps of making some… *other* leadership changes."

What was she alluding to? Did she think he was working up to challenging James for leadership of the pack? And if, gods all forbid, he did, was she offering her *support*?

"I'm sure both of your friendship will be very valuable while I'm trying to get James onboard," Leo said, a touch stiffly. "I'm not sure he has any other changes planned at the moment, though. Not without the full support of the pack."

"The pack comes first," Valerie said sagely, her lips curving in that same close-mouthed smile as she echoed his words from earlier. "Whatever is best for the pack."

"Indeed," Leo said, and then Della was letting them know they'd be starting in a few moments and another vampire was slipping into the seat on Valerie's other side. She barely had the chance to introduce them—Beaufort greeting Leo with an uncomfortably knowing smile that showed off his fangs—before Della was calling the meeting to order and welcoming them all.

He made it through maybe three minutes of watching her command the room before that and her scent—potent to him even with all the other people around them—had need thrumming through his veins. It was as bad as it had been at the last meeting—maybe worse, since now he knew the taste of her skin and the way she stroked her tongue over his own when he kissed her and how her body shook when he made her come. The sex-and-spices scent that was uniquely Della intoxicated him until he was leaning forwards in his seat, eyes fixed on her even once she'd yielded the lectern to another speaker. Every minute he had to wait to get his hands on her felt like it was stretching into an eternity. Leo found himself falling back on the self-control tricks they used for pups trying to manage their first shifts, focusing on his breathing, on the sensations in his body. Clenching and relaxing his muscle groups in turn. It helped, a little, though the breathing just brought more of her scent into his lungs, and every sensation in his body seemed geared towards the lust pounding in his blood.

He could tell she felt the heat of his gaze by the pink in her cheeks and the infinitesimal pause before she took her place at the lectern once more to close out the meeting. Valerie and Beaufort stood with the rest of the crowd once Della had formally thanked them for attending, but Leo stayed seated, pretending to be absorbed in his phone to avoid anyone trying to speak to him. The room slowly emptied until only he, Della and Ian were left.

He looked up when he heard Ian say, "I think that was a great success."

Della shot the warlock a smile. "I think so too. Go us."

"Go you," Ian corrected her. "You had them eating out of the palm of your hand. By the time I spoke, I could have told them our curriculum plan involved bright blue facial tattoos and they would have accepted it without question."

Della's smile turned a little embarrassed. "I really think we're getting somewhere with all the cross-species input," she said. "Anyway, thank you for coming tonight, Ian. Your input is invaluable too."

"Any time you need me here, just give me a call," Ian said, and Leo rose to his feet without consciously deciding to do so. The movement caught the attention of both witch and warlock.

"Anyway," Ian said, "how about we get this place put to rights, and then we can all take off?"

"Why don't you head out?" Della suggested. "You've done so much already. Leo's giving me a lift home, and we can easily manage the pack-down with the two of us. I might cheat and just do it magically," she added with a conspiratorial grin.

"If you say so," Ian said, glancing between Della and Leo, who was still standing stock-still in the midst of the chairs. "Make sure she gets home safe," he added to Leo.

"Always," Leo said, the word coming out with more growl than he'd intended.

And then the other man was gone, and it was just the two of them in the big, empty room.

"If you move out of the chairs," Della said, her voice a touch unsteady, "I can put them all away."

Leo could feel the predatory nature of his movements as he walked forwards to the stage where Della still stood. She only took her eyes off him long enough to flick her fingers at the room full of chairs, which immediately disappeared.

"You could have set them up that easily too?" Leo asked when he stood below her.

Della smiled down at him, her cheeks still pink and growing pinker under his focused gaze. "I guess so. My grandmother always taught me not to use magic for menial tasks, though, so it makes more sense to me for us to set them up by hand. It feels kind of… wrong to use magic to do it. Like I'm cheating. Wasting it, or something, unless I desperately need to siphon some off that day."

"Why did you just do that, then?" Leo asked.

"You know why," Della said, dropping her eyes to the ground.

"Tell me anyway," Leo said. "I want to hear you say it."

"I didn't want to wait as long as it would take to put them all away by hand," Della said quietly.

"Wait for what?" In an instant, Leo had jumped up on to the stage next to her. She started, gasping, but he already had her in his arms and *fuck*, but it felt *so good* to be holding the woman who had been tempting him all night. "Don't want to wait for me to take you home and kiss you goodnight at the door like a gentleman?"

"I don't think you're that kind of gentleman," Della whispered, her eyes flicking up from where they were fixed on his lips to meet his own gaze.

"You're damn right," Leo said, the words coming out in a growl. "I'm the kind of gentleman who'll have his mouth between your legs a minute after you invite me through that door, sweetheart. The kind who'll pleasure you until you're begging before I even think about putting my cock in that pretty pussy. Do you understand me?"

"*Yes*, Leo," Della gasped, her hands grasping fistfuls of his shirt as though she'd drag his mouth to hers right here.

With a colossal effort, Leo stepped back. "Good," he said. "Grab your things, then. Let's get going."

Della's entire body felt like her nerves had been set to 'hyper-drive'. She'd never been more aware of clothing touching her skin, of the temperature in the car, of Leo's hand on her thigh as he drove. If only she'd worn a shorter skirt, she could already be feeling his skin on hers. She cursed the fabric that separated them, but at the same time knew that if he'd actually had his hand on her bare thigh, she probably wouldn't have been able to resist pushing it higher and begging him to give her the same thing he had after their dinner date. And there were two ways that could end—one, he crashed the car and the two of them died a fiery death, or two, he somehow managed to both drive and get her off with the innate competence with which he seemed to do everything and left her even more turned on than she already was. If that was even possible.

Her blood was pounding in her veins, and she could feel how wet and swollen she was between her legs. Everything was hot and cold all at once, and every breath she took sounded loud in her ears, like she was gasping for air.

"I need you to distract me," Leo said suddenly, his voice loud in the heated quiet.

"Wh-why?" Della managed to say.

"I can *smell* you, Della," he ground out. "I can fucking smell how turned on you are and it's killing me not to pull over and bury my face in that needy little pussy *right now*, so I need you to talk about something else and distract me."

"Oh," Della murmured, her cheeks flaming at the idea that he could smell her arousal, but knowing his words were only making it worse. "Oh. Um. What would you like me to talk about?"

"Anything," Leo said. "Work, friends, family. Just get my mind off how easy it would be to fuck you in the back seat."

Della latched on to the first thing that popped into her mind. "My grandmother, who I mentioned earlier, about teaching me not to use magic for everyday tasks—she did most of my magical education after my mother passed away. My dad worked long hours, so I would go over to Grandmother Elise's after school and watch her cast spells. She's a-a bit of a difficult person to be around sometimes—well, most of the time, really, with me—but she taught me a huge amount of what I know about magic. She's a big reason I have the kind of control over my power that I do now, because I started building it at such a young age."

"How old were you when your mother passed?" Leo asked. He was still visibly tense, but he seemed to be a little less tightly strung.

"I was ten," Della said quietly. "Brain aneurysm. She was only forty-two."

He reached over and squeezed her hand but didn't say anything, and she appreciated it. Too many people tried to talk her out of the grief that never truly went away.

The car pulled into her driveway, and they sat in silence for a moment.

"Well, that's one way to kill the moment," Della said with half a laugh. "Talk about your dead mother."

In a blink, Leo was out of his seat and rounding the hood of the car. He pulled open her door and undid her seatbelt faster than she could take a breath and pulled her out to press her body back against the car in a mirror of what they'd done the night they'd had dinner. In a flash, she was as hot as she'd been before they'd started talking about her family.

"You think anything you say to me is enough to kill this

mood?" he asked, pressing the length of his erection against her.

"Leo," Della gasped, and then he was stepping away from her, the loss of his body against hers so shocking in its suddenness that she stumbled. His hands came up to her waist to steady her, and when she met his eyes, the hunger in his gaze was so deep, she felt it in her bones. She had clasped his forearms before she knew what she was doing and felt the muscles clench under her touch.

"Invite me inside, Della," Leo said, and though the words were an instruction, there was a plea in his voice. "I need to make you feel good."

In answer, Della flicked her fingers at the front door, magicking it unlocked and open. She tugged Leo's hands away from her waist but kept a hold on one, pulling him with her up the front stairs and into her home.

The door had hardly closed behind them before he turned her around and pinned her back against it, wrapping her in his arms as he did so. Their lips met at the same moment as the rest of their bodies, and Della felt rather than heard Leo's growl of approval mixing with her own moan. Surely, it was crazy to think she could *taste* the intensity of his need for her— but wait, there was magic at work here, hadn't her spell proven that? Magic beyond what she could control—the magic of the universe. Magic that had her rolling her smaller, softer body against Leo's larger, harder one as she reached up to wrap her hands around his neck, opening her entire body to his touch.

He took advantage, stroking his hands over every curve of her like he was trying to memorise them. When he gripped her ass and used the leverage to work his rigid cock against the covered juncture of her thighs, she moaned so loudly she was pretty sure her neighbours would have been able to hear.

"If someone comes around to check why I'm making all these loud noises," Della managed between breathless gasps, "you're going to have to stop long enough for me to convince them I'm all right."

"Oh, sweetheart." Leo's grin was nothing short of wolfish. "You think that was loud? Just wait until I'm making you scream."

He pulled the collar of her shirt out of the way and sucked on the place he'd bitten earlier, and it was as if the spot had a direct line to her clit. Della's hips bucked without conscious instruction from her brain, and she found herself dragging Leo's shirt up and over his head, forcing him to lean back from her, just so she'd have access to more of him to touch. He was glorious, all thick slabs of muscle and golden-tanned skin, but he didn't give her long to look. Within barely more than a breath, he had her pressed against the door once more, sucking on her tongue with a growl as she ran her hands, her nails, over the broad expanse of his back. She dug them in and he positively snarled, big hands making quick work of the buttons of her shirt and tearing it off over her shoulders. In the same breath, he was yanking her skirt's zipper down and tugging it off over her hips and down her legs, so he was kneeling at her feet when he looked up and got his first glimpse of her in her underwear.

She'd never been so glad she'd worn nice lingerie as she was seeing Leo's jaw drop when he caught sight of it. The set had been another gift to herself after what had happened with Dane, but she'd rarely had the chance or the inclination to make use of them. The fabric was mostly sheer, with applique roses in crucial places making it borderline decent.

From the look on Leo's face, you'd have thought she'd appeared in nothing but the dust of crushed diamonds.

"You wear this for me?" he asked, still on his knees. His voice was rough, harsh.

"Yes," Della said honestly, and then, because he was still kneeling at her feet and staring at her, added, "You like it?"

As if in answer, Leo lunged forwards and covered her fabric-shielded core with his mouth. She could feel him perfectly, so warm and soft and wet, and gods above, what was he doing with his tongue that could feel so incredible even through the fabric?

Della had to strangle a scream, grabbing at his hair—to pull him away, or drag him closer, she wasn't sure.

Leo pulled back a moment later, and even his breath was coming in uneven pants. "I love them," he said between gasped breaths. "I hate them. You look beautiful. Nothing should ever hide you from me." He laid another long lick over her swollen, covered flesh that ended with such perfect pressure on her clit that she thought she might die. "I'll buy you more of these. A hundred of these," Leo growled against her, and then there was a tearing sound and her panties appeared, shredded, on the floor next to her. She might have been outraged if he hadn't gone right back to what he was doing and the capacity for anything beyond pure desperation for *more* left her brain entirely. Leo's mouth was *impossible*, was *everything*, his lips and tongue teasing and caressing her like he had a direct line into her brain, knowing exactly what she needed almost before she did. When he pressed his fingers inside her, she made a noise the likes of which she'd never even *heard* before, instinctively rocking against the perfect combination of his fingers in her pussy and his tongue stroking over her clit.

"Leo," she moaned, her voice coming out high and tight.

He pulled back long enough to say, "Della," before returning to flick his tongue over the sensitive bud of nerves in a way that had Della clenching down around his thrusting fingers.

"I could do this all fuckin' night," he growled. "Spend hours making you scream my name, just from my mouth between these legs." He quirked his fingers in a way that made her eyes roll back in her head. "You going to let me do that, my little goddess? Going to let me get on my knees and worship you all night?"

"Anything," Della said, meaning it with her whole heart. "Anything, just don't stop. Please don't stop."

"Never," Leo snarled against her skin, and set his tongue to stroking over her once more; up and back, side to side, in circles—gods, those perfect, teasing circles—until her flesh was clenching spasmodically against his working fingers and Della was working her hips in time with his strokes, moaning and panting and—

"Leo," she managed. "Leo, I'm going to come."

"Do it," he growled against her flesh. "Come for me, sweetheart."

It shouldn't have been possible for him to work her even harder, but somehow it was, and then she was tipping over the edge and tumbling down, down, into a whirlpool of pleasure that seemed to have no bottom. Words were spilling from her lips that she barely heard, *yes* and *oh, gods*, and endless repetitions of his name, as his lips and tongue and fingers drove her deeper into that whirlpool than she'd ever been.

Finally, flesh throbbing with hypersensitivity, she grabbed at him to stop the endless pleasure waves. Leo drew back, withdrawing his touch from her skin, only to keep her gaze pinned with his as he slowly licked his fingers clean. Pink tried to rise in Della's cheeks, but she banished it. How could she be embarrassed when they'd just done… that?

"You ripped my underwear," she managed eventually, still gasping for breath.

Amusement lit his pure-silver eyes. "I'll buy you more. As many as you like." He rose to his feet until he was towering over her shaking body, then leaned down to lick a path up the side of her neck. "That was one, Della. Enough to take the edge off how goddamn hungry I am for you." He nipped at her earlobe and her whole body shuddered. "But you have to remember, I'm starving here, and you," his tongue flicked out to soothe her flesh from his slight bite, "are fucking delicious."

Another shudder rolled through Della's body, centring on the swollen flesh between her legs. How on earth did she have the audacity to get aroused all over again when she was still recovering from the orgasm to end all orgasms? "Leo," she managed to say, and then words failed her when she beheld the hunger still in his face.

"Good girl," he ground out, hands tracing over her body, soothing and arousing her all at once. "Practice how you're going to say my name when I'm inside you." He gripped Della's hips in his hands and the pressure of his thumbs stroking over her hipbones was astoundingly erotic. "Now you'd better show me where your bedroom is, sweetheart, unless you've got a strong desire to be fucked on your hallway floor."

He must have caught the hint of excitement that rolled through her at his words, because he shook his head with a mirthless laugh. "Next time. I'll take you in every room of this house and the garden under the moon if it makes you happy, but the first time I want to be in the bed where you sleep. I want to leave the smell of us on your pillows, so even on nights you're alone here, you're reminded of who made you scream there."

Wordlessly, Della gestured to the doorway at the end of the hall. Leo gathered her up in his arms without comment, as though she were some fragile, precious thing, and carried her into her bedroom, nudging the door shut behind them. He took a moment to take in the room lit only by the lamp by her bed—her dresser, the window that showed her moonlit garden, her bedside table overflowing with books—before depositing her on the bed. Della sat on the edge, watching as he stripped off his jeans, then his boxers, until he stood before her naked. And… wow. Leo in clothes was a thing of beauty, but a naked Leo could stop traffic. And possibly cause a riot.

"You're beautiful," she managed.

He dismissed the compliment with a small smile, eyes still glowing silver. "Take off that bra for me," he said, his voice still as deep as the ocean. "Show me what I've been dreaming about."

Slowly, Della reached behind herself to undo the clasp, then let the straps slide down her arms until her body was as bare as Leo's own. There was something in the way he devoured her bare breasts with his eyes that was even more intimate than what they'd done out in the hallway now that both of them were naked.

"Stunning," Leo said in a tone barely more than a whisper, and barely looking away from her, he reached for his jeans to grab a condom from his wallet. He moved forwards until he was close enough to reach out and press Della backwards on to the bed.

Instead, she slid off the edge and on to her knees.

For a moment, she wished she had a camera so she could capture the brief look of shock and arousal that slid across his features.

"Della, no," Leo growled.

"You promised," she reminded him. "In the carpark, you said, 'next time when we're somewhere private.' That the first time would be in my mouth. Leo, I want that." Deliberately, she licked her lips, watching as his eyes caught on the movement.

"It's not a good idea," he ground out. "Della, the way I'm feeling right now… I could hurt you."

"Please," she said softly, arousal throbbing in her veins as she spoke. "I'll tell you if it's too much. Even with my mouth full, I have ways of communicating." With a thought, she made the lamp flicker on and off.

"I want to see you with that mouth full of me," Leo growled. Was she imagining it, or had he grown even bigger in the moments they'd been in this room? His shoulders, tensed now with indecision, seemed even broader than when he'd knelt before her.

With a growl, he gave in. "Can't deny you a goddamn thing," he snarled, stepping forward to wrap a hand in her hair. "You have two minutes, sweetheart, until I put you on your back and find out if you feel as good as you taste. And I'm betting the answer is *yes*."

Without a word, Della wrapped her fist around his huge arousal, opened her mouth, and took him deep.

Leo's strangled shout echoed off the walls of her bedroom. She smiled around the length of him, drawing back before taking him all the way to the back of her throat. She stroked her hand up and down the part of his length that she couldn't take, in time with the movements of her mouth. Shallow and deep, shallow and deep, her tongue flicking over his head, learning every ridge and vein. His hand in her hair was a reminder he could control her movements any time he wanted, but instead, he let her decide what she wanted to do to him. His harsh grunts and curses above her told her when she was hitting the right spots, but she was barely cognisant of them beyond her focus on making him feel even just a fraction of the pleasure she'd found under his ministrations in the hallway. Had it been two minutes yet? She slid deep down his length again, tracing patterns with her tongue, then withdrew and sucked hard on his head, flicking her tongue against the underside.

Leo used his grip on her hair to drag her away and she felt a mew of protest leave her lips.

"Enough," he growled, his voice frantic. "Enough, Della, or I'm going to blow down your pretty throat."

"I thought you wanted the first time to be in my mouth,"

Della purred, feeling a surge of feminine satisfaction. "Isn't that what you told me?"

"That was before I knew I'd have the option of this perfect pussy," Leo snarled. He reached down to grip her arms and lifted her effortlessly onto the bed, prowling up over her prone body until she was lying back on her pillows, Leo hovering over her. He kissed her as though he truly was starving and she was the only thing that could sate his hunger, their bodies pressing together as he reached down between them to cover himself.

"Spread your legs for me, Della," Leo murmured against her lips. "Show me where you want my cock. Let me give you what you need. Let me give you *everything* you need."

Heat thrumming through her like her blood had been set aflame, Della let her knees fall open, reclaiming his mouth with her own. For the briefest of moments, she cradled his body with her own, every bare inch of their skin touching, and then he was reaching down to position himself at her entrance.

"Look at me," he said, and Della realised she'd been staring down at their naked bodies. She lifted her gaze to meet his, and Leo pushed inside her.

It was like nothing she'd ever experienced. Like her body has been asleep in every other interaction she'd ever had, and he was bringing it to life. She could feel every inch of him in exquisite detail as he withdrew, then pushed in farther, then farther again. His jaw was clenched so tight, she knew it must be similar for him, knew he must be feeling the same blinding rush of sensation as her hips lifted to welcome him and her feet dug into his backside to urge him deeper, faster.

"You feel," he ground out, then faltered, "I don't even have words, Della. This is everything. You are *everything*."

"Please don't stop," Della begged, her voice almost a sob. "Please, Leo, don't stop. I need this. I need you."

"I'll never stop," he growled, and then his hips met hers and he was fully seated within her, filling her so full she could barely breathe.

"Leo—" she gasped.

"Della," he said, and then he was rearing back and thrusting into her, pressing against pleasure points she never even knew she had, and time lost all meaning. The *world* lost all meaning. Surely, this must be the supernatural magic at work, because nothing natural could possibly feel this good; nothing but the power of the universe at work could have her arching and writhing with her approaching orgasm already. Leo's body pressed down on her own, pinning her to the bed, his hands holding her in place to receive his thrusts. She wrapped her legs tighter around him, her back arching with the strength of her approaching climax.

"Let it go, Della," Leo ordered without pausing in his thrusts. "Give it to me. Let me feel it."

"Leo," Della gasped. "Kiss me."

He covered her mouth with his without hesitation so that a moment later when her pleasure hit its crest and her back arched even further, her thighs locked tight around Leo's still-thrusting body, she screamed, releasing the sound into his mouth. Leo took it like she was gifting him with the elixir of life, swallowing down the sound as he ground himself deep into her body. His movements never ceased, sending her shooting straight from one orgasm into a second, and she screamed again. She didn't realise she had her nails dug into the breadth of his back until he growled out, "*Yes*, Della. Mark me up. Make me bleed. I want to see the marks and remember how fucking perfect you feel. How you get even tighter when you're coming on my dick. I want to be reminded of how good I made you feel."

"So good," Della managed, her voice trembling. "Leo, you feel *so good*." He angled his hips, hitting a spot that had her back arching all over again, and she dug her nails in deeper, hearing him growl at the sensation. He reached between them to run his thumb over her clit, and Della had to stifle another scream.

"Leo—" she gasped out. "Leo, I can't—"

"You can," he growled. "One more. I need you to come with me, Della. I need to know I earned it."

His cock filled her, over and over. His thumb rubbed mind-blowing circles around her clit. His muscles bunched against her bare skin. All of it combined to rocket Della towards pleasure so fast that all she could do was wrap her arms and legs around him and let the whirlpool engulf her once more as Leo roared his own completion above her. He was a thing of beauty in his pleasure, all clenching muscles and golden skin as he drove into her one final time and held, held, her own pleasure magnified as she felt him pulsing inside her.

One of Leo's arms seemed to give out without warning, but he caught himself before he could crush her, and she held him as the last waves of her orgasm ran through her. She felt his heartbeat thrumming beneath his skin where his chest pressed to hers, and in that moment, Della would not have been anywhere else for all the money in the world.

Chapter 9

Given all the questionable things he'd done, both as Beta and in his own time, Leo had been pretty sure he wasn't destined for an eternity in heaven among the gods his kind worshipped. For some reason, though, they'd decided to grant him a glimpse of it when they made Della and had her trust him with her body.

He'd had his share of partners—not an exorbitant number, but enough to keep his wolf quiet. But nothing had ever, *ever*, felt like the first moment he pushed inside her. The taste of her, the feel of her spasming around his fingers had both sated and amplified his hunger for her, and that first moment of having her beneath him, legs spread around his hips, her breasts pressed to his bare chest, her most private flesh open to his as he pressed deeper and deeper into her tight, hot wetness… it was branded on his fucking soul. It was like giving water to a man dying from thirst. It was like being given a gift he'd wanted his entire life but never dreamed he'd truly receive. The first time she came, her sex clenching even tighter around him as shudders rolled through her body, he had to dig his nails into his palms to avoid falling to pieces then and there. Tasting her scream of pleasure as her back arched beneath his body almost undid him. *For her*, he had ordered himself, barely able to keep his body in check. *You hold it together for her.*

And it seemed anything truly was possible, because he'd managed to keep himself from shattering into a million tiny pieces as she hit a second peak, then had driven her to a third. The surge of pride in him from knowing he'd brought her pleasure could have powered Mystic City for a month. And finally allowing himself to come with her… there was no parallel he could draw to the sensation of releasing within her perfect body. Nothing else he'd ever experienced even came close. His wolf had been howling like it was a full moon in midsummer, shouting out to the world, '*Mine! Mine! Mine!*' The heroin addict metaphor he'd given Raj and Emmett suddenly seemed vastly more appropriate; he felt like the deepest craving he'd ever had—to pleasure her, to take pleasure in her, to claim her for himself, to meet every need she'd ever had and ever would have—had suddenly been fulfilled. He'd *served* her. He'd claimed her in the moment that he took her, and for the first time, that prospect didn't scare the living hell out of him.

She was his now. More than that, he was *hers*. He knew instinctually that this craving would be with him for the rest of his life. He would never get over this need for Della Green-branch, no matter what he did or how far he went in an attempt to outrun it.

He could no longer discount his friends' belief in the idea of having a mate—not when he knew no one could ever mean as much to him as she did in this moment, her body so warm and soft where it cradled his own. Wishing he could make this moment last the rest of his life, he rolled off to avoid crushing her, pulling her with him so she was cradled against his side. At this moment, Leo was physically incapable of letting Della go. He settled for stroking a hand down her side, tracing patterns on her skin.

"Well," Leo managed once his breathing had evened out somewhat. "That was… something."

"That's one way to describe it," Della said, her voice uneven. She laughed breathlessly. "Is it always like that with a werewolf?"

Leo couldn't stop himself from letting out a low growl. "I'd advise against you conducting any experiments to find out."

She ran a hand down his chest, stroking the hair there, gentling him with her touch. "Leo. I'm here with *you*. I'm not planning on going out on the prowl for other werewolves like some kind of… groupie for wolves. I'm with you." There was a long moment when he got himself at least partly under control before she added, "Besides, after what we just did? I wouldn't have the stamina. You wore me out, Leo Tyler."

"Good," he replied, his wolf finally calming down from its surge of possessiveness when he added quietly, "It's not always like that. Not even close."

"Maybe it's a witch-and-werewolf thing," Della murmured.

"I think maybe," Leo said in a low voice, "maybe it's just a you-and-me thing."

There was a brief moment when the movements of her stroking hand paused on his chest and she seemed to be deciding how she felt about that pronouncement, but then she burrowed even closer into his side, her hand resuming its movement over his skin. "I think I can live with that," Della said softly. "You know, provided we can do it again to test the theory."

"I think I can probably handle that." Leo laughed, his cock already thickening once more at the thought.

The smile she sent him was pure seduction.

Leo woke up reaching for Della, as if his body knew he'd find the bed empty and wanted to alert him to that fact. Of course, he'd fallen for a woman who was an early riser. And not by the definition that his body was quickly reminding him that *he* fit, surrounded as he was by the scent of them together. Barely pausing to pull on the jeans he'd discarded last night, he prowled off to find her and show her how a morning with the two of them in bed together *should* begin.

Usually, he'd just follow the trail of her scent but, this being her home, it was already on everything, so heavily layered he was hard pressed to tell recent traces from older ones. Plus, if she came in to find him sniffing the seat cushions on her couch, she might find it a little strange.

He found her in a room that was obviously a spare bedroom she'd converted into a study. Papers and books were piled on the unused bed behind the desk where Della sat perusing a document while she sipped at a mug of what smelled like coffee. Pushing down his wolf's frustration that there was a bed in this house where he hadn't yet taken her, Leo closed the door loudly enough behind himself that she'd know he was there.

Della jumped, sloshing coffee over the edge of her mug that she magically halted in mid-air with lightning-fast skill before it could land on her papers. Returning it to the mug with a twist of her wrist, she looked up at him with a slightly embarrassed smile.

"Sorry, I was kind of absorbed in what I was reading. You startled me."

"You've got excellent reflexes," Leo said, prowling closer. He pressed his face into her hair and finally took a deep breath of her intoxicating scent. "But then," he added, pulling back just far enough to tilt her chin up for his kiss, "I already knew that."

Della opened her lips to his and sighed into the kiss. "Good morning to you too." Leo could feel her slight smile against his mouth, and it made him growl with pleasure as he met her tongue with his own.

When they broke apart, they were both breathing hard. "There's coffee in the pot in the kitchen if you want some," Della offered.

"How long have you been up?" It bothered him slightly that she'd managed to leave the bed without waking him. He needed to be more aware than that if he was going to sleep beside her. What if there had been a threat to her safety, and he'd slept through it? Unlikely, in her own house, no doubt surrounded by protection spells, but still. It was the principle of the thing.

"Not long," Della said, then glanced at the clock on the wall. "Okay, slightly longer than I thought. I need to start getting ready for work."

"Take the day off," Leo said, almost without considering the words. "Spend it with me."

Della laughed, but there was a hint of longing in it. "I can't take a day off work just to spend it in bed with you, Leo."

"Then we won't spend the whole day in bed," Leo said, though a large part of him would have loved to. "Do you hike?"

"Hike?" Della asked. "I guess, when I have the time."

"There are some incredible waterfalls at the edge of the pack's territory. I could take you to see them."

He was almost surprised by the way her eyes lit up. "Waterfalls? Really?"

"It's a bit of a walk if you're doing it in human form, but it's worth it."

"I guess I do have some sick days saved up," Della said, clearly wavering.

"I'll take you to the burger place for dinner after," Leo said, trying not to sound like he was pleading. *Spend more time with me. Don't make me let you out of my sight already.*

"It was a really good burger," Della admitted.

"How 'bout it, then?" Leo asked. "Want to get away from the paperwork for a few hours?"

She gave him one of those smiles where half of her mouth lifted fractionally before the other, and Leo's heart almost skipped a beat. "I guess I'll let my boss know I won't be in today." Something seemed to occur to her as she stood. "How long exactly is this hike, if we're not going to be back until dinner?"

"I didn't say what time we'd be leaving," Leo reminded her, feeling his grin turn predatory. "First I have to show you what a morning waking up with me is meant to be like." He lifted her and sat her on top of the papers littering her desk, ignoring her half-hearted protestations. "This is how I'm going to wake you up next time you spend the night sleeping next to me."

Every night, his wolf insisted. *She should be in my arms every night.*

Ignoring the thought, Leo dragged his hands from Della's shoulders down over the curves of her body and pushed her legs apart, then got to work.

Afterwards, having thoroughly disorganised the papers on her desk when he laid her out across it, Leo sat in the chair before it, Della curled up on his lap, practically purring. Hell, if he could make her this content with just the use of his body, he'd have to start waking up earlier to satisfy her before she went to work each day. Gods, only this woman could make him consider getting up early. The idea of her arriving at her job with his scent all over her sent a kind of smug pride running through him. Then *every* male who came close to his woman would know she had been claimed.

What the hell happened to 'casual'? a voice in his head asked.

This happened, Leo told it, shoving the thought away. *Della happened.*

"We'll have to stop by my place so I can change," Leo said, his voice husky from growling her name.

"I've never been to Blue Crescent territory before," Della said. Her body had grown slightly tense in his arms. "Your pack is usually pretty full-on about keeping outsiders away." She pulled away far enough to meet his eyes. "Is that going to be a problem?"

"You'll be with me," Leo said, feeling his canines start to elongate at the thought of one his pack making trouble for her. "It'd be more of a problem for whoever decided to kick up a fuss."

"Part of me would like to see you fight someday," Della said with the air of one admitting a mortal sin. "I think…I think it'd be kind of hot."

Leo wondered briefly if she'd even want to come near him again if she saw him in a state where he let his instincts take over, the half-shift giving him claws and fangs designed for carnage. "Maybe someday," he said non-committally. "My friend Raj is always up for a fight," he added. "You might rethink the 'hot' part after you've seen us spar, though."

"Why?"

"It's not like the kind of fighting you see in the movies. It's messy. And you'd have to see me in my half-shifted form, which isn't exactly cover model material."

"I think I could handle it," Della insisted.

"I'm sure you could," Leo said. "The question is whether you'd let me near you afterwards." He said it with a laugh, but that didn't stop the honest concern that she wouldn't. And there was no way he was risking that.

Della gave a little considering hum noise in the back of her throat and started up from his lap. "I guess I'd better ring my boss, then try to find those hiking boots."

Leo licked his lips. "I might go get some of that coffee. It's delicious… or that might just be because I was tasting it on you."

Leo drove them from her house to his, and Della noticed people watching his car passing as they drove into Blue Crescent territory. The majority looked pleased to see him, some even waved, but others looked almost… scared? She didn't have long enough to assess it before they were driving away.

Blue Crescent territory looked almost disappointingly similar to Avalon Coven territory. Della didn't know what she'd been expecting. Claw marks down the lamp posts and massive wolves prowling the streets? Sure, there were a few more shops with wolf puns in the names, but then, wasn't her favourite café near her own house called the Coffee Cauldron? Who was she to judge?

Leo's house was farther from the centre of the territory than she'd have expected for a pack Beta. His area was almost a little city, full of lively shops and narrow, winding streets.

Leo noticed her sudden silence. "It's the oldest part of the pack's territory," he explained. "Most of my neighbours are about three times my age. I do a lot of handiwork for them, but it's worth it to live somewhere like this."

"It's beautiful," Della said honestly. "So much of my coven's territory is very planned and organised, gridwork streets, carefully selected street trees planted equidistant from each other. This place is a little… wilder. I like it."

A small smile was Leo's only answer as they pulled into the driveway of a house almost completely hidden by trees.

"You must really like your privacy," Della commented.

"You're not wrong," Leo laughed, "but most of these were

here long before I was. I keep them under control, but mostly just let them grow."

"It looks much more like a wicked witch's house than mine does, hidden away like this."

"Doesn't stop my neighbours from coming past when they want a door handle fixed or something. Clearly, it's not as intimidating as it appears at first sight."

"I'm not intimidated—" Della started, but he was already throwing her a wink and climbing out of the car.

The inside of Leo's place was classic bachelor pad, a massive TV, a big couch, and a couple of easy chairs.

"I might have to give you the full tour some other time," he said apologetically. "I can't promise what'll happen if I get you in my bedroom looking like that."

"Looking like what?" Della asked, genuinely nonplussed. She glanced down at herself. "It's just activewear. I'm wearing hiking boots, for heaven's sake."

"You've clearly never seen your ass in those leggings," Leo said with a raised eyebrow. "It's a wonder we made it out of your house to the car without me ripping them off you."

Della felt how high up her eyebrows had risen in surprise. "These are, like, ten-dollar leggings."

Leo sent her a grin as he disappeared through a doorway on the opposite side of the room. "You won't mind when I destroy them later, then."

Shaking her head at the impossibility of males, Della set to snooping around Leo's house. She found a large collection of tools, clearly well-used, and a shelf of old jazz CDs, covered in dust. Crowding the top of a chest of drawers were a series of photos of monuments in various countries, some with a younger Leo in them, some just of the views, the Eiffel Tower, the Colosseum, the Taj Mahal. One picture of him having climbed a trail in the Annapurna Mountain range and looking exceptionally pleased with himself, made her question the wisdom of going hiking with a man who climbed mountains for fun.

Leo reappeared while she was examining a photo of him holding a surfboard at a crowded beach. She only knew he was behind her because he said softly, "That's in Costa Rica. Tamarindo Beach."

Della started, then put the picture back with the others. "When were you there? When were you in… all these places?"

"After I left school when my dad was still Beta. I was learning how it'd be when I took up the role, and I guess I realised that if I didn't see the world then, I'd never have the chance. So, I packed a bag, bought a plane ticket to Paris, and left. It was a couple of years before I came back."

"*Years?*" Della said, shocked.

Leo shrugged. "Honestly, I could have stayed away longer, but my dad was getting sick, and he wanted me home, so I came." A slight smile quirked his lips. "Some of the pack weren't too keen on having a Beta who'd been away from Mystic City for so long, so I think it was also his way of trying to give me time to reintegrate before I had to take up the mantle."

"Do you miss it?" Della asked. "The freedom of it?"

"Sometimes," Leo admitted. "When I have to settle a bunch of stupid disputes or James has me doing something I don't want to do. Sometimes I think about running away all over again. But I couldn't leave the pack."

"They're your home now," Della said softly.

"Yeah," Leo confirmed. "Even the ones who don't much like me know that I'd go to war for them. That's what this job means—more than just solving arguments and handing out warnings, it's about doing what's best for your people. Protecting them."

Something in Della that had been doing its best to protect her heart from this man crumbled to dust.

"Come see the kitchen," Leo said, pulling away. "I'll make us some lunch, and we can eat it at the falls."

The kitchen was almost as big as the living room, with a large wooden table demarcating the eating area.

"Did you make this?" Della asked, running her hand over the table's surface.

"Yeah, that's one of mine," Leo said, getting things out of the fridge. "The chairs, too. You like sandwiches?"

"Who doesn't like sandwiches?" Della laughed. "Maybe I could buy a table from you for my dining room. The one I have is getting to the end of its life."

The breath was knocked out of her when Leo was suddenly in front of her, yanking her tight against his big, hard body with a half-smile that sent electricity running through her. "If you think you're ever paying me for *anything* I do for you, sweetheart, you're about to get that thought very strongly corrected. It would be my goddamn honour to have something I made in your home, all right?" His breath was hot on her neck as he tugged aside the neckline of her t-shirt to flick his tongue over the mark he'd left on her skin yesterday. Her knees went a little weak, and he caught her and made short work of depositing her on the bench beside where he was putting the sandwiches together.

"So," he said mildly, as though arousal wasn't still lighting up her veins from his mouth on her skin. "I can get a dining table done for you pretty quickly. I'll just need to take measurements, and I can take you to choose some timber you like." He held out a piece of cheese to her and spontaneously, instead of taking it, Della leaned forwards and ate it from his fingers, licking them clean for good measure.

Leo's eyes were as brightly silver as a newly minted coin when he added, "But if you want to desecrate this one with me sometime, sweetheart, all you have to do is say the word."

"Desecrate?" Della laughed. "Is that what they're calling it these days?"

"Careful, or I'll desecrate you right here, my little goddess," Leo said, pushing her legs apart where she sat on the bench and letting her feel his swollen bulge against the juncture of her thighs. When Della gasped and rocked her hips towards him, he added, "It's like this all the time when you're around, Della. You make me like this every minute of the goddamn day. Remember that if you ever doubt that this dick knows who it belongs to now."

As she tried to find a valid response to that, Leo winked at her again and went back to assembling sandwiches, whistling jauntily.

They drove out through the remainder of the werewolves' territory to the place it met the edge of the surrounding forest. Della went to offer to carry the backpack that held their lunch, water, and a small medical kit—'*Can't be too careful*,' Leo had said when she raised an eyebrow—but a look from the werewolf had her holding her tongue. Instead, she just cast a spell to make it lighter, and though Leo's muscles suggested he wouldn't have had an issue with the weight of a few bottles of water, he'd laughed and thanked her. They started down one of the trails that led off the gravel area where they'd parked, and though the path wasn't brilliantly marked, Leo seemed to know his way almost instinctually.

"Have you been here a lot?" Della asked.

"A few times," Leo said. "Came down this way a lot as teenagers to see how many bottles of cheap vodka it'd take to get a young werewolf drunk. Witch-spelled powders and pills. Bringing pretty girls out late at night." He tossed her a smile, but the surge of possessive anger that rolled through her must have shown on her face, because he looked immediately taken aback.

"Not recently, I would hope," Della said stiffly.

"Gods, Della, no," Leo said, one of his hands rising as though he'd reach out for her. "Not for… a while now. A long while. And nothing like this, ever."

"Good," Della said, knowing she looked dangerously angry but unable to control it. "Because I know how to turn someone's blood to acid and make whichever *bitch* I had to, burn and suffocate to death at the same time. I'm just saying."

To her shock, Leo responded by pulling her into his arms, stroking her hair soothingly. "Della," he said softly, then repeated the same words she'd used with him before, "I'm here, I'm here with *you*. I don't want anyone else. I hardly even see them anymore because they're not you."

The possessive creature that had reared its head inside her quieted down once more at the frantic note in his voice. She took a deep breath, in, out. In, out. "Sorry," she managed. "I don't know why I responded like that."

"Very wolfish of you," Leo said, a smile in his voice, still holding her close. "How you felt right then—that's the way seeing that Ian guy run his eyes over you made me feel. That's why I responded the way I did last night."

"It kind of makes more sense to me now, I guess," Della admitted. "I guess I'm not used to having those feelings over someone or having someone have them over me. Not in a while, anyway," she added, as the thought of Dane flickered through her mind.

"Hey," Leo said, holding her away from him so he could see her face. She realised she'd tensed up at the thought of her ex-boyfriend. "Where did you go then?" Leo asked.

"It's nothing," Della said, pushing away from him. She'd taken maybe two steps before she felt his hand catching hold of her arm.

"It's not nothing. Not if it takes you away from me."

"It was a long time ago," Della argued.

"That doesn't matter, not if it still upsets you like this." There was a pause as he seemed to put two and two together. "Is this why you got all cold on me last night? Is it the same thing?"

"Leo—" she protested.

"Della," he replied. "I need to know so I don't do it again. So, I can stop hurting you with these reminders of whatever it is."

She pulled her arm out of his grasp and turned away, walking a few paces before she stopped. Was she really going to do this? What if he looked at her the way everyone else did afterwards—like a victim, worthy of pity and needing to be handled like fragile glass, or worse, like it had been her fault, like she deserved everything she got and more? What if after he knew, he didn't want her anymore?

Hadn't she told herself, after Dane, she'd never let herself be controlled by fear again? Didn't she owe it to both of them to be honest about her past, about how it might affect the future of their relationship?

"I'll tell you," Della said, steeling herself as hard as she could. "But can we walk and talk? It'll be easier for me to discuss it that way."

She risked a glance back to meet his eyes as he said, "Of course," and they began to follow the semi-visible trail once more.

"I met Dane as soon as I left university," Della started. "He was a friend of a friend, a human who also worked in government, more than ten years older than me, but in my eyes that just made him look more experienced and worldly—appealing, to a girl who grew up barely leaving Mystic City. I guess I thought I could trust him, because he was friends with my friend and everyone who knew him seemed to have nothing but good things to say about him. He was a human, so there were a few raised eyebrows about that and our age difference, but mostly my friends were just happy to see me happy.

"And I was. He seemed to adore me, seemed to be happy with me no matter what I said or did. He was a little uncomfortable with my magic, so I just didn't use it around him, trying to keep us on an even footing as much as possible. I moved in with him after just a few months, and all he seemed to want to do was take care of me. I still went to work each day—he'd helped me get the job I had before I moved to my current one—but at home, he handled everything. I thought it was symbolic of his devotion, the way he helped me choose my clothes and what I ate and the books I read, and I just let him do it, not realising he was completely taking over my life. We had a joint bank account, but I didn't touch it without his approval. After a while, when I did anything without his say-so, he started to get angry. Throwing things, yelling at me. And still, I was in so deep, I didn't think of it as wrong. He wanted to look after me, he would tell me, and how could he do that if he didn't know where I was, what I was doing, who I was seeing? He needed all the information, all the control over my life, so that he could make it as easy for me as possible. So, I wouldn't have to do anything for myself.

"I didn't realise part of the reason I'd become so biddable was that I was growing weaker. Physically, but mostly in my magic. I barely used it anymore because Dane had never been fully comfortable with it. At first, I thought it was romantic that he loved me even though I had what he might have perceived as a flaw. Even though we were different. But a witch has to expel some power every now and then—it's called siphoning off—or the build-up becomes uncomfortable. So, I encouraged the small garden of his house—our house—and that was it. Slowly, even that small act started to drain me, until I was exhausted all the time. I stopped going out, withdrew from my friends, could barely go to work. I did whatever he told me without question, accepted his words like royal decrees—even when he told me he wanted to start seeing other women, but I could not touch anyone but him, I didn't even question it. I was far too tired to seek out other liaisons anyway. I wondered if I might be pregnant and decided to visit my grandmother to find out, when I had the energy, since I was no longer confident that I was strong enough to reliably do the spell myself.

"He started spending more time with his other women, and less with me, telling me they were more interesting because I was so tired all the time, and I was lucky he hadn't just left me when I stopped being interesting myself. Like a sycophant, I accepted that too. I wanted him to be happy. I loved him, still. His absences turned out to be a blessing, because it meant he was away for dinner some nights, and though he still decided what I ate, he wasn't cooking it.

"I finally had my strength back enough to go see my grandmother, to find out if I was pregnant and ask how it would be different given that I might be carrying a human's child. Regular pregnancy tests don't work for witches; our magic interferes with them. There's a spell we can cast to find out instead, and I presumed she would just do that.

"When she saw me, she started criticising me immediately, but that's sort of just Grandmother Elise's way with me. I was too thin, my skin had gone dull, I looked like I hadn't seen the sun in months. She was almost right. I'd barely had the power to continue encouraging the garden, and that I mostly did in the evenings, when Dane was out, so he wouldn't have to witness me using magic.

"She did the spell on me, and I promptly fainted. When she continued working magic to discover the cause, she locked me in the room I used to use when I slept over. Because she discovered that Dane had been giving me a powder of a plant called freyroot in my food almost since I moved in with him. It can be useful in spells for astral projection if you burn it and inhale the smoke, but if ingested, especially in a powder, it dampens magic and causes an almost hypnotised suggestible state that he used to make me so wholly infatuated with him that I let him do whatever he wanted to me. And with long term use, it starts slowly poisoning the person consuming it. In his quest to increase his power over me, he'd been slowly killing me.

"My grandmother locked me away for almost a week, providing food and water and healing spells in the periods I wasn't frantic with the need to get back to Dane. Even knowing what he had done, I was so wholly indoctrinated that I wanted to return to him. I'd always known he didn't like my magic—why wouldn't he try to find a way to rid me of it, so he could love me more?

"Slowly, as the freyroot was washed from my system, I began to regain a clearer mind. To realise what he had done to me, what he had been trying to do to me. To be terrified of seeing him again in case I fell back under his influence. I hadn't told him I was going to see Grandmother Elise, so he didn't know where to find me, thank the gods, but my work also didn't know where I'd gone. What I didn't know was that he'd told them I was ill, so no suspicion would fall over my absence, at least for a little while, as he tried to find me. What friends I still had were used to not seeing me for weeks or months, so they didn't question it. I had enough time to recover my mind, at least in part, before Grandmother Elise insisted on taking me to the hospital.

"What I didn't realise was that I looked like I'd been in a war camp, I was so thin, so pale and haggard-looking. When she explained that I'd unknowingly been dosed with freyroot powder probably for over a year, the hospital went into high alert. They called the authorities; Dane wound up being arrested. They found his stash of the powder, and after all the tests they'd run on me, it was clear the accusation was true. He was charged with attempted murder.

"The trial wasn't until months later. My entire witness statement was read before the court, every detail of our life together and my failure to notice the signs that something was wrong. I saw him in the corridor just once, under guard, and he just stared at me as I stood, frozen in fear. I was still irrationally scared that just seeing him would be enough to break my mind all over again. But it didn't. He looked at me and I looked at him, and he said, 'I thought you loved me.' I told him, 'You were right. I did.' And then I walked away.

"He was found guilty, and he's currently in prison and will be for years. I begged off from attending the sentencing and went into work instead. Everyone knew what had happened, because it was in the papers, and to them, I had become this great victim figure, fragile and breakable. In part, they were right. It was the best part of a year before I fully recovered from what he'd done to me—physically, at least. Longer, for my magic to recover. And I swore I would never allow myself to become so fully in someone's power again. I must never let myself become someone's object, their possession, allowing them to define what I do or where I go or how I eat or dress. I need to always remember that I belong to myself before anyone else."

Finally, she stopped talking, stopped walking. "And that's my story," she said softly. "I haven't told anyone that for a long, long time."

Leo stood several arms' lengths away from her, and when she managed to work up the courage to look at his face, she almost flinched. She'd never seen that kind of anger in someone's expression before, such livid fury. "I'll kill him," he said without preamble. "Tell me where he is, and I'll kill him. I'll make it hurt, like he hurt you."

"No," Della said, keeping her tone even. "That's not your decision to make. It's mine, and I say it's better if he rots away in jail, powerless and surrounded by the magic he hates, than to have an easy way out like dying. I want him to spend all these years knowing that I am out here, living a good life and using this power I've been gifted however I want, because that will be the worst kind of torture that I could possibly inflict on him. Knowing that in his bid to rid me of my magic, he just made me more powerful, and I will change the world to make sure hatred like his can't fester between species in the same way, ever again."

In the span of a few moments, the fury melted from Leo's features—not gone, but controlled. Instead, the look on his face as he took her in was awestruck. In a blink he was before her, pulling her close and burying his face in her hair.

"You're the furthest thing from a victim I've ever met, Delphinia Greenbranch," he said quietly. "You are a survivor of the worst kind of hell, and I'll always be grateful that the universe brought me to you."

Hearing Della's story had sent Leo deep into what the older werewolves had taught him as a pup was called the 'killing calm'—when one became so angry that it went beyond fury and into a kind of rage so severe it was quiet. In that moment, if the man who'd hurt her had been standing in front of him, Leo would have torn the bastard limb from limb and made him watch his own dismemberment, consequences be damned. But her words made sense—enough that he could leash the fury and focus on *her*, at least. On what it had cost her to reveal this part of her history to him. On how he could possibly find the means to show her what it meant to him that she trusted him this way.

"Thank you," he managed to say out loud as she wrapped her arms around him in return. "Thank you for telling me."

Della buried her face in his chest, and they stood there, unspeaking, surrounded by the sounds of the forest.

"I don't want your pity," she said eventually.

"Good," Leo said, "because I don't have any for you. All you have is my admiration." He felt her smile against his chest. "I'll leash it," he promised. "The werewolf part of me, the… possessiveness. I'll keep it in check."

"I don't want you to be anyone but yourself with me," Della said. "I don't want you keeping parts of yourself 'leashed'. And as we've seen, I have it too, I just—if I react badly, sometimes, now you know why."

"No," Leo said with finality. "I won't do it; I won't do anything that reminds you of him. I won't let myself do that to you. To us."

Della pulled away far enough to meet his eyes. "I know you're nothing like him; of course, I know that. It's just the memories. Most of the time, though, I like it. I like that I mean enough to you for you to feel that way about me." A small smile graced her features. "And I think we've ascertained beyond question that I more than like the ways you show it when we're alone." She pulled his head down so she could kiss him, even the light touch of her lips pressing against his sending lightning through his body.

"We'll work it out," Della said when they broke apart. "I won't let him, or even memories of him, define what I'm allowed to do or enjoy or who I can be with." She took a deep breath. "I know we said we wanted something casual, Leo, but—"

"It's more," he finished for her. "You think I don't feel it too? This is everything, Della. *You* are everything."

"Everything," she echoed softly, and this time it was she who pushed him backwards until his back was against the thick trunk of a tree, her hands tangling in his hair as she pressed their bodies together like she could meld them into one. Her touch raced over him, pushing up his t-shirt and scraping over the flesh beneath, her nails digging lines into his abs. He found himself grabbing at her like she might be taken away from him, cupping and squeezing her breasts, the curve of her ass.

She broke away, panting, long before he was ready to let go of her. "So, these waterfalls?" she asked breathlessly.

"Not much farther," Leo said, catching the look of self-satisfaction that slipped over her face when he had to adjust himself to keep walking.

Perhaps he'd become immune to the beauty of the falls because his quiet appreciation of them was nothing compared to the way Della gasped when they reached the clearing. She stumbled over a rock, she was so busy staring, and when he caught her, she clung to his arm. "Leo, it's *beautiful*," she said breathlessly.

The falls cascaded some forty feet into a pool surrounded by low rocks that was home to fish, frogs and other creatures that could avoid being washed down the small stream they fed. The sun was breaking through the trees of the surrounding forest at just the right angle to send rainbows shooting from the tumbling water. They seemed magnetised to Della, lighting up her brilliant smile with a myriad of colours.

"Can we swim?" she asked.

"I don't usually in my human form, but I don't see why you couldn't," Leo said. His mind flickered to the nights he'd spent here in the past, knowing that they would now always be classified in his head as "before"—before he'd brought Della here and seen the beauty of the place through her eyes.

"I can stand watch if you want to try it without all those clothes on," Leo offered, raising an eyebrow.

"Sensor spells," Della said. "I can set them far enough out

that we have time to get dressed again before anyone comes close." She stripped off her shirt, and Leo was momentarily struck dumb by the sight of her perfect breasts encased in lace.

"Wolves can move pretty fast," he managed.

"I'm familiar with the concepts of time and space, Leo," Della teased. "I'll set the spells far enough away, don't worry." She pulled her leggings down her legs and closed her eyes for a moment, making a spreading motion with her hands. Magic rippled from her. "There. Good to go. Now if you felt like joining me…"

Leo had stripped down to his underwear in a bare moment, revelling in the way she took in his body, in the hungry look in her eyes.

"Why do you still have underwear on?" she asked.

"You do," he pointed out, "I thought that was how you were planning to go in," and wondered if she was uncomfortable being naked around him after her revelations.

"Maybe I was just waiting for you to take them off me," Della offered, and with a growl, Leo was upon her.

He had to consciously restrain himself to avoid shredding her underwear again in his rush to have her bare before him, especially as her own hands were tugging off his boxers. When he had her breasts bared, he leaned down and took each of her nipples in his mouth, just for the pleasure of hearing her gasp and moan. He would never get over the taste of her, the feel of her skin on his tongue. His cock was begging for her touch, but he ignored it as he swung her up into his arms and, with her breathless reprimand of "Leo!" ringing in his ears, jumped into the water. It was cold enough to steal his breath, and when they resurfaced, Della was laughing and sputtering all at once, clinging to him with all four limbs.

"My gods, it's freezing!"

"You definitely feel the cold less when you're swimming as

a wolf," Leo admitted. "I haven't been in here in this form in a long time."

Della kicked over closer to the waterfall itself and ducked under the stream. Leo found a rock by the edge and perched himself on it. When she resurfaced, she returned to him and wrapped herself around him. "Yep, it's even colder under there."

"I could have told you that," Leo said, wrapping his arms around her.

"It was more fun to find out for myself," Della grinned. "I love this place already. It's gorgeous. Thank you so much for bringing me here."

"Can I get you out and into the sun? You're shaking."

"In a minute," Della said, kicking off from him to dive deep under the water. Leo followed her, opening his eyes beneath the water to see her looking like some sort of water nymph, her hair spread out around her head as she explored the depths of the pool. He would have been content to watch her for hours, but soon enough they were both shaking and blue-lipped and Leo dragged her out and onto a flat stone in a patch of sunlight. Della laughed and flicked her fingers, drying them both immediately. The sun warming his bare skin, Leo lay back and soaked in the moment, Della's head on his chest.

"This must be what paradise feels like," Leo mused.

Della replied only with a contented hum, tracing patterns on his chest with her fingertips.

"So, you normally swim in there as a wolf?" she asked eventually.

"I haven't been here for a while," Leo said, "but we used to. You don't feel the temperature so much that way. I'd forgotten how bloody cold it is."

"Good excuse to lie in the sun afterwards," Della pointed out contentedly, her bare skin pressing against his as she shifted. She leaned back to meet his eyes with a smile, then bit her lip. "Do you think I might be able to see your wolf form someday?"

"Of course," Leo said, taken aback. "Whenever you want. I guess... I guess I didn't think you'd be interested in it." *Wouldn't want to see me when I'm so profoundly inhuman.*

"Leo, my job is in youth interspecies integration. You have to know it's not going to upset me to see you shift. You've been seeing me do magic all the time, and it doesn't seem to bother you. Why would your wolf form bother me?"

"Do you want to see it... now?" Leo asked. Despite her words, worry coiled in his belly. What if she didn't want him to touch her once she'd seen him as an animal?

Della sat up, taking his hand, and pressing it to her face. "If you're happy to show me. I don't want to push you."

"I want to show you," Leo said, slightly surprised to find that the words were true. "I want you to see me."

Della sat back, watching him with wide eyes. "Do you have to be naked to shift?"

"No, if you're wearing clothes, they just kind of... disappear as you shift. And then they come back when you shift back to human."

"Magic of the universe," Della said, as though she was confirming something she'd already suspected.

Leo climbed to his feet and across a few rocks, away from her. "Just don't be scared when you see me," he said. "Remember it's still me in there—it's just a different part of me that's leading. Remember I'll never hurt you, no matter what form I'm in."

"I know," Della said. "I won't be scared."

With a brief prayer that she still wanted him the same way afterwards, Leo reached within himself to his wolf and let it come to the fore.

He'd long since become used to the strange, somewhat painful sensations of his bones shifting shape, of his jaw elongating to fit extra teeth, of the fur bursting through his skin. As a pup it had scared him, but now it was second nature to set the wolf in him free and let the shift roll through his body.

He settled onto his four paws and took a deep breath, relishing the improved sense of smell he had in this form. The forest and the water were both deep and green, but mostly he smelled Della—and revelled in the fact that the sex-and-spices scent of her was now mixed with his own scent.

She was staring at him, but not in fear or disgust as he'd been afraid. She was taking in every inch of him, from his nose to his tail, a look of utter fascination on her face. She rose to her feet, the sun gilding her naked skin, and stepped towards him, slowly. The wolf part of his brain, so much more powerful in this form, wanted to howl its pleasure at her approach. He kept it in check, but barely.

"Can I… can I touch you?" Della asked hesitantly, and Leo inclined his head. There were some drawbacks to this form; he couldn't tell her that he'd relish her touch no matter what body he was in. Her hands came up and started with the fur between his ears, stroking down his neck and to his back and sides. She alternated between weaving her fingers into the thick fur and petting him the same way she stroked his chest when they lay next to each other. Leo closed his eyes, revelling in her touch, until she tapped his nose with one finger. The man in him loved that she was completely unafraid of him.

"Could I have human Leo back now, please?" she asked, all politeness.

Leo gave the wuff of breath that passed for a chuckle in his wolf form and shifted back. Della smiled up at him.

"What are you thinking?" he heard himself ask.

"That you're beautiful in that form," Della said quietly. "And deadly, I'm sure. I didn't expect you to be quite so… big."

"Not every wolf is. And the females are smaller." He paused. "You really didn't mind it?"

"Mind it?" she asked, sounding shocked. "Leo, your wolf form is stunning. I want to cuddle it like a huge teddy bear and go to sleep curled up next to it."

A massive laugh burst out of Leo like a balloon popping. "Okay, that is not the response my wolf form usually gets."

Della's laughter joined his own. "I'm sorry, what would you prefer? You're terrifying, so big and scary, I'm shaking in my boots?"

"I mean," Leo said, still laughing, "that is the usual reaction."

"But I know you'd never hurt me," Della said, stepping close enough to run her hands over his pecs and twine them up around his neck. "I have no doubt that you're utterly deadly in that form, as I'm sure you are in this one. But why would I be scared of you when I know you won't hurt me?" She pressed her body against his, her skin warmed by the sun. He tried to hold back the growl that came from their skin touching, and almost succeeded; it came out more as a rumble deep in his chest.

"Sweetheart, unless you're looking to get fucked on one of these rocks, I'd be careful what you do with that body."

Della pressed her lips to his collarbone. "And if I am?"

He wrapped a hand in the darkness of her hair. "Just confirm for me first that this isn't because you're turned on by my wolf. Bestiality is not on my kink list."

"I promise it's not because I want to fuck your wolf, Leo. I just… I love that you trust me enough to show me that part of yourself." She pulled back far enough to meet his eyes, a hint of a smile playing around her perfect lips. "So, what is on your kink list?"

Leo pulled her down onto the largest of the rocks, turning them so his body hit the hard surface. "For starters," he said, rolling his hips against her so she could feel the extent of his arousal, "I want to watch your gorgeous tits bounce while you ride my dick beside a waterfall. Think that could be arranged, sweetheart?"

She licked her lips, sending even more blood shooting to his swollen erection. "Oh, I think we can manage that."

She sat up on top of him, scoring her nails down over his pecs, his abs, all the way to his throbbing cock. The sight of her hands, so much smaller than his own, wrapping around his length and slowly moving up and down in a mind-blowing glide action made his head spin. "That's right, gorgeous, jack my cock. Let me see how much you like playing with it."

Della flicked her fingers and with a ripple of magic, suddenly there was a condom in her hands, drawn from who-knows-where. Had she packed them when they were getting ready? Had she been planning on taking his dick by the water this entire time?

All semblance of thought left his head as she rolled the thin latex down his length and positioned him at her entrance. "This much," Della said, looking like a primitive forest goddess as she rose over him. "This is how much I like it." And without giving him a chance to breathe, to even think, she sank down on him, engulfing him in the tight, hot wetness that he knew in that moment he would happily kill or die for. She bit her lips at the sensation of him filling her, and he couldn't help himself from pulling her down to cover her mouth with his own. She rocked her hips, moving atop him as their lips met, and her tongue flicked over his in sweet strokes matched by the way she took him shallow and deep, her hips rocking against his.

She released his mouth with a moan and pinned him to the rocks with her hands braced on his shoulders as she rose over him once more, using their position for resistance so that she could move her hips ever faster, ride him even harder. Half his instincts said to flip her on to her back and pound the boundless ocean of lust inside himself into her, but the other half was enamoured beyond words with the perfection of her sun-gilded curves, the way her body moved atop his, the sounds she made when he bottomed out inside her, his skin meeting hers. This woman was *his*, his wolf insisted—his heart insisted. And now she was claiming him too, her nails digging into his shoulders as her moans became higher, sharper, her movements even faster.

"Leo," she gasped, meeting his eyes, and then she was throwing her head back as she shuddered around him.

Leo's control snapped. With a snarl, he palmed the curve of her hips to force her to take his thrusts as he arched up off the rock beneath them, dragging her as close as he could as he drove into her over and over.

His release struck him like a blow, and he was almost unconscious of dragging Della down to bury his face in her neck as he roared his pleasure loud enough for the whole world to hear.

They lay there for a long moment, the spray from the waterfall mixing with the dampness of their skin. Feeling Della's breath against his chest, her heart pounding as fast as his, her slick skin pressed to his own... there were no words for the feeling that filled Leo's chest so completely that he half thought he might burst with it. Or perhaps, there were a very specific three.

But surely, it was far too soon to use those words, especially with a woman who'd been so brutally betrayed by someone who should have protected her in the past.

But he couldn't keep himself from muttering into her hair, so quietly she could claim not to have heard it over the rush of the waterfall if she wanted, "I'm yours, Della. And someday, when you're ready, I hope you can say those words back to me."

Della tilted her head back to stare at him, her eyes wider

than he'd ever seen them. Surprise, or fear? What had he just done?

"And if I'm never ready?" she asked, her eyebrows drawing together.

"Then that won't make what I said an ounce less true," Leo said. "I will still be yours, no matter what."

For a long moment, all she did was hold his gaze. And then she bent her head to press a kiss to his chest, right over his heart. Impossibly, the emotion filling Leo's chest expanded even further, making it hard to breathe.

Especially when she pressed her lips back to his and whispered, "Mine."

Chapter 10

All right, so she'd lost her mind. A little, at least. Okay, a lot. Because why else would she, Delphinia Green-branch, claim a man as *hers*? Let alone be sitting in the car with him afterwards as they drove back to his place, because he wanted to stop in there before they went to dinner. No matter that his hand on her thigh made her magic coil and curl within her like a needy kitten looking to be petted. No matter that the feelings she had for him were getting so big, so intense, so quickly, that it was like someone was inflating a beach ball in her chest when she looked at him. A warm, fuzzy, delicious beach ball that she was finding it hard not to get addicted to. Okay, so the metaphor wasn't perfect. Was it her fault when this man—this *werewolf*—was so expertly scrambling her brains with every touch?

As if he'd heard her thought, Leo's hand tightened where he was gripping her thigh. She followed his gaze as the car slowed and realised they were almost at his place, but there were two cars parked in front of the tree-shielded home, each with a werewolf leaning on its hood as they chatted to one another. Their conversation faltered as Leo and Della pulled into the driveway.

"Do you know them?" Della asked. She hesitated, then added, "Should I be worried?"

"They're friends," Leo said, undoing his seatbelt before reaching over for hers. "Idiots, but friends. I just don't know why they're here."

The two wolves leaning on their cars unashamedly stared at Della as she stepped out of the car, pre-empting Leo's move to come around and open her door. Instead, he wrapped an arm around her, holding her to his side as his two friends approached. She tried not to shrink behind him. They might be werewolves—one leanly muscled, the other the size of a semi-trailer and grinning—but she was a witch, dammit. Where was her confidence?

"So, this is her," the massive—well, more massive—one said with what could have been understanding or appreciation in his voice. "I see what you mean about her scent."

"It would be in your best interests to stop seeing it as soon as possible," Leo practically snarled, his arm around her tightening.

Mr. Massive raised his hands in surrender and halted his approach, though the other wolf kept coming until he could hold out his hand for her to shake. "I'm Emmett. The idiot back there is Raj. Nice to meet you."

"Della," she said, accepting his handshake in a brief greeting. Brief, because she felt Leo tense the moment they touched. "I'm Leo's…" she trailed off, not sure what word to use. *Girlfriend* didn't seem to fit right. *Partner*, she knew, carried different weight with wolves and vampires than regular people.

Her cheeks were starting to flush at the expectant silence when Emmett interjected, "He's told us about you. We get it."

She almost questioned his statement, but Raj's voice came from his position behind Emmett.

"A witch, huh, Leo?" Raj asked jovially, still not coming any closer. "How are you going to explain that to James?"

Leo fixed him with a dark look. "Leave James out of it. What are you two doing here?"

"Jesus, Leo," Raj said with a chortle. "Don't be too welcoming. We might not recognise you."

"You don't hang around the front of my house for no reason," Leo said. He relented after a moment, adding, "If you tell me what it is, you can take off, and I can take Della for dinner. Give me a break here."

"Lucky you, paired with the grumpiest wolf in Blue Crescent," Raj joked to Della.

She caught a glance between him and Leo that she couldn't decipher, but was distracted by Emmett saying, "It's James. He's looking for you—wants you to deliver a message for him. When he couldn't find you, he came to us. It wouldn't kill you to answer your phone, man."

"Can't he deliver his own messages?" Della asked without thinking. She didn't want her time with Leo to be cut short because he had to work, as hypocritical as that was.

Emmett and Raj both laughed. "James doesn't really like getting his hands dirty if he can avoid it," Emmett explained.

"Yeah, he's got Leo for that," Raj added.

"All right, message delivered. We're finally allowed to go home," Emmett added, rolling his shoulders. "Guess we won't see you at training in the morning, Leo. Nice to finally meet you, Della. Maybe we can all hang out sometime, next time the two of you come up for air."

"Sounds good." Della smiled at Leo's friends as they retreated towards their cars—Emmett's low and sleek, Raj's a rickety-looking truck. Before they had even turned on to the street, Leo was pulling her inside the house.

"What's going on?" she asked. This didn't have the flavour of desperation fuelled by arousal that she was getting used to.

"I don't know who else James has out looking for me."

"And you don't want them to see us together?" she asked.

Leo stopped in his tracks. "Della, no. But James is—he can be brutal in the way he does things. He'd see you as something to use against me if I get out of line. And I'm trying to buy us time, so he doesn't realise I've got his message yet and expect me to report for duty immediately. I need time to drive you home."

"Won't he know from your friends?" Della asked.

"We've been friends since we were pups," Leo said. "Trou-blemakers tend to gravitate to each other. They'll hold off for a while, give us some time."

Something that had been niggling at her finally fell into place in her mind. "When you say James would use me against you—"

Leo turned away to rummage in a chest of drawers. "You don't have to worry. I'll never let anyone hurt you, Della."

"So, he'd threaten to hurt me?" Della asked, somehow not surprised.

"I told you," Leo said, "I won't let him touch you. I won't let *anyone* touch you."

Something clicked in her head. "Leo. When Raj said James wanted you to deliver a message… how exactly do you send these messages for him that requires you to 'get your hands dirty'?"

"Della—"

"Do you hurt people for him?" she asked, her voice so low as to be almost a whisper. "Is that the kind of thing he has you do? Have you been telling me about fixing fences and settling vegetable garden disputes when really you've been doing *this* for him?" She drifted closer to him and for a moment he looked relieved, until she pushed him aside to peer into the drawer where he'd been digging.

Tape. Bandages. Dressings. A full first aid kit. That's what he'd been digging through while he told her he wouldn't let anyone hurt her. Preparing to go and hurt someone *else*.

This time when she moved, Della was backing away from him until she almost hit the door they'd walked through together. Leo looked somewhere between pained and frantic, his hands outstretched towards her, but thankfully he didn't come any closer. Didn't come any closer, or she might not have been able to stay strong and remember what he'd done. Might just collapse into his arms because she felt so safe there.

But not everyone felt like that around Leo. The occasional looks of fear that had been directed their way as they drove through Blue Crescent territory that morning suddenly gained new meaning in her mind. Were those people Leo had hurt on his Alpha's command in the past? *Messages* he'd delivered in the times they were apart?

"Della, I'm his Beta," Leo said, his voice pained. "It's my job to do what he says. I *have* to. For the pack."

"The same pack that you're singling out members of and *beating* them?" Della snapped. "You really think you're doing the best thing for them by staying as second-in-command to a man who would have you do that? Not taking any kind of action against him?"

"I told you why I'm still here," Leo protested. "I *told* you I can't just up and leave, that there are ways you go about dealing with an Alpha like James, and your kind of political action isn't part of it."

"And your kind of total inaction does *nothing* to help the people you claim to want to protect," Della snapped. "Carrying out his acts of violence isn't exactly looking out for them, is it? Letting him continue to give those orders, even if you weren't the one carrying them out—it makes you just as bad as him." The image of Leo using the body that had held her so close, the hands that had brought her such pleasure, to carry out this kind of mob justice made her want to be sick. She spun for the door. "Don't bother driving me home before you go and deliver his *message*. I'd rather get a cab."

He was behind her before she could blink. He didn't have to speak for her to know he was there; she was so hyperaware of his body she'd know him a crowd of thousands.

"Della, don't go. We can talk about this." Leo sounded desperate.

"About what, Leo? About you beating people up for your boss and using the 'this is how it's always been' excuse to avoid actually doing anything about it?" She laughed mirthlessly. "I can't believe I actually thought you were one of the good ones. God, I can't believe I got sucked in by someone like you *again*."

His body was pressing hers to the door faster than she could reach for the handle, ridges of muscle pinning her to the hard wood. She tried to push away, but he didn't move. "Don't you dare put me in the same category as him," he growled in her ear. "I am *not* the same as the man who hurt you."

"No, you're just hurting other people," Della said, the words coming out like a sob. "When you said he used you like a mob enforcer, Leo, I didn't think you meant literally. But you're letting him make you into a monster and you're doing *nothing* to change things."

"I would never hurt you," Leo insisted.

"I don't care about that!" Della cried, tears now streaming down her face. "Not compared to this. Not compared to who it means you *are*."

"I am who I've always been," Leo protested. "I'm the same man you claimed as *yours* by the falls this afternoon. This doesn't change that."

"This changes *everything*," Della said. "The man I was with today wouldn't let someone else tell him to go and beat someone just to send a message."

"If I don't, he'll go after the people I love," Leo said, quietly as though he was ashamed. "Della, you are my *mate*. How could I not do anything in my power not to protect you?"

"I'm not your anything," Della snapped. "The man I gave myself to would find a way to change things, so he didn't have to hurt people on someone else's whim. He would find a way to do the right thing. Because what happens when the message he has you sending has to be delivered to *me*, Leo? Or someone I love? Or someone *you* love?" She pushed back against him, and this time, he moved. Della cast her eyes back over her shoulder once more, and something deep in her broke when she saw the absolute desolation on Leo's face. He looked… obliterated.

She ignored the tears running down her own face and blindly reached for the door handle. "If you ever find that man again, come and see me," she said softly. "Maybe then I'll be able to look you in the eye again." Without another word, she walked out the door.

Chapter 11

L eo was… not at his best. Actually, it was pretty likely that this could be termed his worst. Ever. He was certain he'd never felt so awful in his life, so that would make sense.

He'd lost her.

She'd been right there, pressed up against him so tight he could feel the ridges of her spine against the front of his body, and he'd lost her. Because of who he was. What he did. What he'd allowed being James' Beta to make him into. Someone who hurt people at another's whim, and didn't even try to change things, just like she'd accused him. Just as bad as the man who had hurt her before.

The part of him that seemed to be connected to Della like a physical tether was always there, reminding him what he'd lost. Sometimes it felt like it was wrapped around his intestines, like he could yank his guts out if he pulled on it hard enough.

The first night he drove past her house, he told himself it was just to be sure she'd made it home from work safely. Then he went home and got so rip-roaringly drunk that he woke up next to the first half of a bad poem he didn't remember penning to her, and no fewer than four empty whiskey bottles that he'd apparently shot-gunned one after another. The second night, he gave the same excuse for driving past her house, but at least had the wherewithal to ring Raj and Em and ask them to come over to prevent any more terrible poetry from eventuating. Not that he mentioned that part to them.

Emmett, who arrived first, took one look at him and knew something momentous was wrong. It probably had something to do with the fact that he hadn't shaved in four days and was likely starting to resemble a yeti.

"So, things went pear-shaped with the witch?" he asked, surveying the living room that Leo had only cursorily cleaned up. Well, at least he couldn't see the detritus of the bender Leo had been on for the last few days.

"Her name is Della," Leo said, unwilling to acknowledge the knife-to-the-heart feeling that came from saying her name.

"Oh, man," Emmett said, surveying Leo and cataloguing his expression, a habit he'd had since they were kids. "You are fucked up over this one."

"You have no idea," Leo muttered, taking a swig of the beer he'd set down to open the door. "She's my mate, Em."

Emmett just about dropped the carry bag he'd been holding. "Are you serious? The way you feel about her convinced *you* of all people that the thing you've been calling the 'mate myth' for years now is actually real?"

"This feeling..." Leo paused, slightly uncomfortable with talking emotions even to one of his oldest friends. "It can't mean anything else. This is more than being in love with someone, it's... belonging, Em. I belong to her. And she doesn't want to see me ever again. She's *ashamed* of me." The words felt like they were burning his throat. Ashamed. Ashamed. Ashamed.

Emmett laid a hand on Leo's shoulder. "Well, don't tell Raj

you changed your mind about the mate thing. He'll never shut up about it if you let him think he got something right."

For the first time since Della walked out, Leo managed to summon a laugh.

"I presume you're talking about me," Raj noted, coming through the door still dressed in the formal clothes he wore as a librarian—a far cry from Leo's own sweatpants-clad form. "What with the discussion of someone being right."

Leo and Emmett exchanged glances.

"It's your little witchy friend, isn't it?" Raj asked, settling on to the couch as he always did when he came over.

"Della," Em and Leo said in unison.

"What happened?" Raj asked. "You two seemed pretty cosy when we saw you the other night."

"It *was* the other night," Leo burst out, abandoning his beer, and storming into the kitchen in favour of something stronger. The others followed. He pulled out a bottle of something he didn't even take the time to identify and took a swig from it. It burned going down, which was exactly what he wanted. Pain was what he deserved.

"You want to give us some more information about what happened?" Em asked hesitantly.

"She knows what I do for James now," Leo said dully, then took another draw from the bottle. "Delivering messages. The threats. The beatings. I hadn't… told her. Not in detail. I just said I didn't like all the things he had me do and left it there. And she doesn't want anything to do with someone who would do that, would live with that, without trying to change it."

The two wolves stood in silence for a long moment, staring at him before Leo broke the standoff to take another swig of undefined liquor.

"She's my mate," he said, hearing how broken his own voice sounded, ringing in his ears. "She's my mate, and I lost her."

"See? I was right about the mate thing!" Raj crowed, then realised they were glaring at him and promptly changed his tune. "That's brutal, man. Are you sure there's nothing you can do?"

"There are plenty of things I could do, but none of them end without someone getting hurt," Leo burst out. "I leave my position as Beta, leave the pack, and James gets to choose someone who doesn't give a shit about the violence to take my place. I oppose him, and he comes down on the people I care about to force me into obeying. He comes down on you guys, on my mum… on Della, if he can get to her. I wait until he dies from a life of bad living, or someone challenges him for the position of Alpha, and maybe they're worse. Maybe I spend my whole life as a glorified message boy for a violent psychopath who doesn't give a shit about the people he's supposed to be leading." He took another swig of liquor, relishing the burn. Hell, at this rate maybe he would be able to drink enough to actually get drunk after all.

"Leo—" Emmett started.

"I just want to see her," he said, focusing on the bottle in his hand. "My wolf is fucking furious and doesn't know why I'd let her get so far away. But I just want to know that she's okay, that she's eating enough, getting enough sleep. I don't even need to have her back in my bed, I just want to know she's taking care of herself." *Because you're not there to take care of her anymore, you stupid prick*, his internal voice berated him. *Because you well and truly fucked that up, now you don't even know if she's back to working through her lunch breaks.*

He wondered if he was going to be sick at the thought and had another drink instead.

"Okay, is your aim tonight to get too shitfaced to remember your own name?" Raj asked. "Because it looks like you're headed that way."

"Leo," Emmett said insistently. "Leo, you know we can

take care of ourselves. We'd take care of your mum. And Della's a witch—a damn powerful one, from what I've heard. She can protect herself too."

"I can't risk it," Leo said. "I can't risk him bringing the wrath of the pack down on the people I care about. The way things are now is bad enough. How could I live with it if I was the reason one of you guys got hurt or ejected from the pack? Or Della? God, she's been hurt enough already. I can't risk bringing any more of that shit into her life."

"What did you think was going to happen between you, Leo?" Raj asked, not unkindly. "She's a witch. You know how James is about keeping the pack clear of other species. Were you just going to hide her away and pretend she wasn't your mate? Keep her clear of the pack and hope she never found out the stuff James gets you to do? That's no way to run a relationship, man."

"I hate to be the one to say this," Emmett said after a beat, "but Raj is kind of making sense here. How did you see it playing out, if you were trying to hide her from the pack, and the rest of your life from her? You really think that would have worked?"

"Great, so it was doomed from the start," Leo said, throwing his arms wide. Liquor sloshed in the half-empty bottle. "I couldn't have kept her apart from the rest of... of everything. Couldn't have made her live like that. No matter what, we end up here. You think that makes this any easier?"

"No, but—" Raj started.

"She is my *mate*," Leo interrupted, feeling something inside him fracture like a punched mirror. "There's only one of her, and I have *lost* her. I had her and I *lost* her." He pressed a hand to his chest, half surprised that his heart was still beating, half wondering why the hell it was bothering.

"All right," Raj said, wrapping an arm around Leo's shoulders. "We're gonna watch a movie to distract you and you can get plastered in front of the TV. Boys' night." He steered Leo into the living room and plunked him down on the sofa. "Everything looks better with some scripted gunfighting onscreen in the background."

"Is that a fact?" Em asked.

"Trust me," Raj replied. "You've already admitted that I was right twice tonight. And good things come in threes." When Leo looked up, he could see them having some sort of communication through glances between him, the TV, and the liquor bottle he still held. He was too emotionally exhausted to take offence at their silent communication. He'd gone from being the strong, competent Beta of the pack to this… this hopeless wreck. Could he sink any further when he was already thinking about Della approximately every other second? When the tether that linked them seemed to be intent upon slowly disembowelling him?

"How much booze do you think you have in this house?" Emmett asked. "Because I don't think I can sit through another one of Raj's movie picks sober."

Leo jerked his head towards the kitchen. "All yours. And bring me another one of these. Anything'll do."

Anything would do. Anything to try to fill the hole that losing Della had made in his chest. Though he had a bad feeling that no matter how hard he tried, nothing was even going to come close.

Chapter 12

D ella was a mess. Her head was a mess, her body was a mess. Worse, people could *tell* she was a mess, because she couldn't sleep properly, and the big purple circles under her eyes were starting to give it away. Her work was suffering. Mags was concerned. She was actually considering going to see her grandmother to ask what happened when one opposed the universe's magic and to ask for a tea that would stop her from spending approximately two-thirds of her waking hours barely able to function around how much she missed Leo.

Doing the right thing had never felt so awful.

And that was the thing, she *knew* she had done the right thing. Knew that, even if so much of her life wasn't devoted to making change in ways that helped people, she wouldn't be able to live with being with someone who not only looked the other way when their pack leader ordered violence, but actually carried it out.

The problem was, she told herself, she had had this image in her head of a Leo who didn't exist. A man who did things he didn't like—like arbitrating fights over vegetable gardens—

but was overall *good*. A man with a dirty mouth and a body built for sin and an impossible pull on her that could only be the supernatural magic Grandmother Elise had talked about, but a man who, at the end of the day, would not stand by while the wrong thing was being done. And she'd been falling for that man. She'd *claimed* that man, on the rocks by the most beautiful waterfall she'd ever seen. She'd let down some—just a few—of the walls around her heart, and he'd walked straight in and claimed it. But it was a lie, it was all a lie. That man, the man she'd almost convinced herself she could allow herself to belong to, wasn't real. And that left her pining and broken and unable to eat or sleep or think properly, all for someone who had never existed in the first place.

And it *hurt*. Being away from him *hurt*. It was like someone had shoved a knife into her belly and was continually twisting it. Truly, the supernatural magic did not like being thwarted. Did not like that she'd run away from the man it was trying so hard to tie her to, heart and soul. Everything she saw was actively reminding her of him. Every room in her house where he'd touched her. Every time she skipped lunch at the office to try to catch up on her workload. Her car, which he'd pressed her against with his body the first time they'd kissed. Even when she chose her clothes for work each morning, she found herself picking things based on what he would think. Sometimes, things he'd approve of her wearing. Others, things that he wouldn't, as though her dressing just on the line of "suitable for work" might drag him out of her imagination to deliciously punish her for being inappropriate, for wearing a skirt like that for anyone but him, for wearing heels this high to the office where anyone could see. And despite the fact that she wished it were otherwise, she longed for the possessiveness of his touch. The way he'd practically set her body aflame with the lightest brush of his hands, his lips. The safety and rightness she'd felt in his arms.

But it hadn't been real, she had to keep reminding herself. That man she'd thought she was falling for wasn't real.

So, she'd spent what little downtime she had to spare trying to convince herself—to convince her aching heart—that going back to him would be wrong. She looked for hospital records of werewolves from Blue Crescent, complaints of violence, but there was next to nothing available, even with her government access. The werewolves really did keep their own business to themselves.

Sometimes, she thought her sensor spells were picking up on just a trace of Leo's presence, as though he was there, but slightly out of range. But when she checked, she only ever saw the taillights of a car disappearing down the road. Clearly, she was officially losing her mind, if her desperation for him was enough to have her inventing signs of his presence when he wasn't even there.

One day, telling herself it wasn't just because she was desperate for information that would convince her stubborn heart to let go of this man, she approached Petra, one of her friends at work who happened to be a werewolf, while they were waiting for their turn at the coffee machine in the staff break room. Petra wasn't Blue Crescent, but Della figured surely, they must share *some* information between packs, even if they didn't outside of them.

After they'd gone through their usual chat about their excessive workloads, the afterschool program, and the fact that Nathan in reception kept checking them both out in a way he clearly thought was subtle, Della launched into her interrogation. "I actually have some werewolf-specific questions you might be able to answer if you have some time later."

"I have time now, if you don't mind using your coffee break for work stuff," Petra smiled.

Della sat forward at the table. "It's about the Blue Crescent pack," she started slowly. "They sent their Beta to a couple of the afterschool program meetings, but I can't work out if they're actually interested."

"They're a very insular pack," Petra said. "I'm surprised you got a representative to attend in the first place, to be honest."

"That's what I've heard," Della agreed. "So, I started looking into them, and there's not much on record. I was just wondering if you knew anything about the pack or their leadership that you might be willing to share. So, I can get a better idea of how to get them to commit to the program, of course," she added, hating herself a little bit for resorting to lying to her friend.

"I don't know how much I know that will be useful to you," Petra said. "They're the biggest pack in Mystic City, as I'm sure you know, but they're very private. Their Alpha, James Norfolk, is kind of… I don't know, maybe racist is the right word? He doesn't like anyone but werewolves. Hardly interacts outside the pack unless he must. And between you and me, if he was my Alpha, I'd be looking for a different pack."

"Why is that?" Della asked, her mouth dry.

"Rumour has it that he's been pretty much ruling the pack like a king from his castle for years now. Doesn't train with his wolves, doesn't get out into the community to help people. Just leaves it all to his Beta and expects everyone to bow down to him, even when he's giving orders like," she dropped her voice to just above a whisper, "actually beating people who don't do what he wants." She cleared her throat and glanced around as though someone else might have heard her. "You didn't hear that from me, okay? I don't want any trouble with Blue Crescent, and neither does my pack. We share a territory border with them, you know. The relationship hasn't been the best the last few years, and I don't need to be the reason it got any worse."

"Of course," Della said. "What about the Beta? Is he just as bad?"

"He hasn't been around nearly as long," Petra said. "He probably doesn't know any different. But I've heard he's one of the good ones—tries to soften James' orders where he can, helps the members of the pack who are struggling. Stuff that a good Alpha would probably do if they had one. Betas are supposed to be backup to the Alpha, a kind of brains' trust to balance them out. But James just uses his to do all the things he doesn't want to do himself—or maybe can't do anymore, if he hasn't been training with the rest of the pack." She smirked. "It's kind of a shame that he's Alpha, really, because as long as he is, I seriously doubt you'll be able to get them into the afterschool programs. And because they're the biggest, a lot of the other packs take their cues from Blue Crescent. So, you might have to wait until they have a change of Alpha to get the werewolves involved in the program." She smiled sympathetically at Della.

"A change of Alpha?" Della prodded. "What, do they retire at a certain age or something?"

Petra laughed. "Retire? No way. I mean, an Alpha can abdicate his position, but that almost never happens. Only if they know they can't win the fight and they want to avoid the shame of losing."

"The fight?" Della asked.

"If someone challenges the Alpha, the two of them fight for the position. Normally, the Beta acts as the Alpha's Second, though, so even if you've got a weak Alpha, like," she lowered her voice, "*James*, you'd also have to beat their Beta to win."

"That's seriously how werewolves decide their leadership positions? By beating each other bloody?"

Petra shrugged. "We're not so much like you witches, all politics and popular vote this and council session that. We're old-fashioned, and this is the old way. Traditions are important to us. I must say, it's a nice change from all the hoops we must leap through here for proposal approval or grant funding. It's simpler."

"But the Beta position? That's inherited, right?"

The other woman nodded. "Parent to child, usually. If a Beta dies childless, or abdicates the position, though, the Alpha can appoint a new one. Not that abdication ever happens, really—the Beta takes an oath, and breaking it is a mark of great dishonour."

"So, the Alpha just chooses someone? There isn't any process to it?" Della asked. "Nominations, or a selection process?"

"Only if you're the Alpha," Petra said, laughing like Della had just told a hilarious joke. "God, you witches. It must take you years to get anything done."

Della thought about arguing, or even taking offence, but the truth was she was just too tired from so many days of heartbreak-induced insomnia. Add to that, she was pretty sure nothing she said could possibly change Petra's mind.

"Well, that about answers my questions," she said with a smile, draining the last of her coffee. "Thank you for being so open with me, Petra."

"Any time," Petra grinned. "And for what it's worth, I really do hope we manage to get some werewolves involved with the program. So many of our pups drop out of school and take up jobs in the pack and never realise there's more to the world than the limits of pack territory. I think some inte-gration with other species would be really valuable for them."

"I think the rest of us could learn a lot from the were-wolves, too," Della said honestly. "I might not agree with your leadership selection process," she added with a laugh, "but there is plenty I'm sure you could teach us. And that's half the point of these programs, really. To try to get everyone to engage with each other and learn, so there's less mystery and less fear between the species."

Petra hesitated. "I heard about what happened to you, Della—with that human bastard. And for what it's worth, I think it's wonderful that you're doing things to work against it ever happening again."

Della gave Petra the most genuine smile she'd managed in days. "Thank you. I just… I just couldn't stand by and do nothing to change things, knowing that was the kind of result it produced. Knowing more people might be hurt."

Petra finished her own coffee and stood. "You're a good person, Della. But a word of advice?" Della nodded. "Get some sleep. You look like you're about to drop."

Leo usually saw his mother once a month when they had dinner together. She didn't seem to mind that his busy schedule kept him from visiting much more than that—it meant she always had several weeks' worth of gossip to impart from her craft club, her bridge club, the training group she'd started for older members of the pack who weren't comfortable at regular sparring practice anymore. Sometimes he thought she mostly attended all these groups just to hear what everyone else had been up to—and to determine who had age-appropriate daughters that she could encourage Leo to take out on dates. Then he'd come to one of her Christmas parties one year and realised she just loved the friendships she formed through all her extracurricular activities, loved having people around in a way she'd been missing since the loss of Leo's father and his constant stream of Beta duties-related visitors. Clearly, they had not passed this desire for constant social interaction on to Leo, who made a point of conducting as much of his work as possible outside his house. So that he could have a place where he got a break from it, or so he could pretend he wasn't carrying out the worst of James' orders, he wondered grimly as he drove over to his mother's house. Maybe he'd been trying to hide from the guilt and shame of being the kind of man who had driven Della away ever since he took up the mantle.

He tried to shake off the thoughts as he parked out the front of his mother's cheerful house, but clearly didn't do a good enough job, since she seemed to scent his ongoing misery on him the moment she opened the door.

Laura Tyler was a pretty, round-bodied woman, with reddish-brown hair now streaked liberally with grey and a penchant for brightly coloured fabrics. She was also the most perceptive woman Leo had ever known. The first time he'd ever carried out a beating for James, he'd found himself driving here afterwards, and she'd taken one look at him, sat him down on the couch and fed him fresh-baked scones until he was too full and tired to think. He'd woken the next morning covered in scone crumbs and a fluffy pink blanket, to the sound of his mother humming to herself as she made breakfast in the kitchen. When he'd reluctantly opened his mouth to explain, she'd simply laid a hand over one of his and said, "It was sometimes hard for your father as well," and never asked him to talk about it any further.

This time, she surveyed him for a long moment before pulling him into a tight hug. "Well?" she asked as she led him into the house. "What's put that look on your face, Leo?"

His childhood home was largely unchanged, the postcards he'd sent his parents in his time travelling still stuck to the fridge, his father's winter coat still hanging on the back of the front door. Leo knew his mother had turned his childhood bedroom into a sewing room, but that was about the only change in the house that Leo was aware of since he'd moved out.

He took a seat at the kitchen bench, knowing she'd turn him down if he offered to help with dinner prep as she finished putting together a salad. Seeing his slumped shoulders, Laura paused. "Maybe we can talk about it in a minute, then," she said kindly. "Francine from bridge said her daughter and her partner have decided to have a baby. Isn't that lovely? It wasn't easy for Francine and Les, so they're getting started early in case that's carried through to their daughter—Roxanne, I think her name is. And Daniel and his partner—that's Daniel Court, not Daniel Bloomfield from training group—have decided to move from that big old house of theirs to one of the apartments in the building that got renovated on Suffolk Street in the centre of town. Though I wish them luck trying to sell the house; it'll take a certain kind of person to want to manage a garden of that size!" She went on, listing the life events of people Leo knew only peripherally through the pack or his work as Beta. They had moved to the table and were halfway through the meal when she suggested the first single young woman Leo might like to give a call, and he couldn't help himself. He flinched at the thought of even trying to make date conversation with someone who wasn't Della, let alone putting his hands on her.

"Oh, Leo," his mother said, interrupting herself. "It's about a girl, isn't it?"

"She's not just a girl," Leo said, his voice hollow.

"What's her name?" Laura coaxed gently.

"Della. Delphinia. Greenbranch."

"A witch, then?" She sounded cautious.

"Yes, she's a witch," Leo said. His tone was harsh, but he couldn't control it. "She's… she's my mate."

His mother's eyes widened. "Your mate? But, Leo, you've always said—"

"I know what I said," Leo said. "But this can't be anything else. I've never been so sure of anything in my life. She's…

she's everything, Mum. She's so smart and beautiful and kind and I wanted her from the second I caught her scent. Her *scent*, it's like—" He caught himself before he said anything explicit in front of his mother. "I can't even describe it. It's incredible. *She's* incredible."

"And you're worried about what James will do when he finds out your mate is a witch?"

"No, it's not... I mean, yes, that, but it's worse. Her whole life is about making things better for other people, about changing things so people don't get hurt by the way the system runs. And she found out about what I do for James—all the things I've hated but lived with, because that's just the way things are, instead of trying to change anything. All the violence, the threats, the intimidation. And I've done nothing. I've just let him keep sitting in his restaurant headquarters judging everyone in the pack like some kind of goddamn king, and I've done nothing to stop him hurting people. Having *me* hurt people."

Wordlessly, his mother stood up from the table, came around and wrapped him in her arms, fitting his head beneath her chin like he was a child again. "Oh, Leo," she said, sighing deeply. "My little boy. My baby boy has a mate."

"That's really not the biggest part of this," Leo pointed out, his voice muffled by her floral cardigan.

"I know. But let me deal with this one thing at a time, all right? First, I'm coming to terms with the fact that you found your mate. And I'm so happy for you, Leo. I thought you didn't even believe in those stories."

"Neither did I, until I met her," Leo admitted.

"And then, we come to the... other part," Laura said hesitantly. "Leo honey, James has been in decline as an Alpha for a long time. It wasn't as bad before your dad died, I guess because he didn't have a Beta as physically... intimidating as you are. Your father knew it, but he also knew he'd taken an oath to be Beta of the pack and he couldn't break it, even as his Alpha was becoming more and more tyrannical. We had hoped we might get a new Alpha in your father's time, but it never happened; I guess things weren't bad enough for people to make that kind of change. And with you as James' Second, no one is going to challenge him now. So, unless James manages to drink himself to death, Leo, I don't see that things are going to change around here. I don't see how they can." Sadness was as deep as a well in her voice. "So, you're not doing anything wrong, by living the way you are. You're simply fulfilling your oath to the pack as Beta. And if this Delphinia can't understand that, then maybe, mate or no, you and she are just too different to be together."

Everything in Leo rebelled at the very suggestion. Just accept that he and Della weren't meant to be together? Accept that he'd never again hold her in his arms, kiss her, touch her, wrap his body around hers? Just thinking it felt like drinking acid.

Suddenly, a thought occurred to him. If no one had challenged James because Leo, as Beta, was bound to be his Second... that meant that there were people who had wanted to. His packmates, seeking a new leader. Looking for change.

So, he wouldn't be betraying them, doing something they didn't want, if he gave it to them.

And if Leo wasn't James' Second...

"Mum," he said into the silence, "I have to go."

"Why?" she asked, her eyebrows pulling together in concern. "Is everything all right?"

"I have to talk to Raj and Emmett," he explained.

"What? Why?" his mother asked, looking put out.

"To work out which of them will be my Second when I challenge James to be Alpha of the pack," Leo said.

Laura blinked at him twice, then fainted.

Chapter 13

Della was exhausted. So many nights of troubled sleep plagued by memories of Leo, combined with throwing herself into work and her duties to prepare for the next meeting of the Council of Witches, had finally caught up with her. In a way, it might be a blessing, if collapsing into bed the minute she got home meant she might finally be able to sleep for more than a few minutes at a time without Leo invading her mind.

This time, she got a full couple of hours—more than she was averaging in an entire night most nights if she was being honest with herself—before she woke up. This time, though, it wasn't memories of Leo's hands stroking over her fevered flesh that brought her to the surface, but rather her ringing phone. She'd neglected to take it out of her pocket before lying down on the bed, fully clothed, and passing out.

It was Petra. Della groggily picked up the call. "Hello?"

"Della." The werewolf sounded frantic. "I'm sorry, I know it's late, but I need your help."

"What's wrong?" Della asked, immediately wide awake.

"You know how I was telling you my pack and Blue Crescent haven't been on great terms the past few years?"

"Yes," Della said hesitantly.

"There are wolves lining up along their side of the border between our territories. A hundred of them, at least. Della, I think they're going to invade."

"Invade?" Della repeated, disbelieving. "Surely, that's not legal."

"I told you," Petra said, "werewolves stick to the old ways. And this is very, very old. There hasn't been a true invasion in centuries. But back before there was a city here, how do you think Blue Crescent territory got to be so big? They conquered the territories of smaller packs, and Della—I think we're next on the list."

"What do you need me to do?" Della asked, already looking for the shoes she'd kicked off upon her arrival home.

"Anyone who might be willing to come and stand with us, anyone you can think of, *please* call them in. We can't stand against Blue Crescent otherwise, and if we look like easy pickings, I don't think they'll bother trying to negotiate. I think they'll just attack."

"I'll make some calls," Della promised, running through a list of witches in her head who might be willing to ally themselves with the Apex River pack. "Where are we meeting?"

"Outside the apartment building on Brook Street, where the territory border runs. You'll know it when you see it. Plus, there's a huge crowd of werewolves here. You can't miss us."

"I'll see you soon," Della promised as she grabbed her car keys.

Petra was right; the crowd of werewolves outside the apartment building was unmissable. So was the air of menace emanating from the significantly larger pack on the other side of the four-lane road. Surely, there were hundreds of wolves on the Blue Crescent side, and on the Apex River side... well, significantly fewer. There was a rumbling of chatter on both sides when Della joined the Apex River group, but Petra quickly found her and wrapped her in a hug. "Thank you so much for coming."

"Of course," Della said. "And I was able to call in another nine or ten witches. They should be here soon."

Petra looked like she might cry. "Della, I can't tell you how much this means to us."

"But, Petra..." She gestured at the crowd on the other side of the street. "Will it be enough?"

"It's a statement that we have allies," came a voice from behind them. Della turned to see a dark-haired man with the single wildest beard she had ever seen.

Petra stood back. "Delphinia Greenbranch, this is Alpha Simon Bennett of the Apex River pack."

"We are indebted to you, Delphinia," the Alpha said. "Apex River will not forget this."

"Just Della is fine," she said, extending a hand with what she hoped was a convincing smile. "And when I heard that this was what Blue Crescent were planning, I couldn't not come and help."

"They haven't made any aggressive moves yet," the Alpha said, with the air of someone admitting to a flaw.

"Except send a massive pack of wolves to gather on your border," Della pointed out. "I'd say that's a pretty clear threat."

Simon inclined his head. "I'm glad that's clear to more than just us. You see why we need to respond to this show of strength with an indication that an attack on Apex River is going to affect their pack's relationships with more than just us. Your presence, and that of any others you were able to rouse, is more powerful than you might think."

"Do you think they'll really attack?" Della asked, looking

between Simon and Petra.

The two werewolves exchanged glances, and then Petra shrugged. "Maybe," she said. "No one can really predict what their Alpha is going to do. But if they do, it'll be a clear act of war."

"I won't put the wolves of this pack in jeopardy," Simon said quietly. "If they launch an attach we can't repel, I'll surrender to their son-of-a-bitch Alpha. I won't let my people get hurt when I could save them by giving in."

"There are more witches coming," Della said. "Powerful ones. You don't have to think like that."

"I'm the Alpha," Simon said without preamble. "I always have to think about what the best and safest thing for my pack will be."

"You don't have to give up," Della said, hearing the note of desperation in her voice. "We can fight with you. Together, we'll be enough."

"We shall see, Delphinia," Simon said, turning away. The weight of his duty to his pack showed in his slumped posture and dark expression. Della's heart went out to him, and her disgust with the Blue Crescent Alpha only grew.

The other witches arrived one by one, joining the Apex River Pack still collecting on their side of the street as the Blue Crescent wolves waited in near silence. A rumble of mutterings rolled through the Blue Crescent Pack each time another witch joined the Apex River contingent. *Good*, Della thought. *Be worried. Be intimidated. Fear our power.*

Clearly, they feared them at least a little bit. Because after the tenth witch arrived, one of the threatening Blue Crescent werewolves strode to the line demarcating the middle of the empty street, two others behind him like a security detail. In response, Simon and two of his own wolves went forwards to meet them. Clearly, everyone was being careful not to cross the centre line that must have indicated the shared border of their territories. This meant that they were standing at least six feet apart, and their projected voices meant Della could hear every word they exchanged.

"Would you like to explain what the hell is going on here?" Simon asked.

"Our esteemed Alpha, James Norfolk, sends his greetings," said the other wolf, with the air of one repeating a memorised phrase. "Under the ancient laws of our people, he requests that you surrender your territory, your position as Alpha and the sovereignty of the Apex River Pack to the rule of the Blue Crescent Pack."

"You can tell your esteemed Alpha he can suck my—" one of the wolves behind Simon snarled, but his own Alpha silenced him with a look.

"And if I don't?" Simon asked.

The wolf on the other side gestured widely to indicate the members of his pack arrayed behind him. "Our pack is easily twice the size of yours. This is far from a full contingent of those of us trained to fight. If you really want to watch as your own pack is beaten into the ground, well." His eyes flashed silver so brightly, even Della could see it from where she stood, and his savage grin showed that his canines had elongated into fangs. "We're more than happy to turn this street into a bloodbath. It's been ages since I had a good fight. I can drag you before James by your shredded skin if that's what you'd prefer," he added. "But I thought an Alpha with such a reputation for being reasonable might consider putting the lives of his pack first in this kind of situation."

"I doubt you have any idea what a responsible Alpha would do in this situation, seeing as you have no real experience with one," Simon said, so calmly it took a minute for the insult to sink in. When it did, both the backup wolves on the Blue Crescent side of the street stepped forward, growling. The two behind Simon moved closer to their Alpha, who stayed them with a raised hand. The whole time, the Blue Crescent spokesperson remained unmoved, a faint smile on his face.

"You have an hour to consider your response," he told Simon. "After that, we will consider this territory ceded to Blue Crescent and will cross the border at will. Any resistance will be dealt with as an act of internal terrorism." He turned on his heel and walked back to his gathered packmates, and after a long moment, Simon did the same.

Petra was among those who rushed to their Alpha as he returned to the crowd of Apex River wolves. "You can't surrender to them," she said without preamble.

"What about the honour of our pack?" someone else asked.

"There are too many of them," Simon said. "I won't risk your lives in a fight we'll only lose."

"We have the witches!" another wolf cried out with a grateful look at Della's gathered brethren. "We could win!"

"And who are we willing to sacrifice for that?" Simon asked. "You, Zeke? Do I have to go to your wife tomorrow morning and tell her I let you die in a fight we have only the faintest hope of winning, for the sake of pride?"

"When you became our Alpha, you promised to do what was best for our pack," Petra said.

"What's best for our pack is to *survive*," Simon insisted, his voice strained. "No matter whether it's under a different name."

"That asshole Alpha of theirs won't let you stay in his pack," a tall blond man pointed out. "And with the shame of a surrender to your name, who else will accept you into theirs?"

"That's a price I'm willing to pay to keep you all alive," Simon said quietly.

"Alive and *shamed*," Petra said. "Alive and forced to bow to an Alpha who rules with violence and threats. Apex River might have a reputation for being reasonable, but we're not weak, Simon. I'd rather meet this threat fighting, with no promise of victory, than put our noses to their boots like a pack of shamed dogs. This isn't just about pride, it's about who we *are*."

There was a chorus of agreement from the other wolves.

"I'd rather go down fighting with my honour intact than bow to their tyrant Alpha," another wolf said. "Apex River to the end."

"To the end," several others echoed, then several more, until a wave of the words was moving through the crowd.

"You really all feel that way?" Simon asked.

An affirmative chorus sounded.

The Apex River Alpha took a long, deep breath. "Then I guess we tell them to go fuck themselves," he said simply. "Apex River to the end."

Della looked at the other witches gathered around her. Most wore the same expression of moderately intrigued shock that she could feel on her own face, but there was some horror mixed in there as well.

"Is this really how werewolves do things?" one of the witches Della knew from the council asked. "No, I don't know, committees? No reasonable discussions between parties? They're just this *aggressive* about territory disputes and solve it all with violence?"

"This isn't a territory dispute," Della said. "It's an invasion. And from what they're saying, I think it's an unheard of thing to do in modern times. The territory lines have been set for as long as Mystic City has existed. The Blue Crescent Alpha is an asshole, though, and it sounds like he's made this archaic decision to expand the territory he rules over."

"Are they really planning on killing each other over this?" one of the warlocks from Della's coven asked.

"I don't know if it'll go that far, or if they'll just injure each other," Della said. "If you want to leave, Wes, no one will judge you."

"I'm not good with violence," Wes admitted, looking pale. "I can't even watch action movies without feeling sick."

"I'll see you at the coffee shop on Monday and tell you what happened," Della assured him kindly.

"Are you sure you won't get hurt?" Wes asked. "They won't attack you?"

"And risk starting a war with every coven in the city?" Della asked, putting more certainty in her voice than she felt. "They wouldn't dare."

In the end, five of the witches Della had called in stayed. Vivian and Lucille, twins with whom Della had gone to school, Troy and Normandy, who Della knew from the council, and Adele, a family friend who brought Della cookies every time she baked. Not the most overwhelming alliance, but enough to make a dent in this attacking wolf pack. She hoped.

Della found Simon in the middle of a group of werewolves, outlining battle plans. She quietly joined the group, considering the strategy they were putting together.

"Where do you want the witches?" she asked when conversation lapsed.

"You're staying?" Simon asked in surprise. "When some of them left, we thought—"

"You have six of us," Della said firmly, refusing to apologise for those who had departed. "Viv and Lucy will do best if they're placed together. Adele is strong but doesn't have much stamina. She'll need backup beyond the initial clash. Normandy is best with elemental manipulation—fire, water, you know. Troy can manipulate emotions well. You'll want to put him somewhere a healthy dose of fear will do some damage to the attackers."

To his credit, Simon hardly missed a beat. "And you?"

Della shrugged. "Whatever you need me to do." Abandoning modesty, she added, "Someone tried to take my magic away once, and it just made me more powerful. And the Blue Crescent wolves can't hurt us in case it starts an all-out witch-werewolf war."

She could see Simon turning that information over in his head. "All right," he said eventually. "Here's what I'm thinking. We use the witches' power to force a bottleneck. Funnel their attack into where we're strongest. Place some of the pack along the line so if the magic breaks, we're still protected, but the bulk of our fighters stay in the centre. That way, we control the playing field. They might outnumber us, but that won't matter if they can only attack a few at a time."

Out of the corner of her eye, Della was aware of the Blue Crescent wolves arraying themselves along the territory border. Their hour was almost up.

It was nearly time.

Chapter 14

Leo's friends were surprisingly unsurprised when he told them he was planning on challenging the Alpha.

"Shit, finally," Raj said, stretching out on the couch. "I've been waiting for this for ages."

Leo just stared at him. "What?"

"I mean, it has seemed pretty inevitable," Emmett explained. "To us, at least."

"I literally never considered it until maybe an hour before I rang you two," Leo said.

"People have been getting sick of 'Alpha James' for years," Emmett said, the title dripping sarcasm in a way he could only do inside, away from potential listening ears. "The only reason he hasn't been challenged half a dozen times by now is because he had you as a Second, and before he got sick, your dad. You'll be a pack hero once you take him down."

I only want to be her hero, something in Leo said, but he shoved away the thought. He couldn't afford to be distracted by Della right now.

"Tonight," he said out loud. "I'm doing it tonight."

"Why?" Em started, then clued in. "Oh, right. Full moon."

"I'm not waiting another month to make this right," Leo said.

"You could always be a tiny bit less adherent to the traditions and challenge him on a night that isn't a full moon," Raj suggested.

"I'm doing this right, so he can't challenge the result," Leo insisted. "It has to be tonight." He swallowed. "And I know it's a lot to ask, and I won't be upset if you say no, but—"

"Hell yeah, I'll be your Second," Raj interrupted.

"Now wait just a minute," Emmett said. "Who said he was going to ask you?"

"I beat you last time we fought," Raj pointed out.

"I had just finished another fight, and you were fresh," Em protested. "That was hardly a fair contest."

Raj shrugged. "I still won."

Leo thought perhaps it was time to intervene before things got ugly. "I actually was thinking Raj. Em, you ran two training sessions this morning. Plus, we have the same fighting style. If Raj comes in as my Second when I go down—"

"If you go down," Raj interrupted.

"If I go down," Leo acknowledged, "then it'll force whoever James picks as his Second to totally change their style when they're already worn out."

Emmett considered that for a moment, then acknowledged the validity of the point with a slight incline of his head. "All right. But I would've won that fight if I hadn't just finished sparring with Julian."

"Whatever helps you sleep at night, man," Raj drawled. "All right, when do we leave? I'm guessing you want to get it all done before everyone comes back from the Apex River thing, to reduce James' choices for Second?"

"Hold up," Leo said. "What Apex River thing?"

Emmett and Raj looked at each other. "Dude, how out of it have you been?" Raj asked. "I mean, I know the whole Della thing has messed you up, but the pack's been talking about this for days."

"About what?" Leo asked, ignoring the stab of pain that hearing Della's name brought on.

"James is making a bid to take over Apex River territory tonight," Emmett explained. "He's sent more than half the pack's fighters down there to ensure they surrender."

Leo had leapt from his chair before he could think. "Is he insane? No one's tried an invasion of territory in... what, two hundred years? And why would he need to? We're already the largest pack in the city." *And why the fuck didn't he tell me?* Leo thought. *I'm his Beta. I should surely know when he's planning a fucking invasion. Or did he, and I've just been so out of it that it didn't even register? Have I failed this pack as their Beta by letting this happen just because I've been consumed with my own goddamned heartbreak?*

"Hey, snap out of that," Raj ordered, snapping his fingers in front of Leo's face. "He probably didn't tell you because he knew you'd say it was a stupid, narcissistic, imperialistic thing to do, which it is."

"But what if—" Leo started.

"What if nothing," Emmett took over. "Leo, you're going to be a thousand times better as an Alpha than James is. This is the best thing for the pack. Now let's get it done, shall we?"

"Midnight," Leo said. "We lay down the challenge at midnight. You can bet James will be at Horatio's at that time on a full moon night. And the whole thing will be over by sunrise, one way or another."

"No one way or another about it," Raj said, full of confidence. "We're going to kick their asses, James and whatever fighter he chooses as his Second. We've got this, Leo."

"Yeah," Leo said, unwilling to let himself be convinced. He needed to be prepared for anything. For James pulling someone out of the woodwork who could somehow take down both him and Raj. For this mystery fighter doing serious damage to him in the process. For James winning and ejecting him from the pack, forcing him to leave his friends and family behind. Maybe even leave the city, because who would accept a disgraced former Beta who failed in a challenge of his Alpha? Who would even dare anger the city's largest pack—even larger, if they absorbed Apex River tonight—by taking in their former Beta? For Raj being hurt in the fight as his Second. For James punishing his friends and family for his sins once Leo himself was gone.

He had almost talked himself out of the whole endeavour when Raj clapped a hand on his shoulder. "Hey. Get out of that place in your head," he ordered, his tone a stark contrast from his usual goofy good humour. "This is the right thing to do, Leo. It's time and past that we show James we won't tolerate his bullshit anymore. You and I, we can take anyone he throws in our path. We can bring this role—this pack—back to where it's meant to be. We can stop the people we care about living in fear of pissing off the asshole in Horatio's. We can change things for the better around here."

His words were so like those Della had voiced that Leo felt the tether that eternally linked him to her jolt, tugging on him. Raj was right. It was time to be a better man—one who didn't tolerate violence and brutality without trying to counter it.

One who Della wouldn't have run away from.

"Yes," he said out loud. "It's time."

There must have been some invisible signal to the wolves in the Blue Crescent Pack when the hour Apex River had been given was up, because they came at the barrier the pack had formed like a rolling wave of fur, claws, and fangs. Della had only seen a werewolf in wolf form once, that day with Leo by the waterfall that she wouldn't let herself think about, and the sight of dozens of them shifting on the fly and streaming across the territory border towards her was an entirely different experience. Unlike Leo on that sunlight-drenched day by the water, these wolves were geared to attack, to wound, maybe even to kill, the pack she was protecting.

She raised her hands and pressed down into the well of her magic. She drew it up in tendrils and sent them out at the attacking wolves, freezing them in their tracks. She kept them still long enough for the Apex River wolves to dart between them, doing damage that made her sick to think about. Enough to stop them fighting, but nothing permanent, Simon had ordered, and she didn't want to look closely enough to confirm they were following his orders.

Instead of watching the fighting exclusively, Della checked on the other witches. Lucy and Viv had hesitated at the sight of the onslaught of wolves, but quickly joined their power to create a wall of solidified air that the attackers crashed into. Adele was doing well at holding the wall to Della's right, as Troy sent waves of fear and despair into the invading pack. Normandy had not only erected an eight-foot-high wall of ice but was also sending darts of flame forwards beyond it that left their attackers dodging and reeling. It was working.

The wolves they'd funnelled into the space at the centre of their magical wall met Simon's fighters, some in their full wolf forms, others half-shifted and making the most of their teeth and claws. It was brutal. This was violence as she'd never seen it, had never even considered it—bloody and brutal and unchoreographed and *real*. That was real blood she was seeing spilled on the already-slick tarmac, real cries, and howls of pain as each pack fought for supremacy.

Some fell. A couple did not get back up.

With an effort, Della refocused on her section of the witches' wall. Wolves from the Blue Crescent side still ran at the portion of solidified air she'd created, only to find themselves frozen in place for the Apex River wolves to prowl forward and ensure they were unable to continue fighting. The issue was once the Apex River wolves were on the other side of her wall, they had to fight their way back to the safety behind it. Even with her depth of power, Della couldn't immobilise every wolf that attacked one who belonged to the pack she was protecting—not when she didn't know how long she'd need to hold this wall, anyway. So, she was forced to stand and watch, as the Blue Crescent and Apex River wolves tore each other to shreds in front of her, throwing out a magical bolt every now and then when she could see it would make an important difference.

"Della!" Adele, with whom Della was holding the wall this side of the bottleneck gap, yelled to her over the wolves' growls and snarls and howls of pain. "I can't hold this much longer!"

"Step back!" Della yelled back. "Regroup! I can hold it!"

As Adele drew her flickering power back from the wall, Della drew from the deep well of magic within herself and extended her defence to cover the other witch's section. After all Dane had done to her, the toll the freyroot had taken on her, she'd feared it would cut her off from her power forever. Instead, over the course of months and years, she'd found that the power within her grew greater and greater, as though the magic was responding to the assault on it by growing ever stronger. She'd never tested the depth of this well of reinvigorated power, never pushed herself to a burnout, or even close. Her magic was just always there, no matter how much she used it, deep and powerful and purring like a needy kitten for release.

It revelled in the moment of liberation when she extended her area of defence to cover Adele's, almost as if it were a separate being to her, a leashed animal within her that had suddenly been given free rein. She extended her wall to cover Adele's space with almost surprising ease, feeling as much as seeing the Blue Crescent wolves who thought they'd dodged her area of influence slam into it and find themselves frozen at the mercy of the Apex River wolves who fought to reach them, to ensure they were unable to continue fighting.

The Blue Crescent attackers were thinning, concentrating on the bottleneck gap. Their plan was working.

But the witches couldn't hold the wall much longer. With the constant challenges of wolves slamming into their defences, their power was fading. Della could feel it in the echoes of power from the other side of their wall. Troy was all but burnt out, but still sending weakening waves of terror into the Blue Crescent wolves who still fought through the gap in the wall. Viv and Lucy were visibly leaning on each other, holding their portion of the wall, while Normandy was struggling to keep her ice barrier frozen.

Some part of Della that was more than the identity she knew reached down into the well of her power. Down, down, down. And still, she did not reach the bottom.

She could do it. She could hold this wall.

"Troy!" she yelled, her voice magically amplified. "You're too close to burnout. Step back and recharge, I'll hold it."

"Can you?" he called back.

"I've got this!" she shouted. She pushed her magic across the bottleneck gap, where wolves were slashing at each other with teeth and claws, and covered Troy's section. Her magic revelled in the unfamiliar degree of extension, and the euphoria rising in Della almost made her question what she was doing. This sheer joy of testing the limits of her magic… surely, it was out of place in a territory war. Surely, she shouldn't be gaining this much satisfaction from every attacking wolf who slammed into her wall of power, who found themselves immobilised by her magic. But as she extended herself to cover for a burnt-out Normandy, then Lucy and Viv, until it was only her holding the entire defensive wall, the well of magic in her rejoiced. Finally, it seemed to call, she was diving down into it, exploring the depth of magic given to her like a gift to compensate for the years of Dane's abuse.

Della held the wall. Standing to the side of the bottleneck battle, muscles straining against an invisible force, Della held. Wolves crashed into her defences, trying to break through, and she immobilised them with darts of fire and ice and solidified air made as sharp as a blade. The magic in her pulsed and rejoiced, seeking an outlet, seeking freedom, revelling in the moment it was released. She sent out her magic to cover the Apex River werewolves as they burst through the bottleneck gap to engage the final standing Blue Crescent wolves, and something in her wanted to howl at the moon as they did when they defeated an opponent, wanted to become the most primitive version of herself that she could, relishing this release of her power overcoming an enemy.

She was so deep in her magic that she hardly realised when no more attackers were hitting her wall. She hardly noticed that she was no longer immobilising the Blue Crescent wolves, until a tap came on her shoulder, and she slammed back into her physical body, breathing deep into lungs that felt suddenly starved for air, dropping her aching arms. Finally seeing through her wide-open eyes—seeing the fallen combatants surrounding her like a halo of carnage, the Apex River wolves howling their victory. The attackers limped away from the place they'd been beaten. Wolves shifted back into their human forms, their fur disappearing to reveal slashed skin on limbs and abdomens, some needing to be carried away from the battle ground.

It was Simon's hand that had landed on her shoulder, bringing her back to herself. He certainly looked like he'd been in a war, blood running down his face, slices marking both his arms.

"Della," he said, his voice awed. "Della, it's done. You can stop now."

"Are you sure?" she asked, looking at the retreating wolves around them.

"Don't worry," Simon said, his hand still on her shoulder. "I have guards in place along the perimeter. If they try to launch another attack, we'll be ready. But I don't think they will."

"Why not?" Della asked.

"They've already been defeated once," Simon said, a glimmer of satisfaction in his eyes. "No one wants to lose two fights in a row. And we've just shown them that with our allies," he gestured to her, "they'll have to do better than that to beat us."

"I can't believe we won," Della murmured, the muscles along her spine finally relaxing so she sagged.

"Me either," Simon admitted quietly. "But before we take the time to celebrate, there's something I need to do, and I was wondering if you'd come with me."

Chapter 15

J ames was right where Leo expected him to be, sprawled in his customary seat at Horatio's, surrounded by sycophants. Leo strode into the bar, Raj and Emmett at his heels, just like he'd done a thousand times before, and his ease with what he was about to do was almost unsettling. He'd come to terms with it, with the risks inherent in his actions. He wished he'd been able to tell his mother he loved her once more before coming here. Just in case. In case he lost and was thrown from the pack, and she spent the rest of her days being punished—ignored, socially isolated, looked down upon—for bringing him into the world. In case he lost, and he never got the chance to again.

He couldn't think like that, he told himself, the same lesson he taught in pack training sessions. Go into a fight with the wrong outlook and you're already setting yourself up for failure.

He steadied himself, accepted the pats on the back from his friends, and moved to stand before James' chair. The table separated them, but he could feel the arrogance radiating from James like the light of a small sun. Usually, when Leo

was forced to interact with James formally in a public setting
—receiving instructions from the Alpha or making a report
when his orders were carried out—he did his best to maintain
an air of at least respect, since he could hardly manage defer-
ence. Tonight, would be the first time he'd ever allowed
himself to let that mask of public courtesy slip, to show his
true contempt for the man and the way he led the pack.

"Leo," James greeted him with some gusto, presumably
thinking he was here in his usual capacity. "Did you have
something you needed to tell me?"

"Yes," Leo said, bracing himself. "And it's long overdue.
For too long, you've led this pack like the world belongs to you,
with no repercussions for your actions. For too long, I've
allowed myself to be part of the brutality you've used to keep
our people in line. But that ends here."

"If you're got something to say, *Beta* Tyler, get on with it,"
James ordered, his eyes flashing silver. His face was hard. Did
he know what was finally coming?

Leo took a deep breath. "I, Leo Tyler, Beta of the Blue
Crescent pack, hereby challenge you for the position of
Alpha."

The room, despite its many occupants, was so silent you
could have heard a pin drop.

James laughed. "You know, Tyler, I've thought you had
ideas above your station since you took over from your father.
But I'll bet the old man is rolling over in his grave to hear you
disrespect your Alpha like this. I'll give you one chance, son, to
retract that challenge, and I'll even let you stay in the pack—
stripped of your position, of course, but surely it's better than
being a packless Omega with the stain of 'oath breaker'
against your name."

Murmurs echoed through the room as James rose from his
seat to stand at his full height. Leo so rarely saw him out of
that chair that it was easy to forget the Alpha could stand

almost eye-to-eye with him. James was no longer the muscle-bound young man he had been, but there was bulk to him that showed that giving up the pack's training sessions and spending his days drinking at Horatio's might not had disadvantaged him as much as Leo had been thinking.

"Well, son?" James asked. "What'll it be?"

Leo tried, and failed, not to picture Della's face as she walked out on him that night. *The man I gave myself to would find a way to change things, so he didn't have to hurt people on someone else's whim.*

This is me being that man, Leo told the vision of her face. *This is me making a difference, being better. For you. For us. For them.*

"Choose your Second," Leo said simply. "I will not back down to you again."

The door to the room slammed open, and suddenly every person in the room was on their feet as a man Leo vaguely recognised stormed through the door, blood on his face from a cut on his forehead dripping down to soak into his massive beard. Behind him were no fewer than five werewolves, all looking similarly battered, and—

Holy shit.

Della.

Della and another witch he didn't recognise, who stood among the wolves as though they belonged to their pack. Della, here in front of him, looking somehow tired and yet energised at the same time, her hair breaking free of its tight braid to frame her face with dark tendrils. Her hands were clenched into fists, like she was steeling herself for this encounter. Or preparing to have to use magic to get out of it.

Instantly, James' demeanour shifted, from angry and threatening to a kind of nauseating lazy welcome.

"Is this a bad time?" Beard Man asked.

"Never," James drawled. "You know you're always welcome, Alpha Simon."

"I felt significantly less welcome when you sent your wolves to invade my territory tonight," the man replied, keeping his tone impressively calm. "For the record, *Alpha* James, under the diplomatic treaties that govern Mystic City, if you or your wolves harm me or mine on this visit, the might of all the city's forces of justice will be arrayed against you. And considering what my pack did to yours with the assistance of just half a dozen witches, I don't imagine you particularly want the might of the combined covens arrayed against you." He folded his arms over his chest. "I'm sure your emissary will be back to give you a full report of their defeat, just as soon as he can limp home."

For the first time, James looked slightly uncomfortable. "Politics isn't personal, Simon."

"It felt pretty fucking personal tonight," Simon shot back. "I came here to give you one chance to explain before I take this before the City Council."

"This is wolf business," James snapped. "Those government assholes have no place in our affairs."

"They do when you threaten my people," Simon said coldly. "One chance, James. Give me a good reason not to take this further."

Leo had never seen James look so scattered. Not that he was really looking at his Alpha; not when Della was standing so close, he could smell her sex-and-spices scent. He was barely capable of noticing that there were even other people in the room.

She had fought with Apex River? Every part of him rebelled at the idea of Della in any kind of combat situation, any kind of dangerous situation. Fighting wolves who were out for blood, the wolves of *his* pack. But clearly, his woman had held her own, if a smaller pack like Apex River, with the assistance of only six witches, had been able to take down the bulk of the Blue Crescent fighting force.

James had started speaking while Leo was fixated on Della. "—be glad to have this conversation, but first I'm afraid there's something of an insurrection around here that needs to be put down. My Beta here was just explaining that he thinks he's better suited for the top job."

Leo felt Della's gaze snap to him like she'd run her fingers up his spine. He tried to drag his attention back to the situation at hand, but it fought to remain focused on her. He clenched his jaw and fixed his gaze on James and Alpha Simon's conversation. The other Alpha was looking at him.

"Leo Tyler, if I've heard right," Simon said with a nod of acknowledgement. Leo returned the gesture but said nothing. He could feel Emmett and Raj as tense as stone statues at his back.

"So, you'll forgive me if I take care of this before engaging in your *conversation*," James added to the Apex River Alpha before Leo could reply, rising from his chair once more. The change in position revealed a man perhaps slightly beyond his prime, but his body had far from sunk into the shameful state Leo had expected. Apparently, even sitting in a chair for the vast majority of every day wasn't enough to make an Alpha lose all his muscle; not that Leo had any similarly sedentary wolves to whom to compare him. James was still a threatening sight as he rose to his full height. Leo had been a fool to discount him as an opponent, not to mention whoever he chose as his—

"Seconds," James announced loudly, clearly enjoying the degree of attention focused on him and his role as master of the show. The sycophants surrounding him seemed to swell in their places, jostling for attention. Whoever James picked as his Second, after all, had a fair shot at being named Beta if Leo was evicted from the pack. Even the risk of getting beaten up by someone like Leo was a small price to pay for such a chance—especially since it was something many of them were already familiar with from pack training.

"But first, to run the show…" James continued. "Simon, would you be so kind as to adjudicate? We'll pair you with one of our wolves as well, of course. How about… Emmett O'Neill?"

Leo tried to keep his surprise off his face. So, James must have thought he was going to pick Em as his Second and was taking him out of the running. Well, he couldn't allocate Raj to adjudication as well, and more fool James, since the three of them had already decided that the bigger wolf would be a better choice for Second anyway.

Emmett broke away from the miniature pack the three of them had formed before James' chair with a clap on Leo's shoulder and went to stand beside the Apex River faction. Leo caught a brief glance of his friend's face, looking as though he was picking up a strange, unfamiliar smell, and tamped down on his immediate anger response that he might be catching Della's intoxicating scent.

"I hereby name as my Second," James continued, interrupting Leo's thoughts. He followed the traditional script unheard of for decades now—though if Leo remembered correctly, didn't the challenger usually name their Second first? And then James took a deep breath and switched his cocky smile from Leo to the wolf behind him and said, "Rajesh Lewis," and Leo felt his eyes go wide.

He swung around in time to see Raj's face completely lose its colour, and then returned the see James' deeply self-satisfied grin that he made no effort to hide, even from the disgruntled followers still surrounding him. Oh, the Alpha was good. He'd seen right through Leo's strategy and shot it straight in the heart. In addition, he'd put one of the pack's fiercest fighters—and one against whom Leo had lost as many times as he'd beaten him—in his own corner.

Plus, he'd all but isolated Leo on his own. Who the hell was he going to name as his Second now?

"Leo," Raj said from behind him, sounding desperate.

"I know," Leo said, clapping a hand on his massive friend's shoulder. "Good fighting, buddy. You'll need it." He forced a smile on to his face. "Don't cry too hard afterwards."

Raj managed something of a rictus grin of his own before slowly stumbling over to join James' side of the room.

"And your Second, Tyler," James asked pointedly, clearly revelling in the way he'd upset Leo's plans.

Scanning the room and still completely undecided which of these wolves he judged good enough in a fight to hold up against Raj, Leo started, "I hereby name as my Second—"

"Me."

The voice that came from behind his was not loud, but it carried through the entire room. Even without looking, Leo would have known it in his sleep, in a coma, from beyond the goddamn *grave*. And even if he hadn't, the hush that ensured would have told him what had just happened. Told him that Della had moved into position to support him, his challenge, and declared herself his Second in a fistfight against *James and Raj*.

Ignoring the myriad watchers, Leo turned to look at her. She was dirty, sweaty, worn from the fighting alongside the Apex River wolves. She was beautiful, beyond anything he'd ever seen before. More precious than the most valuable treasure. There was no way he could put her in danger like this.

Della had moved forwards to stand behind him, quietly supporting him. Well, as quietly as she could in a room full of people now staring at them.

"Leo," she said, and every one of his muscles tightened. How long had he been waiting for her to say his name? It felt like forever. Forever since he'd heard her voice, heard the way she said his name. Forever since he'd held her in his arms.

Since he'd felt her breath against his skin. Every instinct he had was telling him to grab her, hold her close, use his body as a shield to protect her from the coming conflict. How could he force himself to allow her to put herself in danger on his behalf?

"Della," he breathed into the silence between them. "You're here."

"I'm here," Della said. Her eyes were wide as she took him in. "Let me help, Leo. I'm powerful. I've just proven I can take on a ton of your wolves and win."

"You've just fought in a territorial war," Leo protested. "Della, you must be drained. I can't ask you to put yourself in danger for me—put yourself in front of *Raj* for me."

"You're not asking," Della said evenly. "I'm telling you, Leo. I can do this—better than Emmett could have, better than anyone else. I still have more than enough magic in me to take down a wolf or two. Don't make me prove it on you."

Leo reached for her hand, and to his surprise, she wrapped her fingers around his and held tight.

"What kind of man would I be," he asked quietly, "if I let you put yourself in danger over me?"

"The same kind who knows you never would have made this challenge and put *yourself* in danger if it wasn't for me," Della said. "The kind of man who won't force me to endure that from the sidelines. One who will let me help you make a change, here, today, now."

Awe ribboned through Leo in bright streaks. How had he ever lived without this woman? Every inch of his life before her seemed so dark and meaningless compared to the sensation of having her back in front of him. This was Della, putting herself on the line to change the world for the better. Putting herself on the line for *him*.

"Tell me something first," Leo demanded. "Is it just because you don't want to feel guilty over me getting hurt? Or is this because if I can do this differently, if I can make changes in the pack so no one's getting hurt unnecessarily—maybe, someday, you could see a way to forgive me for living with it for so long. To give me a chance to make this right. To be with me again."

Della's eyelids dipped to cover those beautiful eyes and he wanted to shout at the loss of her gaze. "Leo," she breathed, and then met his eyes again. Was he imagining it, or were hers wet? Was she tearing up because she was about to tell him there was no chance for them, no matter how he tried to fix all the damage James—with Leo's help—had done to this pack?

"It's because I can't watch you put yourself in danger and do nothing," she said, her voice as soft as if they were completely alone, back in that sunlit afternoon by the water-fall. "It's because I am done being too scared to embrace my power and make the world better. It's because I protect what's mine. So let me protect you, Leo."

There was no fraction of a second for processing. The moment she said the words, Leo's wolf was howling, roaring, wanting to rip open his chest and hold his beating heart out to her in his hands in offering. She already owned it, after all. Owned every part of him.

That's why she was doing this. Because she knew he belonged to her—and wanted to fight to protect him. Because Della Greenbranch was done being scared, and Leo had never loved her as much as he did in that moment, as she stood before him with bright eyes and power flickering over her skin.

He straightened his shoulders and turned back to face the impatiently waiting Alphas. Well, James looked impatient. Simon just appeared vaguely amused. Where Leo's own Alpha was clearly spoiling for the fight to begin—and the upset he'd forced upon Leo's plans to come to fruition—the Apex River Alpha just seemed content to watch this unexpected turn of events play out.

"If you're finished with this truly heart-warming reunion," James drawled, "Perhaps we could get on with it? Some of us have things to do, and," he added, drawing closer to Leo, "I've been waiting a long time to pummel you into the ground, Tyler. I'm going to enjoy every minute of bringing you to heel and casting you out of the pack in front of your little witch bitch girlfriend."

All Leo said in reply was, "Bring it on, old man." His head filled with memories with James telling him to get Della "out of his system," whatever it took, and the rage simmering beneath his skin began to boil.

"I hereby name as my Second," Leo said, looking directly into James' eyes, "Delphinia Greenbranch. And when she wipes the floor with you, maybe it'll finally teach you some fucking manners."

James snarled, moving as though to lunge at Leo, his fingernails already extending into claws, when the nervous-looking proprietor of Horatio's stepped between them.

"Gentlemen, gentlemen!" he said, the joviality in his voice clearly forced. "Perhaps we could take this outside? There's a lot of furniture in here that might get in the way… and my paintings… and the crockery…"

James visibly reined himself in with a nod, his fangs retracting slightly on a growl. Knowing he was only taunting the beast, Leo turned his back on James to exchange nods with Emmett and take Della's hand, leading her out of the restaurant into the street beyond.

"This will get messy," he told her quietly. "They'll call in the Seconds only if the primary fighters are beyond continuing. The fighting is done half-shifted, teeth and claws only, but it could get bad, Della. I need you to be safe, no matter what. Raj is, like, three times your size. Don't let him get his hands on you."

"Don't worry about me," Della said softly, as the rest of the inhabitants of Horatio's spilled out into the empty street, James at the back like the most anticipated float in a parade. Raj walked beside and behind him, looking pale and sickly. Leo had no doubt that his friend would fight to the best of his considerable ability, though; called upon by the Alpha, he really had no choice. If Leo wasn't on his A-game, Raj alone could grind him into dust.

"Very well, combatants," Alpha Simon said, stepping forward into the circle of onlookers and easily slipping into the role of adjudicator. "This contest is to decide the outcome of the challenge issued by Beta Leo Tyler against Alpha James Norfolk of the Blue Crescent Werewolf Pack, with Seconds Delphinia Greenbranch and Rajesh Lewis. The fight will involve natural weapons only. No full shifting. The Seconds will be called in only if their fighter is unable to continue or at risk of death. We are not aiming for casualties today, people," he added with a stern look at James, who only grinned, showing his elongated fangs. Simon continued, "We'll call it when the Firsts are down, or they can tap out, and the same for the Seconds. Any outside interference," he glanced at James' small group of rowdy followers, "will not be tolerated. Are we clear?"

"Clear," Leo muttered.

"Clear," James said loudly, stripping off his shirt.

Simon stepped back so he was standing next to Della as Leo and James moved into the empty space in the group's centre. "Good fighting," the Apex River Alpha intoned. "You may begin."

James lunged for Leo's throat.

Chapter 16

D ella had seen fights before tonight. Of course, she had; she grew up in Mystic City and went to school with werewolves. She'd even been involved in a few, not that she'd readily admit it these days. But she'd never seen anything like the way James and Leo fought, even between the werewolves on the territory border earlier that night. This was savage, brutal, not just aiming to disable a fighter or get past them, but to kill, despite Simon's proclamation that that wasn't the point of this fight. James had a point to prove, it appeared, and he was using Leo's flesh to prove it.

They fought half-shifted, two werewolf creatures that wouldn't be out of place in a nightmare, elongated fangs, razor-sharp claws and eyes glowing as silver as the full moon above. What parts of their skin hadn't sprouted fur were quickly covered in blood. A slice of Leo's claws down James' abdomen had the Alpha howling as he again tackled Leo to the ground. James' plan seemed to be to get Leo pinned, then use his greater bulk to keep him down as he brought the fight to what would no doubt be a bloody, brutal, and possibly fatal end. Leo was having none of it. Time and time again, James threw his full half-shifted weight against Leo's body, sometimes even succeeding in bringing him to the ground. Leo regained his feet each time, throwing James off before he could do more than draw blood. And draw blood he did—they both did —ripping and tearing any flesh they could reach with claws and fangs until both werewolves' fur was matted with blood. Though Leo was clearly the better fighter, James' lack of restraint and unbridled rage had them almost evenly matched. Leo was just trying to make the Alpha tap out, that much was clear. James was prepared to kill. He went for Leo's throat, for his eyes, for his abdomen in long, deep swipes that, if Leo hadn't managed to dodge lightning-fast, would have spilled his intestines all over the road's surface.

Was she insane, to get involved in this? She had no doubt that if it was her standing before him, James would show similarly non-existent mercy. And Raj, should it come to that, was easily twice her size, maybe more. She just couldn't stand there while Leo was forced to choose a Second he didn't have faith in after the option of his friends was lost, couldn't watch him struggle. Still, this might have been the stupidest decision she'd ever made. Yes, she had magic, but…

Leo threw James off him so violently, the watching crowd let out a host of different sounds—some shock, some awe, some disapproving. James skidded across the tarmac before rising to his feet once more and spitting out a mouthful of blood. The Alpha was starting to tire from his consistently rebuffed violent attacks, that much was visible, but he refused to stop or change his tactics.

"You think you can beat me fighting like this?" James demanded, stalking close once more. "Being the Alpha requires more than playing defence, Tyler. You have to be ruthless. You have to be strong." As he spoke, he took swipes at Leo with his impossibly elongated claws. Leo blocked them each time, but the Alpha still ripped slashes into his forearms more than once. Blood speckled the road surface, blood from both of them. As James continued speaking, his teeth—those not elongated into protruding fangs, at least—were red with it. "You have to put the pack before everything. What happens when you have to choose between the wellbeing of your wolves and your piece of witch ass over there? Why do you think I told you to get that Delphinia bitch out of your damn system?"

That broke something in Leo. With a snarl, he attacked. It was suddenly abundantly clear just how much he'd been holding back. His blows broke through James' defences as though he was just casually batting the Alpha's hands aside, scoring lines down his face, his chest, even his throat. He threw himself at James with a growl so loud, it seemed to reverberate through the very ground they stood on, pinning the Alpha to the ground with his knees on James' chest and his hands trapping the Alpha's arms as he struggled.

"You keep her name out of your fucking mouth," Leo spat down at the wolf trapped and struggling beneath him.

James growled a laugh despite his position. "If it's just werewolf cock she's after, maybe I'll use my mouth for something else on your little friend."

Leo curled up his fist and punched the older wolf in the jaw so hard, Della winced. And then kept going, blows raining down on the felled Alpha's face. Without his claws involved, Leo was clearly just aiming to punish James, to damage him, rather than to kill the way the Alpha had been. Della heard the crunch when his nose broke. Then again when Leo's fist ploughed into a cheekbone. Bone and cartilage shattered as Leo struck again and again.

James' limbs relaxed and his head lolled back, and still, Leo kept hitting him, even as he began to shift back into his human form beneath the blows.

"Leo!" Emmett yelled. "Leo, he's down! Lay off!"

Leo drew back as though he'd only just noticed that James had gone limp beneath him. He got to his feet, slightly off-balance, as James' followers rushed forwards to collect his prone body. One of them snarled at Leo, but the others seemed to be cowering away from his obviously still incandescent rage.

Once James had been removed from the circle of onlookers, presumably to receive medical attention for his destroyed, swollen and bleeding face as well as the numerous wounds to his body, Della looked to Simon next to her. "Is it over? Has he won?"

"Not yet," Simon replied. "Emmett's giving him a moment to regroup, then he'll call in the Alpha's Second. Usually, this is where the Beta fights for their Alpha—finishing what the Alpha started. That way, the challenger can't win with a lucky shot—they must be able to take down two of the wolves who are supposed to be among the pack's best fighters. Plus, it's a show of unity in the pack leadership. But clearly, that's not the case today."

"Clearly," Della agreed absently, but her eyes were on Leo. He was favouring one of his legs, the other streaming blood from a deep gouge to the thigh. His chest was heaving, but he stood proud before the crowd. Waiting.

"How long do they normally get before the Second comes in?" Della asked.

"They don't," Simon admitted. "Emmett's giving him a chance to get ready before unleashing the big guy on him."

"Is that—"

"Not normal," Simon said, "but I don't blame him. I'd do the same for a friend who had to fight that guy, especially as a Second." He gestured towards Raj, who was standing on the edge of the circle, surrounded by James' followers and looking determined—unhappy and slightly ill, but determined. He and Leo made eye contact and Della saw Leo take a deep breath, then crack his neck, grinning to reveal his bloodied teeth and fangs.

Had she once thought she'd enjoy watching Leo fight? Whatever the opposite of enjoyment was, that's how she felt about the prospect of seeing Leo and Raj go head-to-head. That bloodied grin—it had been one of permission, of forgiveness, of understanding that Raj would be honour-bound to do his best to grind an already-wounded Leo into the ground.

"Raj," Emmett said quietly, and the massive wolf stepped into the ring.

Leo didn't fall back to the defensive approach he'd had with James. He attacked. Was he still riding the high of taking out the Alpha? Della barely had time to wonder before the two wolves were at each other's throats. Claws flashed; blood sprayed. Whose? She couldn't even tell as the two wolves grappled, Leo fighting to avoid getting pinned under Raj's bulk. He fought to his feet and took a step back, leading Raj in a chase around the circle of onlookers that the larger wolf entered into without question, a savage grin on his half-shifted face. Without a word, he dove for Leo, forcing the gathered onlookers to scatter as the two of them rolled across the road's surface. Leo managed to drag his claws down Raj's face and the larger wolf reared back with a sound halfway between a snarl and a howl. Leo had half got his legs up to shove Raj off him when the bigger wolf landed a closed-fist blow to his abdomen—right over the slice where James had caught him with his claws. Leo half doubled over in his position on the ground and Raj followed it up with a strike to the face that Leo half-dodged, so it caught him only a glancing blow rather than the full force of the punch, which, Della thought, defi-nitely would have knocked him out. Leo responded by bending one of his legs up to kick Raj full in the stomach, but Raj was fresh to the fight where Leo was already battered, and he noticed the wound on Leo's thigh that had clearly weakened the kick and slammed his hand against it even as Leo managed to scramble out of the bigger wolf's grasp. His leg clearly borderline giving out beneath him, Leo limped out of Raj's reach, panting.

"Sure you don't want to give up yet?" Raj asked as he rose to his full height, the blood dripping down his face and neck making him look like a creature from a nightmare.

"Against you?" Leo laughed, as though they were just two friends sparring for fun, ignoring his own obvious wounds. "Not a chance, big guy. Bring it on."

"Well, since you asked so nicely," Raj said, raising an eyebrow, and lunged. He'd worked out how to force Leo to move relying on his injured leg, and it crumpled beneath him, sending him down to one knee. Raj was on him before Della could even breathe, wrapping Leo in a bear hug that pressed his back to Raj's chest, one of his arms around Leo's neck. Leo fought the hold, his claws tearing Raj's forearms to shreds, but Raj held him despite the bellow of pain he let out when Leo's claws found purchase in the muscles of his arms. He lifted until Leo's feet were off the ground, his kicks quickly losing power as he lost consciousness.

"Della, get ready," Emmett ordered. "I give it five seconds, then you're in."

Della felt her eyes widen in terror as she reached down into her significantly depleted well of power. She could do this. She had to be able to do this. For Leo. *For Leo.*

Leo stopped kicking, and Raj dropped him back to the ground. Groaning, Leo, barely conscious, rolled over and fought his way into a sitting position, raising his fists in front of his face as though he expected to keep fighting. With a growl, Raj drew back a fist to deliver what would surely be a massive blow, and—

Della stepped into the ring. "Don't you fucking touch

him." She barely recognised her own voice as she used a wave of raw power to shove Raj backwards. The big wolf looked almost comically shocked to find himself pushed away from his target. Leo, still barely conscious and with his face bleeding from every place a man could bleed, stared at her.

"Della," he rasped. "No."

"Get out of the way," Della ordered. "Emmett called it." She felt the power rippling over her skin as she added, "This one is mine."

"You want to play, little witch?" Raj asked, stalking forwards with surprising grace for a man his size, half-shifted to wolf. "Oh, we can play."

He lunged for Della, and she stepped forwards to meet him, lifting her hands to throw up a wall of solidified air that he hit full force with a grunt that did not cover the crunch of his nose breaking.

"Jesus fuck," Raj managed, leaning over to spit out a mouthful of blood.

"Come on, then, big guy," Della heard her own voice say as he straightened, power crackling over her sweaty, dirty skin. "Let's play."

Her magic, depleted though it was from earlier, leaped to her bidding like a happy kitten. Only this kitten was tiger offspring, all claws, and razor-sharp teeth, ready to meet the big wolf's every attack. Her magic had had a taste of victory and it wanted to fight, not to freeze her opponents for others to take out but to eliminate them herself, to exchange blows the same way Leo had with his opponents, wanted to swipe across Raj's skin like a blade and make him *bleed* for touching what was hers.

What was *hers*.

She flung an arm out as he made to approach her again, this time unable to restrain herself from making the magical blow *hurt*. But Raj was ready for it, and he regrouped lightning-fast and dove for her again, almost faster than she could rally her magic into a defence. The burst of raw power was barely controlled, and it struck him right in the chest, once again throwing him backwards. He skidded across the ground, and she caught a strange look of almost... pleasure in the strike, as though he was glad that she was able to defend herself this way, to keep throwing him off. As though he was relishing the pain.

He climbed back to his feet, and Della readied herself for his next attack. He approached like he was about to lunge for her again, but the words he spoke were for her ears alone. "This is going to last a long time if you just keep pushing me away," he growled.

"Unconvinced of your own stamina?" she asked.

"Fight me properly, or end this now," Raj demanded, and while she was distracted by his words, he lunged for her.

Della tried to get her hands up to form another defensive wall, but he was too fast. He had her arms pinned by her sides and held her tight the same way he had Leo, trapping her against him and cutting off her air. She tried to stomp on his instep the way she'd been taught as a teenager, but he lifted her too high off the ground. She couldn't shove him away with her power without risking injuring herself; and besides, the repeated bursts of pure magic were quickly burning through her reserves.

Burning through.

And in that moment, her brain slowly losing oxygen, Della knew what to do. She set herself aflame.

She covered herself in a layer of fire burning hotter, hotter, hotter, shielding herself from the heat but offering Raj no such protection from the column of flame she became. He let her go with a bellow of pain, the fur covering much of his half-shifted body igniting.

Fire still sparking over her skin, her ragged clothes smouldering, Della faced the big wolf, who was now looking at her with a mixture of respect and fury.

"End it?" Della asked, her rasping voice a taunt, then repeated his own words from earlier. "Well, since you asked so nicely."

She raised her hands once more and, with a growl that rivalled any the wolves had given tonight, summoned the dregs of her power and dragged the energy from his body.

It slammed into her like a tsunami, enough that she felt like every part of her had succumbed to her earlier flame, had caught alight and was burning. She was barely conscious of Raj dropping like a stone as she felt more than saw an impossibly bright white light racing over her skin until she was glowing like a star. She felt her feet leave the ground as her body fought to burn through the unfamiliar energy, felt the scream leave her throat as the last of her magic was drained away and she dropped to the ground, completely burnt out.

Leo was there within a fraction of a moment, pulling her battered body into the protection of his own. His wounds were already healing—werewolf power, she supposed distantly.

"Della," he was saying, over and over, yelling her name in desperation. "Della, Della, please, Della."

"For you," she managed to reply. Then she fainted.

Chapter 17

Della had been unconscious for fourteen hours. Not that Leo was counting or anything—he was just hyperaware of every second that passed as he sat beside her hospital bed. He'd left only to have his own wounds checked and to check on Raj in a room down the hall, who was thrilled with the outcome of the fight despite technically losing because, in his words, "It doesn't count if you lose because your opponent can literally drain the life from your body."

Given that he was already almost healed—one of the benefits of fighting as a werewolf—all they could really do was set his broken nose, which meant re-breaking it, and he'd likely always have the bump on the bridge to remind him of what had happened. To remind him of Della stepping into the ring to fight for him when he was barely conscious but still terrified for her. Terrified that she'd be injured trying to protect *him*, to support *his* challenge.

He'd had no idea how powerful his woman was. This was underscored by the tale of the Alpha of Apex River, who had come to check in on her sometime around hour four and wound up staying to talk for several hours after that, the two of them discussing the relationship that they could form between their packs now that Leo was officially Alpha.

That was a concept he was doing his best not to think too hard about. Though talking to Simon about it had made the idea significantly less intimidating. That was partly what had kept the Apex River Alpha there for so long—discussing the way he led his pack—so Leo had an example he could try to follow that wasn't just "What would James not do?". A few of the Blue Crescent wolves had come by as well, shifting their requirements for leadership from James to Leo without a moment for hesitation. He was starting to wonder if he was making this hospital room his base of operations the way James had Horatio's. He also wondered how long he could insist on being by Della's bedside before the nurses—especially Della's tiny human friend Magnolia, who had been popping in and out regularly since her shift started a few hours ago and made an impression on Leo to say the least—officially kicked him out. He couldn't stand the thought of leaving, though. Couldn't stand the idea of Della waking up without him there. As his skin and bones slowly knitted back together, he couldn't stop seeing the moment she'd pulled the energy from Raj's body into her own, her skin lighting up like her power had turned her incandescent, her body rising from the ground like she was the Messiah returning from the heavens. And then the moment when that blinding glow had winked out and she'd fallen, collapsed in a heap in the centre of the circle of gaping onlookers, and he'd barely been able to drag his broken body to her.

For you.

Simon had told Leo what Della had done earlier in the night, how she'd held off the full force of the attacking wolves on her own as the other witches had flagged one by one. Clearly, his woman was far more powerful than he had realised—to be able to do that and still have the power to hold off Raj without permanently injuring him. It wasn't something he'd put a lot of thought into, how powerful a witch he'd fallen so desperately in love with, and he questioned his own wilful blindness on the topic, how he'd barely even acknowledged her magic beyond the times she'd used it in front of him, until he realised the reason for it. The fact that Della was phenomenally powerful made no difference to him. He had loved her before he knew she could drag the energy out of his body with barely a thought; he loved her now that he had that knowledge. Della's strength made no change to the way he felt about her, beyond being even more impressed by her.

He was jolted from his thoughts by the door to the room opening. He'd come to expect the quiet knock of the nurses or his pack members hesitant to interrupt his mooning over Della's unconscious body. The woman who entered the room showed no such hesitancy. She walked in like she owned the entire building, long grey hair streaming behind her, and went immediately to Della's bedside, all but ignoring him beyond a quick assessing glance before she took Della's hand in her own.

"Hello," Leo said hesitantly. "I'm Leo."

"The one the universe chose for Delphinia," the grey-haired woman said without looking up. "I know."

"The universe?" Leo echoed, his sleep-deprived brain struggling to process her words. "What?"

"She came to me to see if I could explain the unfamiliar magic drawing the two of you together," the woman said, still holding Della's hand and assessing her with her gaze. "You werewolves call it a mate bond. Witches know it as supernatural magic."

"Isn't all magic supernatural?" Leo asked slowly.

"I didn't come here to debate semantics, Alpha," the woman said. "My granddaughter is in a fragile state and having your anxious energy constantly in the room is likely not helping."

"M-my energy?" This woman was Della's grandmother?

"Della drove herself within inches of complete and total burnout," she explained. "If she'd pushed herself any further, she might not have been able to return to us at all. She's been depleted like this once before, when that piece of scum was dosing her with freyroot, but active burnout is different."

"Are you telling me what she did for me is like... like what *he* did to her?" Leo asked, horrified.

"In a way," Della's grandmother said evenly, finally meeting his eyes. "In this case, by dragging someone else's energy into her body, Della forced her own magic to rebel. It had to burn up that outside energy in any way possible—it's toxic, otherwise, to have the wrong person's energy transferred into your own body. Because she was already so depleted, that used almost all her reserves. Which is what put her in *this* state." She shook her head. "That is precisely why we tell young witches not to do that exact thing. Still, I suppose one has few other options when facing a werewolf in hand-to-hand combat."

For a brief moment, Leo flashed back to Della rising into the air like a glowing angel, a scream tearing from her. "Will she be all right?" he asked, knowing he was moments from begging.

"Her body needs time to rejuvenate," Della's grandmother said. "Her magic is very slowly replenishing—it'll be several days before she's back to full strength. Her energy levels are a different story. In layman's terms, she's just very, very tired. It'll be another day or two before she regains consciousness, I suspect, and then some time after that before she is fully recovered. I can't tell you how long that will take—think of it as her body recovering from a severe illness."

"Another *day* or two before she's even conscious?" Leo gaped.

"Burnout is not a simple state," Della's grandmother said. "We warn witches very early on to avoid it at all costs. The price of pushing one's body and mind so close to that precipice is a steep one indeed. I wouldn't be surprised if she was very weak and tired, even after she awakens, for some time."

"I'll look after her," Leo rushed to say. A part of him almost revelled in the fact that he'd be *able* to take care of her. That he'd have a chance to look after this woman who had pushed herself to the cliff's edge for him. "I'll do whatever she needs."

"I would expect no less," the old woman said evenly. "And once she's back to being able to handle herself, the two of you will come around for a meal."

"That sounds… lovely. Thank you." Had he just taken an order from this woman? Something about her made it very easy to imagine her as a kind of Alpha in her own right, the Elder of a coven perhaps? Maybe that was why she had this aura of command about her.

With gentle hands, she pushed Della's hair back from her forehead. "Silly girl," she said, so softly Leo wasn't sure he was meant to hear it. "Silly, brave girl." She pressed a kiss to Della's forehead, then straightened, her hard gaze on Leo again. "All this for love?" she asked.

"For her?" Leo replied, his heart in his mouth. "Anything."

He thought he caught a trace of a satisfied smile on the witch's face as she walked out the door.

Della floated. She was tired, so tired, and the floating took care of at least some of the exhaustion. It took the weight of feeling her wiped-out body off her hands. So, she drifted in and out of a darkness that was both light and heavy at the same time, feeling herself returning by increments. She was aware of people around her, checking on the function of her apparently dangerously depleted body, having conversations—many of which revolved around her. And Leo. Always, always Leo.

She recognised Emmett's voice, one of the times she was almost present within her body. But her eyelids were too heavy for her to lift them and greet him.

"I was going to say we're going to have to redefine the rules of a challenge so only werewolves can participate, or after the way she took out Raj, everyone will want to bring a witch as their Second," he was saying. "But if this is the cost of it, somehow I don't think the witches will exactly be lining up to play along."

Leo's laugh sounded almost painful, like it was torn from somewhere deep in his chest. "She'll be fine," he said. "It might take a while, but they said she'll be fine."

"Of course, she will," Emmett agreed. There was a pause. "So, you know, if it's going to be a minute before she wakes up, it might not be a bad thing for you to come and deal with the uproar the pack is in right now. Raj and I have been covering your ass pretty well since he got on his feet again, but people are starting to wonder when their Alpha's going to make an appearance."

"I need to be here when she wakes up," Leo said, his tone brooking no argument.

She wanted desperately to open her eyes and look at him, to tell him that she was here, that she understood, that he should go and take care of his pack. But her eyelids were as heavy as boulders and her body didn't respond to her commands. Floating, floating.

She heard the door open and prepared herself for the

assessing touch of the nurses, but it was Petra's voice she heard. "My gods, Della!" Her hand was pulled into a tight grip. "How could you let her do this to herself?"

The sound of a throat clearing, and Petra stepped away, dropping Della's hand. "Sorry, Alpha."

Simon's voice now. "We didn't mean to interrupt."

"You didn't," Leo said. "Em was just leaving."

"I need to speak to the Alpha, man to man," Simon said. "Petra, if you wouldn't mind waiting…" There was a pause. "Petra?"

"Yes," Petra said, her voice sounding slightly confused. "Waiting. I-I'll be outside."

"I'll talk to you later, Emmett," Leo said. Then, slowly, "And thank you."

"Yes," Emmett's voice said. He, too, sounded distracted. "You're welcome. I'll, um… I'll just go, then."

There was the sound of the door closing, and then a pause. "Did you just see that too?" Simon asked.

"I don't know what it was, but something just happened," Leo said. He cleared his throat. "So, Alpha, what can I do for you?"

The darkness reclaimed her. Floating, floating, weightless, and pure. It gave her time to think, the darkness. Time to consider what she had done, and what it might mean.

She'd thrown herself in front of the proverbial bullet for Leo. Jumped in the ring with the largest werewolf she'd ever seen, on a day that she'd already thrown herself into the middle of a conflict between two packs. On a day when she'd worn her magic down to far from full strength. A day when she'd discovered that, despite what Dane had done to her those years ago, she was far more powerful that even she had realised. She still almost couldn't believe she'd held off the Blue Crescent wolves for that time all on her own, as the other witches' magic had faltered and failed. What did this mean? That she'd need to be far more deliberate about siphoning off bits of her power to keep it under control, now she knew how deep the well inside her ran. More than just encouraging her garden to grow and keeping sensor spells around her house. Now that she'd come close to touching the bottom of that well, it would likely be far more insistent about being used regularly. She'd need to find some way she could regularly drain part of her overflowing river of magic, ideally some way that would do some good in the world, to keep it from breaking its banks and bursting out of her without warning, the way it did with inexperienced young witches.

And, she supposed, on some level, what she'd done would mark her as a threat. Despite her involvement in local government and the Council of Witches, she'd always been politically unassuming. They'd put her on the council in part because she was something of a public figure following Dane's trial, and in part because she was powerful once she'd recovered from the freyroot poisoning, but she was certain no one had known how powerful.

I am here, her magic seemed to whisper in the weightless darkness. *I am waiting. I am here.*

Now… now, she'd lost that veil of anonymity. Surely by now, every witch on the council knew about the one who had held off an entire wolf pack's attacking force, then gone on to defeat one of them in one-on-one combat. Had dragged his energy into her body on an almost totally depleted supply of magic, burned it up and lived to tell the tale. She'd be viewed as a force to be reckoned with on the council now, a power in her own right, to be courted or avoided when there were decisions to be made. Not to mention how the werewolves would view her. Would there be a punishment meted out for meddling in their affairs? Gods, she hoped not—she'd been specifically asked to come and show her support for Apex

River, after all. She'd done nothing she hadn't been explicitly invited to do.

Except volunteer as Leo's Second. That she had done entirely of her own volition. As if in answer to that thought, the tether between them tugged, deep in her belly, drawing her back into an awareness of her own body. The same bond that had seen him in peril and known she had to act, even if it meant putting herself on the line in a werewolf conflict once more. Because Leo was... important. Vital. *Hers.* Hers to protect, to cherish. She felt him beside her every moment she had even partial awareness of her own battered body. Waiting for her to return from this weightless darkness, and for what? To tell her she shouldn't have done what she did? To tell her he'd missed her? To ask her not to leave him again, after she'd just shown she'd do anything to keep him safe?

In truth, even if she'd wanted to, she wasn't sure she would have had the strength to walk away from him again. This man who had taken her criticisms on the chin like a broken boxer in the ring, knowing full well that the only way to make the changes she so arbitrarily demanded was to put his literal life on the line going up against his Alpha... and then *did it*. This brave, beautiful man, who had tried to keep fighting when he couldn't even stand, just to keep her from stepping into the fray. Who the universe's magic had driven her towards and refused to allow her to stay away from.

When Simon had told her he was going to see the Blue Crescent Alpha that night to demand an explanation, she'd known she'd accompany him even before he asked for her to join the group. Known she couldn't turn down a chance to see Leo again when it was dropped into her lap like that, even if they were on opposite sides of the Alphas' dispute. Even if it was just a glimpse of him across the room, even if it had been with him fully supporting his Alpha's actions. She couldn't keep denying the part of herself that unceasingly dragged her back to him.

She couldn't stay away from the man she loved, could not have refused, after all this, no matter what issues they needed to work through, to even try.

He was hers, and she was his, and they had already shown that they would fight for each other. The tether in her belly pulled as though in approval of her thoughts. No matter what the world threw at them now, with him as pack Alpha and her a force to be reckoned with among the witches, they would face it together.

Della floated. And she knew, when she awoke, it would be to him.

Chapter 18

After all the hours he'd spent by her bed as she lay unconscious, leaving only when it was vital, of course, Della woke up when Leo was outside her room on the phone, dealing with a pack dispute involving one of James' sycophants who was hesitant, to put it delicately, to respect the rule of his admittedly so far somewhat absent new Alpha.

The nurse who had ducked in to check on Della while he was out in the corridor poked her head out the door and simply said, "Leo," and he knew.

"I'll call you back," he blurted down the phone and jammed it into his pocket without waiting for an answer, then raced back into Della's room.

Her eyes were open, and just being able to meet her gaze again sent a wave of relief through Leo that was so strong, he stumbled. She was fighting her way into a sitting position, laughing with the assisting nurse at her own weakness, when he burst through the door. The sound of her laughter was better than any music he'd ever heard, and when she turned her gaze on him and smiled, he fell to his knees by the bed, hands fumbling desperately for hers. Quietly, the nurse excused herself, but Leo hardly noticed. He was too focused on Della, the soft happiness on her face, the way she gently squeezed his fingers.

"Hi," she whispered, her voice hoarse from disuse.

"Hi," he replied.

"Leo—" Della said, at the same time as he started, "Della—"

Hearing their mingled laughter made him feel like there was golden sunlight running through his veins.

"You're okay," he managed. "They said you would be, the doctors, and your grandmother, but—"

"Grandmother Elise was here?"

"She stopped by a few days ago," Leo said. "Didn't exactly stop to give her name."

"Yeah, that sounds like her," Della said with a smile. "I thought I felt her here, but I figured I must have imagined it. She almost never leaves the coven's territory."

"She came to check on you. And to say some confusing things about supernatural magic of the universe and mate bonding."

"Mate bonding?" Della asked.

"It doesn't matter," Leo said quickly. "We can talk about it later."

"Leo, tell me," Della said, as serious as he'd ever seen her despite the hospital room and the gown she wore—or perhaps because of them?

"There's… a story we tell pups," he said slowly. "About finding the one person you're meant to be with, and the tie between you is so strong, you can't stay away from them. You'd do anything for them." He swallowed. "And I always thought it was just that, a story, and then I met you. And as if the bond wasn't enough, I fell in love with you on top of it. And suddenly I knew what they meant. About having someone you'd do anything to keep."

"Is that why you challenged James?" Della asked.

"I challenged James because it was the right thing to do, for the pack," Leo said, feeling the truth of the statement deep in his chest. "But I wouldn't have seen that, wouldn't have recognised that I had to do something about it, if it wasn't for you." He paused, glancing down at his hands grasping one of hers like a precious treasure. "Was part of me hoping it would go some way towards fixing things if I could show you I was willing to change, to be better? Yes, of course. But Della, I never expected you to get involved. Never expected to see you facing off against a werewolf three times the size of you, for my sake." The memory of it sent a rush of cold through him. "I would have fought Raj until I was a pile of bones on the ground to stop you from having to put yourself in that situation."

"I needed to do it," Della said simply. "I may not be a werewolf, Leo, but I still have the drive to protect what's mine."

It took a moment for her words to sink in, but when they did, Leo had to stop himself from pitching forwards to prostrate himself at her feet and swear every moment of his life to the service of her.

"Della," he managed, after a long moment. "Della, I-I know there are still issues. I know I have a lot of work to do. But I swear to all the gods, if you'll have me, I'll put every part of myself into making sure I deserve you."

"Funny," Della said, eyes shining, "I was just thinking the exact same thing."

Leo could no more stop himself from launching forwards to kiss his woman than he could lasso the moon. Though if she asked it of him, gods only knew he would try.

"I love you too," Della said when they finally broke apart, laughing at the frantic beeping of the heartrate monitor. "I have loved you, I love you, I will love you. So, we find a way through the issues because, Leo, I don't want to be without you anymore. This bond… I think it goes both ways. So, what you're feeling, I feel it too. I feel all of it too."

"Thank the gods," Leo said and kissed her again.

Homecoming. Heaven. That's what having his lips on hers felt like.

The sound of someone clearing their throat had them breaking apart again.

"Mags!" Della cried, her cheeks colouring. "You're… am I in your hospital?"

"You sure are," the diminutive human said with a smile. "Good to see you're back with us, girlie. Now if you're going to keep celebrating in this way, would you mind if I turned down your heartrate monitor? Not that the entire ward hasn't already guessed what's going on in here."

"Oops," Della said, glancing at Leo.

"Maybe you'll get lucky," Maggie said as she dealt with the machine, "and they'll just think you're having a heart attack." She paused, raising an eyebrow as she met Leo's eyes with an uncompromising gaze. "Because there will be no other getting lucky while you're in my hospital, capisce? Keep those paws to yourself until my girl is back at full strength and out on the streets, werewolf." She shot them both a grin as she turned to leave, drawing the curtains around the bed. "All right, as you were."

"Once you're back at full strength," Leo muttered for Della's ears only as the door closed behind the nurse, "These *paws* are going to have to re-memorise every inch of your body, Delphinia Greenbranch."

"You've forgotten it already?" Della laughed.

"When it comes to you, I clearly have a very poor memory," Leo said with a grin. "I think I'm going to have to remind myself regularly."

"You know what?" Della said, wrapping her arms around his neck to draw him close. "I think I can live with that."

Epilogue

Della was running late. Today, of all days, would, of course, be the day that she couldn't leave work on time, in addition to the fact that she was still being hounded by the council to take a more active position after the revelation of the extent of her power. Power that she now almost unthinkingly siphoned off to do things like rearrange her schedule so she'd be free for tonight's housewarming; though that didn't mean, apparently, that other people wouldn't book meetings in without checking if there was a reason her afternoon was clear.

So, she was late. Late to get ready for her own party, even though she'd "encouraged" some speed cameras not to notice her car zipping past them in a way that was almost definitely illegal. But considering she'd specifically asked Leo this morning to make sure he was home on time tonight, it felt a bit rude to be rolling through the door a bare twenty minutes before people were due to arrive.

Being late was one of the very few downsides to Della and Leo's relationship, especially since moving in together. And it wasn't solely the fault of her two jobs and his demanding role as Alpha; ever since she'd been discharged from the hospital, it seemed that her wolf couldn't be alone in the same room as her for more than thirty seconds at a stretch without finding a way to make her scream his name with pleasure. And she was equally eternally starved for him, for the rush of bringing him satisfaction.

So, they were late for things a lot.

It was worth it.

But she'd really done her best to ensure she'd be on time tonight. She should have been home and doing her best Stepford wife impression an hour ago. Instead, Leo was probably already there and—

Her phone rang as she turned onto his street—their street; since, as Alpha, Leo needed to live within Blue Crescent territory. She hadn't minded when they floated the idea of moving in together in bed one morning and he'd somewhat apologetically suggested his house.

"I know it'll be a pain to have to move," he'd said, "But we can stay here, or we can find somewhere new. You can change anything about it that you like. Hell, knock it down and rebuild it if you want."

"You just want to have a new set of rooms to defile." Della had laughed, but the sound was cut off by his mouth covering hers.

"Who said I need anything new involved to defile you?" Leo had growled, sliding between her thighs, and then it was a while before either of them was capable of continuing the conversation.

Afterwards, gasping for air, Della had managed to say, "I like this house. I don't think we should knock it down. Plus, it would make my commute shorter on the days I'm in the office."

"I don't care about the house," Leo said, equally winded. "I just want your things mixed in among mine. I want to know I'm coming home to you every night."

"Moving is a lot less painful when you can do it all with magic," she had added with a smile. "Besides, with your garden, the house already looks like it belongs to a wicked witch. We might as well fulfil the impression it gives."

"You're not exactly a wicked witch." Leo had laughed, gathering her close.

"Oh, haven't I shown you in enough detail how wicked I can be?" Della asked with an arched eyebrow.

"Woman, if you show me in any more detail, I might not survive it."

She had done it anyway.

The persistent ringing of the phone as she pulled into the driveway dragged her from the remembrances. She picked it up without checking who it was.

"Hello?"

"I'm so sorry," Leo said without preamble. "I lost track of time. I'm turning into our street now. Sweetheart, I'm so sorry. I'll make it up to you—why are you laughing?"

She climbed out of her car to see Leo pull in behind her and saw on his face as he realised what had happened.

"Work run overtime?" he asked as he came over to kiss her.

"A little," she admitted. "Good thing I know a witch who can get the house ready for guests in a flash." She flicked her fingers, directing her magic to ready the house for visitors.

She saw the twinkle in Leo's eye a fraction of a second before he swept her up into his arms. "Well, that leaves us with a good fifteen minutes to fill before anyone is due to arrive," he said, his lips against her skin. "Good thing I know a wolf with a couple of ideas."

Della could feel their combined laughter through their touching bodies as Leo carried her across the threshold.

She was home.

Sophia Martin

Sophia grew up in Australia as part of a big family. She started telling stories before she could write, and writing before she could spell. Her early works consist almost entirely of misspelled fairy stories. As a teenager she would hand-copy the steamy scenes out of her favourite books to enjoy later, and this naturally led her to romance.

After a brief stint in non-fiction writing with a university paper, she returned to her origins and started writing fiction again. When not writing, she can be found pole-dancing very poorly, completing her university degree or terrorizing her two dogs.

Find her on Instagram: @sophiamartinwrites

Don't miss these exciting titles by Sophia Martin and Eclipse Press!

Blue Crescent
Bewitching the Wolf

Shepherd's Creek Series:
He Comes Home
Taking His Time
Belonging to Him
Claimed by Him

Exposed